THE HUNT FOR MADOFF'S TREASURE

SEMI-FINALIST
2019
Royal Palm
Literary Award
Competition

ISBN 978-1-7335443-4-4
Library of Congress Control Number: 2019930184

PANDA PROMOTIONS, INC.
4255 US HWY 1 South, Ste 18-125
Saint Augustine,
Florida 32086

This is a work of fiction. Names, characters, places and incidents either are the product of the author's imagination or are used fictitiously, and any resemblance to actual persons, living or dead, business establishments, events or locales is entirely coincidental.

THE HUNT FOR MADOFF'S TREASURE

PHIL SILLS

Panda Promotions Inc
Saint Augustine, Florida, USA

Dedication

To my wife and life partner Jackie, my sons Chris and Mike and their spouses, Josh and Jenna.

In loving memory of Max XIX, our beloved Cavalier King Charles Spaniel.

Acknowledgment

First and foremost, the author must acknowledge the time, patience, and encouragement his wife Jackie provided in the monumental task of writing a book.

In addition, the author wishes to thank, Jessica Hatch of Hatch Editorial Services in Jacksonville, Florida. Her insightful proofreading and line editing guided me through the editing process, and some of her comments were priceless.

The author wishes to also recognize the contribution of Landon Osteen for his creative web design.

Last but not least, the author followed the recommendations of the prestigious Alliance of Independent Authors and selected Russell Phillips (russellphillips@authorhelp.uk) a seasoned professional who understands the ins and outs of book production and delivers exactly what every author desires...a book to be proud of.

Prologue

"Buzz... Buzz... Buzz."

The small, innocuous alarm clock in his office startled Clarence from his morning trance. He'd been up late last night watching his perennial last-place New York Mets lose to the upstart Dodgers in Los Angeles. Clarence had detested the Dodgers' management ever since their owner, Walter O'Malley, hustled the team out of Brooklyn to Los Angeles in the dead of night. The "Brooklyn Bums," as they were reverently referred to back then, were the heart and soul of the borough, and the thought that the owner put profits above fan loyalty enraged the local populace.

"Buzz... Buzz... Buzz."

Clarence had less than thirty minutes to fetch the city's guest in Cell #107 for his appearance in Courtroom 3A. Cell #107 was located in the bowels of the Brooklyn Federal Courthouse on One Center Street. This particular courtroom was usually reserved for high-profile celebrity trials.

At sixty-four years of age, Clarence Brown was a man who had seen it all. His maternal grandmother raised him after his father and mother died of tuberculosis. After graduation from Tilden High School in Brooklyn, he'd tried to enlist in the army but was turned down when he tested positive for TB. The Health Department then grabbed him up and quarantined the eighteen-year-old in the prison ward of Kings County Hospital for the next two years until his TB was considered noncontagious. A deeply religious man, he was taken under the wing of his local minister who encouraged him to seek employment in the city's civil service system. With his minister's tutoring, he was one of four hundred black candidates to pass the civil service exam that year with high marks. He then applied for and was hired by the New York City Criminal Court Division.

Over the years, Clarence Brown had won the respect of his colleagues, court officers, judges, and prosecutors. Today was the culmination of his long career. He was chosen to escort America's Public Enemy Number One to receive his sentence in Courtroom 3A. It was time that Clarence, looking stately in his navy-blue uniform and starched white shirt, was seen by his fellow Brooklynites in all his glory.

Clarence, knowing that he would be in court for several hours before he could excuse himself, stopped at the men's room to relieve himself and checked for spinach in his teeth when in walked his tight-assed boss, Deputy Director Chuck McNair.

"You got it under control?" McNair asked while presenting his manhood to the nearest urinal. McNair, ever the jaunty sophisticate, was careful not to wet his highly polished black loafers.

"Everything's A-OK," replied Clarence as he stepped to the sink to wash his hands.

"Make sure he looks good for the press... don't want to be accused of roughening him up. You know what I mean, there're hundreds of people out there who would like him cut up and fed to the fish."

"Roger, boss, he'll be spit-shined for them cameras," Clarence said, handing McNair several paper towels.

Both men proceeded to the exit with McNair hesitating a stride so as to allow Clarence the privilege of opening the door for him.

"Oh yeah, one more thing. Sugarman and Titus will be waiting for you on the third floor as your entourage to Courtroom 3A," McNair said.

"Roger, boss," Clarence replied automatically.

He watched McNair enter a courthouse elevator manned by a security officer, then, after checking his pocket watch, made his way to a large steel door with a sign that said, "AUTHORIZED PERSONNEL ONLY."

Clarence pressed a red button adjacent to the door and stepped back to look at the video camera mounted on the wall. "Clarence Brown to collect prisoner in #107 for appearance in 3A."

A few seconds later, he heard the door's steel bolts disengaging, allowing him to enter the court's holding cell area. Clarence stopped at a window, similar to a bank teller's cubicle and signed the obligatory paperwork releasing the prisoner in Cell #107 into his custody.

The officer behind the glass perused the form and asked, "Shackles?"

"No, not this time," replied Clarence, whereupon he was issued a pair of handcuffs and a key.

He then made his way down a long row of cells. A smile came to his face as he contemplated how many prisoners he'd taken into his custody over the years. Hundreds, no, probably thousands, he thought to himself. He also knew the rules called upon him to serve the sentence of a prisoner in his custody if they escaped. Hmm, he murmured under his breath, if he added them all up, collectively it might be a prison sentence over five thousand years. Clarence stopped in front of Cell #107, and after tapping on the reinforced steel door with his handcuffs, opened a three-by-seven inch window in the door to check on his prisoner.

Glancing through the window, he saw a balding, seventy-one-year-old man with a gray demeanor and pasted smile sitting on a twin-sized cot. For his court appearance, #107 was dressed in civilian clothes: gray slacks, white shirt open at the neck—ties, belts, and shoelaces were not allowed in the lockup—and a pair of faux black leather loafers. On the cot next to him was a navy-blue sport jacket.

"Open #107," said Clarence as he pressed the intercom button next to the cell door.

A moment later, Clarence heard the familiar sound of the lock motor retracting the bolts from the doorframe. Reaching for the lever, he eased the door open. As he did, the lights flickered, and the room seemed to shudder as the sound of thunder ripped through the building. Dazed, Clarence and Prisoner #107 looked at each other until Clarence broke the ice by saying, "That must be an omen from the gods of what's in store for you. Now stand up and let me see how you look."

The prisoner slowly rose to his feet, twisted his body to get the kinks out, and responded, "How do I look?"

"I say you're ready for prime time, #107. Now, put on your jacket, I gotta cuff you," Clarence said.

The prisoner slipped on his jacket, adjusted his shirtsleeves, and put his hands out for Clarence to snap on the handcuffs.

"Okay, we're going to take the elevator up to the third floor of the courthouse, and there will probably be a crowd waiting for us. Now, you hear me, if you're a good boy and don't create a fuss, I'll get you that coffee ice cream you like from Jahn's for dessert tonight," Clarence said.

"That'll make my day," said #107 as they walked side by side out of the cellblock to the elevator. When the elevator arrived, Clarence nodded to the security officer running it and asked to be brought to the third floor.

The guard nodded at #107. "No shackles?"

"No, not this time. It's not our first date," Clarence said, flashing a toothy smile.

The ride to the third floor took only seconds, and as the doors opened, Officers Sugarman and Titus were there to escort Clarence and his prisoner past a scrum of reporters, photographers, and curious bystanders all waiting to see America's Public Enemy Number One get his comeuppance. After some pushing and shoving, the security officers formed a phalanx clearing a path to Courtroom 3A. Once within the safe confines of the courtroom, Clarence removed his prisoner's handcuffs and directed him to the defense table where his lawyer, Ken Bernstein, was waiting.

Then, from a side door just to the right of the judge's platform, the bailiff strode into the courtroom and theatrically bellowed above the chitter-chatter. "All rise, all rise, the Supreme Court of Kings County is now in session, the Honorable Alfonso Gennetti presiding." On cue, the judge in his black robe entered the courtroom from that same side door. As he ascended to his chair, #107 took the opportunity to turn and face the prosecution table, the spectators, and those chosen to give victim impact statements.

Nowhere, nowhere in the mass of people was there a single friendly face. Everyone was there to witness this Americanized form of retribution. The only thing missing were the vendors selling hot dogs and beer. Yet, in a way, #107 was happy that the charade was finally over, that the circus would be packing up and moving to another venue. It was also so, so anticlimactic. His lawyer had cut a deal ages ago with the Feds that spared his family. The rest was to be determined by the judge today, since there were few guidelines and precedents for the length of his sentence.

Gennetti began his presentation by outlining a litany of laws the prisoner had admitted to breaking. The estimated amount of money stolen from his victims, which #107 had used to engorge himself and his family. The steps the government had taken to recover his ill-gotten gains from various entities. Finally, after a twenty-minute presentation of #107's crimes, the judge announced that several people had been selected to give brief victim impact statements. The bailiff called these people, one at a time, to a microphone set up on a podium next to the prosecution table. Limited to three minutes each, the victims, most fighting back tears, told of how #107 took all their savings, leaving them destitute in their old age.

During their testimony, #107 sat on the edge of his chair, hunched over the table, his head buried in his hands. The last one to give a victim impact statement was his Aunt Ida. She said that he was always a scumbag and a lying, good-for-nothing cheat, and that he had caused her husband's death, whereupon #107 sprang to his feet to denounce her testimony.

"Ida, you're full of shit. Your fuckin' husband begged me to. 'Make me some money, make me some money,' he said, 'and don't let Ida know.'"

Crash, boom, bang went Judge Gennetti's gavel.

"Sit down and shut the hell up," the judge snapped at #107.

Clarence, seeing his cue, grabbed #107 by the shoulders and pushed him back in his seat.

"You did, you did... you son of a bitch," Ida continued.

"That's bullshit," #107 said, looking at Ida. But the judge's gavel couldn't stop him this time. "I gave your husband ten percent of his investment, under the table, every year, year after year for over twenty years... tax free!"

Finally, his lawyer, Ken Bernstein, in desperation grabbed #107 by the arm and whispered in his ear, "Don't go there. He'll vacate our deal to protect your family."

"Attorney Bernstein, please advise your client that if I hear one more outburst from him I'll have him brought back to his cell," the judge said.

"Thank you, your honor, I have advised him to do just that," said Bernstein.

"Mr. Madoff, if there's anything you would like to say on your behalf, now's the time to say it," the judge said, pointing his gavel at #107.

#107 slowly rose to his feet. With a smile on his face, he looked up at the judge and said, "Is that all? 'Cause I want to get back to my cell. The Mets are playing the Dodgers today."

Not amused, Gennetti told #107 to sit down and be quiet while he opened a three-ring binder, which contained his ruling and the length of #107's sentence. The judge went to great lengths explaining the rationale for the sentence based on his interpretation of the law, with an eye towards deflecting future appeals from the defendant. At the end of his presentation, the bailiff asked #107 to rise to hear the sentence of the court.

Both the defendant and his attorney rose and faced the bench.

"It is the ruling of this court that you, Mr. Bernard Madoff, are sentenced to a term of 150 years in prison. That you will be taken to a federal penitentiary where you will spend the rest of your life."

With that being said, the judge slammed his gavel down, scooped up his papers and swiftly left the courtroom. Madoff and his defense lawyer shook hands as Clarence came over to place him in handcuffs. Clarence then took him by the arm, with Sugarman and Titus in the lead, to return the prisoner to his cell.

However, just before they left the courtroom, Clarence came face to face with #107 and said, "I warned you...you were a bad, bad boy... no ice cream for you tonight!"

Smiling, Bernie rose on his tiptoes to whisper in Clarence's ear, "No problem. It'll taste better when I get out of prison!"

Meet Max Rosen

Max Rosen was never known to be a morning person. His idea of starting off the day was to sleep late, snuggle up with a beautiful woman, and get a little loving. So, when he got a call at six-thirty on Sunday morning, before he had an opportunity to get a leg over his partner, Margery, he felt that the call had better be important. As it turned out, it was. The caller said that Sy wanted to see him at eight-thirty at the corner of Pell and Mott Street in lower Manhattan.

Awake and leaning on one elbow, Margery asked, "Who was that?" Rubbing the sleep from her eyes.

"Just Sy," Max murmured, heading to the bathroom to shave and shower.

"Do you have time for breakfast?" she called after him.

"No, I'll pick up something around the corner," he said through the bathroom door.

One of Max's favorite haunts was a kiosk about a block away that served fresh, toasted bagels with thick gobs of cream cheese.

For the past several years, Max has been a fixer, a freelancer, a gofer, you name it, for Sy. After Max was unceremoniously given his walking papers from his job at a Madison Avenue advertising agency, Sy became the source of his off-the-books, post-employment income. Sy was a childhood acquaintance of Max's older cousin Howie Shapiro. Sy and Howie grew up in the same dilapidated tenement house on Pennsylvania Avenue in Brooklyn and had been classmates at Jefferson High School in Brooklyn, where they were as thick as thieves in creating mischief and mayhem. Nary a week went by that either or both sets of parents weren't called in to see the principal for one of their children's pranks— whether stink bombs in the bathrooms, Elmer's glue on the science teacher's chair, spraying a film of motor oil on the basketball court, or setting off the fire alarms during Halloween.

One would think that their parents would have had them drawn and quartered in front of Jefferson High School, but luckily for Sy and Howie, they were the only children of dotting Jewish parents who indulged their inappropriate behavior with the blanket explanation of "boys will be boys."

So Howie had introduced Max to Sy when he fell on hard times. In the beginning, Max did little things for Sy: getting tickets to Broadway shows and sporting events, greasing politicians' palms in return for their votes on legislation, even organizing trips to faraway places for clients with hookers. Then he graduated to more lucrative endeavors like laundering money for the rich and famous.

Sy would often remind him that he was merely a messenger boy. "Pick up whatever they give you and deliver it to Rosebud Limited, farshteyn?" (Farshteyn means, do you understand in Yiddish)

Rosebud Ltd. was located near the docks in a nondescript warehouse on West 28th Street. Invariably, Sy would send an escort to shadow Max while making the pickups and deliveries. Everything that Sy did was redundant by necessity, or maybe paranoia.

So, with his jacket collar turned up against the elements, Max positioned himself against a brick wall on Pell Street, between a Chinese grocery displaying Peking ducks hanging upside down by their legs in the window and a clothing store offering knock-off designer handbags. Max stood there, like a soldier, nervously sipping lukewarm coffee from a Styrofoam cup. This was not the first time Sy had arranged a meeting at some ungodly hour, but it was the first time a Chinatown rendezvous was chosen. Usually, their meetings were uptown in a more civilized section of Manhattan, in or around Fifth Avenue and East 57th, where Max's instructions were given while they rode through the greenery of Central Park.

As the appointed hour approached, Max had an uneasy feeling that this new, sleazy meeting place marked a deviation from the norm and that Sy was ratcheting up the ante to more and more dangerous assignments. That said, Sy was the man, the president and CEO of G.C. Waverly Investment Bank, one of the largest brokerage firms on Wall Street that, legally or illegally, juggled billions of dollars of investors' funds each day with the sole purpose of increasing their own bottom line. They had perfected the art of separating investors from their money by telling them, as the bottom fell out of the market, "Don't cash out now, let it grow. You're in it for the long run, right?"

They also had an uncanny influence over every segment of the market, so much so that, when all the major brokerage companies lost hundreds of billions of dollars during the hedge fund and credit default swap fiasco, G.C. Waverly reaped in massive profits. Their mantra was, "Too big to fail? Bullshit, too big to touch."

Like J. Edgar Hoover, they had a book on every politician, past and present, that, if made public, would send shock waves throughout the country. No, Max thought, throughout the world.

As Max glanced at his watch, a black limo turned onto Pell Street and proceeded slowly towards where he was standing. He instinctively emptied his coffee into the gutter and tossed the cup in the direction of a storm drain. As the limo glided to a halt alongside him, a solid-looking man with a crew cut, dressed all in black, exited the passenger side clutching an X-ray wand in his hand.

"Max, you know the drill," the man said in a lazy, matter-of-fact tone.

He was one of Sy's bodyguards and most likely an ex-Secret Service agent. He patted Max down and checked him out with the wand. Satisfied that Max was not carrying a concealed weapon or a bug of any kind, he motioned to the driver to unlock the back door, whereupon Max slid into the seat alongside Sy, who had just finished reading something on his laptop. Sy was dressed in his Wall Street uniform: gray pinstriped, worsted-wool trousers; brown Gucci leather loafers; a starched white shirt with French cuffs; solid gold cufflinks; a yellow silk Dior tie; and powder-blue suspenders. Max couldn't see what type of belt he was wearing, but being the CEO of G.C. Waverly Investment Bank, it probably was made of rattlesnake skin. Sy told the driver he wanted some privacy, and a bulletproof glass partition rose from a compartment behind the front seats, effectively sealing off the front of the limo from the back. Satisfied that their conversation could not be overheard, Sy tapped on the glass partition and the limo took off for the FDR.

Sy looked over at Max and, without any pleasantries, got right to the point of the meeting. "I want you to spring Bernie Madoff from the Butner Federal Penitentiary in North Carolina," he said as if he were asking Max to pick up a loaf of bread.

Stunned, Max's first thought was, 'Did he just ask me to... to bust Bernie Madoff, the Ponzi King, out of a maximum-security federal penitentiary in the heart of Dixie? Is he fuckin' crazy?'

"Max, did you hear me?" Sy asked. Max sat there, unable to speak, staring at the bulletproof partition, wondering if it were a harbinger of things to come. If things went south, he'd be staring through a similar partition in a federal penitentiary.

Sy, sensing that Max was overwhelmed by his request, decided to take it down a notch. "Listen, I want you to come up with a plan, a comprehensive plan of how you—assuming you had all the money and resources at your disposal—would get Bernie out of jail. Do you understand me? Farshteyn, bubelah?"

The use of the word bubelah was uncharacteristic of anything Sy had ever said to him. It was a word he hadn't heard since childhood, a word of affection he'd heard from his grandmother.

"Yes, I'll come up with a plan," Max said automatically.

"Good," Sy said, tapping his arm. "I want you to drop everything you've got on your plate." He shifted gears. "Max, you're a creative guy. That's why I've chosen you for this assignment. I need someone who thinks outside of the box," he said this in as sincere a way as a cold-blooded CEO could without laughing.

"I also know that what I'm asking you to do could conceivably land you in jail for a very long time...or worse. On the other hand, if you can pull it off, you'll be a very, very rich man," Sy said, displaying his white-capped, toothy smile.

Once on the FDR, a nine-mile parkway that skirts the East Side of Manhattan, the limo sped north. Sy used the time to send messages to his office, while Max sat, staring at the river, trying to process his new assignment. He wanted to ask Sy some follow-up questions but didn't know where to start. Bernie Madoff was serving a 150-year sentence for running a Ponzi scheme that defrauded thousands of investors out of billions of dollars. To make matters worse, he was serving his time in a federal penitentiary manned by professional correction officers who were equipped with all the modern bells and whistles.

Passing under the Queensboro Bridge, the limo took the ramp leading to the East 63rd Street exit, then banged a left and headed down Sutton Place South, a cluster of high-rise apartment buildings overlooking the East River. Suddenly Sy pushed an intercom button on his armrest and told the driver to pull over and park.

"Privacy!" ordered Sy. The driver and the security officer exited the limo and took defensive positions, one in front and one in the rear of the limo.

"Here," Sy said, reaching into his shirt pocket and removing a small, foil envelope. "Here, take it," he insisted, handing it to Max.

"From now on, the only way we will communicate is by email. This is an encryption device that plugs into your computer's USB drive. I have a similar device on one of my computers. Everything you need to communicate with me, my email address, sign-ons, and handshakes are preprogrammed. All you have to do is access the Internet, plug in the device, and wait for the prompt to enter the password, which is on the enclosed card. After you memorize the password on the card, burn it. From then on, you and I will be the only ones that can read our emails."

Sy paused. "Is that clear?" he asked, looking directly at Max.

"I understand," Max said.

"Okay. If for any reason, you're in a situation where the device may fall into the wrong hands, you must destroy it. Just step on it. It contains a drop of acid that will erase the code."

Sy then waved to his men to return to the limo. A few moments later, the limo pulled to the curb in front of Max's apartment building.

Just as Max was preparing to exit the limo, Sy reached over and grabbed Max by the arm. "Give me something by this Friday."

Max managed to eke out a faint, "Yes, sir." Sy nodded to him and the limo faded away into morning traffic.

Meet Joe Mancuso

Later that day, on the Upper West Side, Joe Mancuso was waiting on a dark leather couch in Trevor Eisenstaedt's outer office, nervously thumbing through a magazine of luxury yachts. Eisenstaedt was Joe's boss and vice president of operations for A. J. Waters, an international investigation organization with offices in every major capital. The organization's exact number of employees was unpublished, but a close guesstimate would be around 27,000.

Joe looked down at his shoes and, noticing they were in need of a polish, wondered if he had time to run to the bathroom and spiff them up with a little water. No, if he did that, he was sure Eisenstaedt would walk out and find him gone. In his position, that would be the kiss of death. Waters had recently hired him when no one would touch him with a ten-foot pole. He was a defrocked NYPD detective who was caught with a kilo of coke in the trunk of his car. After sixteen years on the force, twelve as a patrolman and four as a vice detective, he was kicked out the back door without a 'see ya later.' No pension, no benefits, no back pay, no unemployment insurance, nothing. Just the order to "clean out your locker and don't look back."

But it was his own fault; he was asking to be busted. If he'd been told once, he'd been told a thousand times, "Leave the gun, take the cannoli," or as it pertained to the vice squad, "Leave the dope, take the cash."

With a wife and kids in the burbs and a sugar baby on the Upper East Side, Joe thought he had it all. After all, he had all the coke he could stuff up his nose. Just pound a dealer—what are they going to do, call the police? But now he had to play "Mister Clean" at a high-priced detective agency. If it weren't for Mo, a fellow detective, he'd be washing dishes in a Chinese restaurant.

Mo had said, "Clean up your fuckin' act, stay off the junk, and I'll put a good word in for you." This turned out to be not so difficult since Joe didn't have a dime to his name and the drug dealers were itching to get a piece of him now that he wasn't wearing a badge.

Checking the time on his iPhone, he wondered what the big boss wanted. He'd been squeaky clean for over six months during his probation period. He'd attended all the classes on rules and procedures, interoffice communication, working with federal agencies, court testimony, weapons training, the official employee handbook, and more.

In addition, as part of his probation period, he was subject to spot checks for drug use. He must have pissed in every cup in the building in front of a security guard.

"Just leave it and walk away," he was always told.

During this period, he was shuttled from one department to another without any comment as to what they had in store for him. On the employment questionnaire he'd filled out when he began at Waters, he'd listed white-collar crime as his preference, thinking that it sounded aloof and completely different from his years on the police force...and a good way of changing the subject.

Joe shifted on the couch and started thinking that maybe they found out about his sugar baby, Mary Baures. Did he have to stop seeing her? Maybe they were following him and noted that he occasionally spent the night with her. They probably had some rule in the employee handbook, 'The No Fuckin' Around Rule,' and he was being terminated. He knew he should have checked the handbook under 'proper mistress decorum.'

The door opened, and Eisenstaedt came walking out of his office with a smile on his face. Eisenstaedt was a tall, impressive man in his fifties whose handshake could crush a Ford pickup. "Come in. I was on a call," he said pumping Joe's hand.

Joe felt relieved. They don't smile if they're going to can you, he said to himself.

"Sit over here," the boss man said, tapping on the back of a chair in front of his desk.

He had a green folder on his desk and took a few moments reviewing the information it held. Looking up, he told Joe that he was pleased with his classroom performance during his probationary period and that he had an important assignment for him. He thought that they'd try him out on a famous white-collar crime that they had been pursuing for some time the Bernie Madoff case.

Hearing this Joe sat back and wondered what the hell they wanted him to do. Bernie was in prison for life what more did they want from the guy? Eisenstaedt explained that A.J. Waters was hired by a group of interested investors who lost a great deal of money and wanted their assistance in recovering it.

"What kinda money do they think he has?" asked Joe.

Folding his hands on his desk, Eisenstaedt smiled and said, "They claim that Bernie's got a treasure stashed away someplace. And yes, it's in the billions. B as in Bunko," he said closing the folder and standing up.

Joe realized that the meeting was over and that finding the alleged money was now his problem. Eisenstaedt walked around the desk and handed the green file to Joe as he opened the door, pausing briefly to tell him that someone, he didn't give their name, would brief him on the case. As Joe walked back to his cubbyhole, he got a sense of how Eisenstaedt assigned cases. Take the cases that float to the top and give them to the low man on the totem pole— yours truly, Joe Mancuso.

On his way back to his desk, Joe stopped to grab some coffee in one of the many employee kitchens. He began reading the file while the machine belched out a cup of steaming hot coffee. At first glance, it looked as if most of the entries in the file were merely surveillance notes, written by an investigator named Sam Craven, on the comings and goings of Bernie's wife, Ruth. 'Went to Bloomies with O, went to shrink with O, went to hairdresser with O.' It went on and on —and who the hell was this O? Research-wise, there was nada, zilch.

"This is bullshit," Joe said to himself. Looking at the dates, he realized that the file encompassed over two years of work with nothing of any substance except for the billable hours in red ink at the bottom of every entry. This wasn't a case of looking for a needle in a haystack; he didn't have a clue where the haystack was!

Oh, if there was ever a time for doing some coke, it's now, Joe thought. Now that his probationary period was over, he momentarily wondered if they were going to continue the unannounced drug testing. No better play it safe, he thought.

Joe decided that if he couldn't do some coke, spending quality time with his sugar baby would take the edge off. Man, she was amazing in the sack, he thought. He tried calling her a few times but only got her answering machine. Joe never left her a message because she was being kept by some rich dude and didn't want him to be aware of who was also given her some loving in his absence. If he had his druthers, he'd have the wife in the morning and his sugar at night.

Meanwhile, with nothing on his plate, he decided to contact the current Waters investigator on the Madoff case, one Sam Craven. After Joe identified himself as his replacement on the Madoff case, Sam asked him to come to his office. However, when he got there, Sam greeted him at the door, holding a folder in one hand and his suit jacket in the other.

"Sorry, place is a mess," Sam said, steering Joe toward the elevators instead. "Let's get some air."

When the men hit the street, Sam said, there was a little bodega a couple of blocks down where they could get a bite and talk. Both men ordered panini sandwiches with meat, cheese, lettuce, tomatoes, and hot sauce. To wash it down, they took cans of Dr. Brown's Celery Soda from a cooler and sat at a small table against the wall. After scarfing down the sandwiches, Sam and Joe felt abundantly satiated, allowing themselves long drags on the celery soda, which brought up loud satisfying belches.

Sam handed over his Madoff notes he had brought with him. "Joe, there's not much to say. Bernie's wife Ruth is barricaded in her apartment on East 66th and rarely goes out."

"Who's this person you refer to as O in your reports?" asked Joe.

"Oh yeah, that's Otto Klein. He's her live-in bodyguard," Sam said.

"A boy toy?" Joe asked.

Sam smiled at the question and said, "No, no he's a pro, ex-Mossad and, from what we know, an assassin. He also carries a licensed 9mm Glock semiautomatic."

Joe asked if Waters had tried to bug Ruth's apartment, but Sam said that it was impossible. The apartment was under surveillance by the feds 24/7. In addition, Sam said that the feds were probably monitoring all of Ruth's phone calls and e-mail. "They've thrown a blanket over everything," he said.

"Why all the fuss?" asked Joe.

"Because she knows where the money is," replied Sam. "Wait, I almost forgot, we did plant a GPS bug in her Mercedes. It's parked in a garage over on West 76th. If it rolls, we can track it anywhere it goes."

"It must cost a bundle, who's paying for all this?" asked Joe.

Sam went on to tell him that a couple of years ago some guys that lost a bundle put together what was internally referred to at the agency as "the group of pathetic losers." These guys had ponied up some cash and hired Waters to find where Bernie buried their investments, which made no sense.

"Look, even if Bernie did stash away a zillion dollars and we dug it up, what the fuck do you think we'd have to do with it? It all goes to the feds, the bankruptcy court. They decide who gets what, and I'll bet you dimes to dollars that the feds will keep most of it for tax evasion," Sam said, taking another gulp of soda.

"So why are they spending all this money on a fool's errand?"

"Because they had more money than God and wanted more. Because there was never enough money for them. Their lives revolved around making money. Now they're pissing away more money like they did years ago when they gave it to Bernie. They just can't accept that they made a mistake," Sam said in frustration.

"Oh, and guess what?" he added. "One of the 'big losers' wants to see you at his place at eleven-thirty tomorrow morning." Sam slipped a card to Joe where he had scribbled: Angelo Spatuzza, Hotel Majestic and Casino, Atlantic City, New Jersey, 609-555-1661.

Joe looked at the card for a moment and then a light went on in his head. "Is this the" he began, but before the words left his mouth, Sam put up his hand and nodded yes.

Joe sat back. An eerie chill seemed to engulf him. Angelo Spatuzza was reputed to be one of the most ruthless crime bosses in New Jersey. A man who was allegedly responsible for most of the bodies recently dug up in the New Jersey Meadowlands.

Chapter 3: Max

At first Max could only stare aimlessly at the limo as it picked up speed heading downtown, taking Sy to his next appointment. As he turned towards his building, he felt dizzy and stopped to take a deep breath, which made matters worse. The doorman, Ralph, came over to him, flashing a broad Irish smile, and inquired if he could be of assistance. Embarrassed, Max put an arm around Ralph to steady himself and told him that it was probably a case of low blood sugar.

"Thanks, Ralph, I need some fresh air. I'll go for a walk," Max reassured him, pointing to the footpath that skirts the East River.

It felt good to be out walking; the air was sharp and clean after the previous night's downpour. Every so often a launch would pass by carrying passengers to and from Roosevelt Island, just a half-mile off Manhattan's eastern shore. On a nice day, the footpath was rife with nannies pushing expensive baby strollers, tourists taking photos using the river as a backdrop, young and elderly couples walking hand in hand, and the obligatory jogger in his red, white, and blue Speedo.

Up ahead, Max noticed a father holding his daughter above the railing as she threw breadcrumbs to a pair of iridescent blue-green mallards. The little girl giggled as the ducks scurried to snatch each morsel of food. As Max watched the choreographic nature of the ducks, it came to him. He envisioned how to get Bernie out of prison. It was a eureka moment, and, in his excitement, he blindly turned, bumping into an elderly couple and nearly sending them to the ground. He apologized for his thoughtlessness before racing home to finalize the plan.

Anxious to put the plan to paper; the seven-floor elevator ride seemed to take forever. Once inside his apartment, he called out for Margery without a reply. He went over to the frig, their official message board, to see where she was.

"Gone to studio—lunch? Call me, Love U," Margery had left scribbled on a yellow Post-It.

Max decided that he needed to spread things out, so he cleared everything off the dining room table and gathered what he needed: a couple of notepads, his address book, adding machine, telephone, plenty of Post-Its, a calendar, his laptop and printer. Then he put on some classical piano music and got to his task.

To simplify his task, Max envisioned his role as the writer, director, and producer of a movie. It was his job to outline the plan, hire and direct the actors and crew, design and order the costumes and props, research and choose the locations, purchase the materials, estimate the costs, and then make a presentation to his investor, Sy, by Friday. Max knew that in order to get Sy's approval, all the I's must be dotted and all the T's must be crossed. He quickly dismissed the thought that Sy might be shopping the job around or looking for ideas. That would be too dicey, too dangerous because there was always a chance of a leak.

Realizing that he had to assemble a professional crew, Max listed the various roles and assignments for the job on one side of a ledger, and on the other side, he added the names of people he had worked with in the past, people he felt he could depend on. The problem was, of course, how many would be available on short notice? What's more, how many had enough time to devote to the enterprise to carry out their parts?

He also realized that he couldn't reach out to them until he got the okay from Sy and knew what the estimated timetable was for the extraction. He wasn't sure if Sy wanted to launch the plan in a few weeks or a few months.

Even as he immersed himself in the work, a recurrent thought kept bothering him. "What the hell am I doing?" he kept asking himself.

Max didn't mind living on the edge. It was exciting and rewarding sometimes, but this, even if they were successful in getting Bernie out of prison, where could they hide? Could he live with the fact that if the shit hit the fan, everyone would be in jail or worse? He didn't want to be theoretically glib as to the consequences of his actions.

Max pushed back from the table and went into the bathroom to splash some cold water on his face. Toweling off in front of the mirror, he looked at his reflection and thought to himself that he'd come a long way in the past several years. Back when he worked at the advertising agency his role model was his boss, Hank Oscar, a high-pressure account executive, a smooth-talking, hard-drinking, John-Barrymore-looking playboy. With a trophy wife and perfect children ensconced in the tony village of Greenwich, Connecticut, Hank cut a wide path up and down Manhattan's East Side, seducing the crème de la crème. When it came to women, Hank considered himself a carnivore whose motto was, "Select only well-heeled, aged cuts. Don't waste my time on the young stuff. Gimme a rich, middle-aged dame anytime." Hank was also known to take his subordinates under his wing when he needed a new sidekick to troll for women, preferably a young, good-looking stud he could use as bait on the shark-infested streets of the Upper East Side.

"You gotta move to Manhattan, boy. What's this shit about living in Brooklyn?" Hank often said. "You want to be where the action is, and that's Manhattan's Silk Stocking District." Then, pausing for effect, he said, "Tell ya what I want you to do. Run an ad in the Times, y'know 'Young Ad Exec Seeks Furnished Apt Upper East Side' Blah, blah, blah."

After a few days Max had received a phone call in response to his query from a woman who said she had an apartment for rent. However, when Max told Hank of the phone call and where the apartment was located over lunch, Hank could only laugh. He told Max that it was a prank call.

"She's shitting you," he said. "50 Sutton Place South, my ass, that's the ritziest place in the city. I mean, fuckin' governor, Mario Cuomo used to live there," Hank said, spilling his martini.

Well, Hank Oscar could not have been so right and so terribly wrong at the same time. Yes, the apartment building at 50 Sutton Place South was a homestead for Manhattan's royalty, but the offer was genuine. The owner, Ms. Margery Ramsden Martin, was sincere in her desire to rent her six-room, fully furnished luxury apartment to the right gentleman. What she hadn't planned on was falling head over heels in love with her new tenant.

It was love at first sight for both Max and Margery, and the ensuing grasping, kissing, ripping of clothes off each other, and the myriad of lovemaking positions and sites boggled the mind. In the height of passion nothing was spared, the overstuffed leather couch, the Jacuzzi, the Henry-the-Eighth mahogany dining room table, the Berber carpet, the adjustable king-sized bed It was the Kama Sutra, Brooklyn style.

And yet, two people could not have been so dissimilar. Margery was forty-three years old; her mother Grace had died when she was six years old. Her father, George Ramsden Martin, was a Member of British Parliament with a grand estate in Cheshire. Margery had attended Woldingham, an exclusive English boarding school in Surrey, as well as art schools in England and Scotland before meeting and marrying a dashing RAF pilot twenty years her senior. The couple had moved to Egypt to launch an airfreight cargo company that ferried khat, a narcotic plant, from the Horn of Africa to England. Their company flourished as the drug became a source of payment to African workers in Liverpool and Manchester. However, after Parliament reclassified the plant as a 'Class C Narcotic,' khat was banned in England, essentially putting them out of business. Soon after, Margery and her husband separated after seven years of marriage with Margery moving to New York and her ex-husband, Brad, remaining in Cairo with his mistress and the two children he'd had by her.

Max, on the other hand, was thirty-four years of age. His father, Ben, was a printer and his mother, Etta, worked as a clerk at the Board of Education. They lived in a three-room apartment in the rough and tumble Brownsville section of Brooklyn. Max found work at various factories in Manhattan to supplement what money his parents could afford to loan him for college. He graduated with a bachelor of the arts Degree from the City College of New York, which prepared him for nothing in particular.

After graduation Max got an offer from a fellow classmate whose father was opening a film production studio in Manhattan. The production company, MPO, had won many awards for their commercials and documentaries in the Baltimore-Washington, DC area. They were noted for their flair and outside-the-box approach. The term 'refreshing' was often used by the media to describe their work.

In a short time, Max, became an important part of the production company's growth. They put Max in a suit, gave him an attaché case, some business cards, sample reels of their work, and he'd hit the sidewalk looking for business. Max's plan, if you could call it a plan, was to ignore the small-time hustle and concentrate where the big money was being doled out —the advertising agencies. In a short while, it became common knowledge that Max was a born hustler, and

Madison Avenue soon came calling. After entertaining some offers from boutique shops, one of the largest ad agencies in the city, Emerson Advertising, requested a sit-down meeting.

Max had heard of Emerson and how difficult it was to even get an interview. The agency was inundated with job applications from all over the world, and here was this nebbish from Brooklyn, no less, invited to their corporate headquarters on Madison Avenue. He went ballistic; it was jumping-up-and-down time. Max decided the morning of his appointment at Emerson that he wouldn't refuse any reasonable offer they made. His mantra was, "Get in the door and claw your way up." So, when they mentioned that, "the successful candidate would have to go through a one-year training program," he stood up, put out his hand, and said, "When do I start?"

Chapter 4: Joe

Joe stopped to relieve himself in his second-floor bathroom before coming down the stairs to the kitchen. His wife, Patty, was sitting at a small, midcentury modern Formica table in the kitchen, cradling a cup of tea while watching the morning news on a small television. Joe nodded in her direction as he opened the refrigerator door, looking for milk for his coffee.

Unable to find any he glanced disapprovingly at Patty who beat him to the punch, saying, "The kids finished it."

"You got any of that powdered stuff?" Joe asked, slamming the door in disgust.

"Don't go breaking the—" Patty started to say.

"Y'know, I don't need this attitude," Joe responded heading back upstairs.

"Where you going?" Patty inquired. When Joe didn't answer her, she followed him up the stairs. "What does this mean? You disappearing again?"

Joe ignored her and began getting dressed.

"You think I don't know what's going on? You come home when you decide to come home, smelling like those cheap whores," she taunted him.

"Don't start that shit with me again. I've told you that's what I do. That's what puts bread on the table," he replied.

"Yeah, and that explains the lipstick on your jockey shorts. You think I'm stupid?" she cried out in desperation.

Joe hurriedly finished dressing, grabbed his cigarettes and wallet off his dresser, and started to leave, with Patty following him down the stairs.

"What time will you be home?" she asked, lighting a cigarette.

"I'll call you," Joe responded looking for his car keys, which he usually placed on a table near the front door. Unable to locate them, he turned to Patty.

"Where's the fuckin' keys?" he asked, moving closer to her.

She instinctively moved back at Joe's approach.

"Give me the keys, Patty. I'll only say this once," he threatened.

Patty reached into her bathrobe and, waving the car keys at Joe, tossed them at him, hitting him in the face. Joe took one step towards Patty, raised his hand as if he was going to strike her, then looked around the floor for the keys. He bent down to retrieved them, then pushed past Patty on his way out the door.

Patty took a long drag on her cigarette, then deftly flicked it in Joe's direction as she slammed the door, murmuring to herself, "And don't come back."

Glancing at his watch, Joe had about two hours to get down to Atlantic City and his appointment with Angelo Spatuzza. He was cutting it close, but if the roads were clear, he could make it. He told himself that he had to calm down, he was letting every little thing set him off—work, wife, girlfriend—he was getting that itch and the only way to scratch it was the white powder. He could have gotten some last night at the club but passed on the nickel bag he was offered. Now he had the shakes and no way to control them. He stopped at a Burger King on the turnpike and bought a cold bottle of water. He then went into the men's room, grabbed some paper towels, and with his head over the sink, poured the bottle of water over his head, much to the chagrin of the other patrons in the restroom. The shock of the cold water stopped the shakes, though, and he was able to continue his trip to Atlantic City.

Looking in his rearview mirror he saw a tired, disheveled man with wild hair and bloodshot eyes. When he ran his hands through his wet hair in an attempt to make himself look presentable, it didn't work. He looked and smelt like he had climbed out of a dumpster. Hitting the strip at eighty miles per hour, he jammed on the brakes just short of passing through a red traffic light. Then, after what seemed like an eternity, the light turned green, and Joe proceeded looking to his right and left for the Hotel Majestic & Casino's entrance. Finally, at almost the end of the strip, he saw the flashing neon sign of the Majestic Hotel.

Leaving his car with the valet, he hurried to the concierge desk and asked for Angelo Spatuzza. The concierge picked up his phone and, after conferring with someone on the other end, told Joe that someone would be down to get him. After only a few moments, one of Angelo's soldiers came up behind Joe and motioned with his head for the investigator to follow him. Once in the elevator, the soldier positioned himself behind Joe and patted him down. The ride up to the fifteenth floor took only a few seconds, opening to the rooftop pool and spa. Joe followed the man into the spa where they were met by another soldier, who instructed him to disrobe and join Mr. Spatuzza in the steam room. At first Joe didn't know what to make of his instructions until they emphasized that it was not a request, it was an order. One did not refuse Mr. Spatuzza's orders.

Joe stripped down and tied a towel around his waist, leaving his clothes in a heap on the floor. He paused at the large glass door leading into the steam room and glanced back at the two men who motioned for him to enter. The first thing that hit Joe was the searing heat that momentarily took his breath away. Bringing his hand up to his eyes, he tried to cut through the mist by fanning himself. It had little effect.

Out of the fog, a voice said, "Come, come. I've been expecting you."

Joe turned to his right and saw a little fat man wearing what looked like a toga sitting on a white throne. He rubbed his eyes in disbelief, but as he got closer, he saw that it was in fact a bald man wearing a toga and waving a two-foot bejeweled ivory scepter in the air.

"I am Angelo Spatuzza, prefect and commander of all that one can see," he said in a singsong fashion.

"I'm proud and, and, happy to meet you," stuttered Joe.

"Have you brought me my money?" asked the so-called prefect.

"I'm trying to I mean, I'm working at it," replied Joe.

Spatuzza cut the act for a second, dropping his voice into a normal register. "Have you been here before? I don't remember you."

"No, your highness, I come from faraway to find to return what is yours," Joe said.

However, this didn't register exactly how he thought it would. On the contrary, it made matters worse. The prefect rose to his full five-foot-five stature and, after peeing in his toga, marched out of the steam room.

After he had left, Joe removed the towel from his waist and mopped the sweat from his face. He didn't know whether he should laugh or cry.

A few moments later the door opened, and someone said, "You can come out now."

Joe put his towel back on and made his way out of the steam room. There waiting for him was an impeccably dressed, tall, thin man who introduced himself as Signore Sergio Leone in a thick Italian accent.

"You dress, and they will take you to my office, yes?" he said before turning and marching away.

So far, this has been a very interesting and unusual day, Joe thought. "Did I get this right? That little guy in the toga, he's the reputed mobster that cuts up people to feed to his fish? Am I fuckin' crazy or what?"

The boys, soldiers, or maybe the king's guard, Joe mused to himself, took him down a flight of stairs to Sergio's office. His first impression of the office was one of opulence. It was right out of what you'd see in a villa on Lake Como. Everything was gold and red and expensive.

Sergio motioned for Joe to sit in an armchair directly opposite his desk and told the soldiers to wait outside. He began by cautioning Joe to never relate what he saw and heard in the steam room to anybody. If it ever got back to the signore that he said something, Spatuzza's family would slaughter him, his family, his friends, his neighbors, and their pets.

"So, you understand?" he asked Joe as if it was no big thing, something they regularly did to those who disobey their orders.

"I saw nothing, I heard nothing," Joe said.

To this, Sergio put his hand together in sort of a prayer and nodded his approval.

"Tell me, where are your people from?" he asked.

"The south ah, Reggio Calabria," Joe replied.

"Bene," replied Sergio knowingly. "Have you ever been there?"

"No, I've always hoped to go, but no," Joe said truthfully.

"The money, our money," Sergio emphasized, touching his chest, "do you know where it is?"

"No, but it's my job to find it," Joe said.

Sergio sat there expressionless.

"Signore Leone," he continued, "I have just been assigned your case only yesterday. It looks like there's been very little progress through let's say using the regular channels. Most of what I've seen are surveillance reports of Bernie Madoff's wife, Ruth."

"What do you mean by regular channels?" Sergio asked.

"Banks, credit reporting agencies, real estate records, travel agencies, federal and state agencies, that kind of stuff," Joe said.

"So, what do you need?" Sergio asked with a smile.

Joe sat back and said, "I need her psychiatric file."

"And who has this?" Sergio inquired.

"She's seeing a psychiatrist on East 78th Street in the city," replied Joe.

"And what do you think you'll find in his records?" Sergio asked.

"Don't know till I look," said Joe.

He proceeded to tick off things he hoped were in the file. "If he's like most shrinks he'd first delve into her past, when Bernie was setting up his Ponzi scheme. Look, Bernie's smart, but he needed help putting the software programs together. I need the names of the programmers who did it. She might know them and might have mentioned them during one of her sessions. Another thing she might have mentioned is the international connection. Bernie must have had someone help him get the money out of the country—you know, someplace safe, with no disclosure and definitely no extradition to the US."

Sergio held up a hand. "Joe, before we go any further, I want you to understand our position, so to speak. The money, I don't know exactly how much we gave to Madoff, but let's say it put us in an embarrassing position. That can't happen, it makes us look weak, capische?" Sergio let what he said sink in.

Joe nodded slowly. "So, can you get me the files?" he asked.

"It can be arranged. And what do I get in return?" asked Sergio.

"What do you want?"

"I want information," Sergio responded.

"What kind of information?" Joe asked.

"Let's say I want some information in a police file. Can you get me that?" Sergio asked.

"If it's not highly classified, I could," said Joe.

"What is considered highly classified?" Sergio asked.

"That would be in a file that our company was prohibited to retrieve," Joe said.

"How would you know the file was highly classified?" Sergio inquired.

"It would probably say I'm denied access."

Sergio sat forward. "Let's do this. I'll give you some names, people's names you tell me what you can about them and I'll see about getting you Ruth Madoff's psychiatrist's file, okay?

"One more thing, we never communicate by phone, text, or email. We use runners, couriers. When we send you something, there must be a handshake; you must go in person to our office in New York to send and receive your messages. The company name is Globe Express on 140 Mulberry Street. When you're there you'll ask for Tina. They will call you if there is something for you. Do you understand my instructions?" Sergio asked.

"Yes. When I receive the names you want run, I'll give Tina the shrink's name and address," Joe replied.

With that, Sergio pushed a button, and the two soldiers entered the room. He rose from his chair and extended his hand to say, "Arrivederci."

On his way to get his car, Joe thought of what had just transpired and how it was going to change his relationship at Waters. After all, he was now working for both Waters and the Mob.

Chapter 5: Max

After briefly explaining to Margery that he was working on an assignment for Sy, Max spent the next twenty-four hours methodically organizing elements of the plan to spring Bernie Madoff from the federal penitentiary in Butner, North Carolina. Now it was time to send it to Sy. Max plugged the encryption device into his computer's USB port. After entering his password, the device automatically logged onto Sy's computer, and a message appeared on Max's screen.

"Are you ready to send or receive?"

Max clicked send and instantly the complete plan, all twenty-six pages of documents, photographs, drawings, timetables, budget estimates, and summaries, was encoded into an unbreakable format and forwarded to Sy's computer, which had the unique ability to decode the message.

Exhausted, both mentally and physically, Max awaited Sy's response for one hour, two hours, three hours. Just as the fourth hour was beginning, the screen informed Max that he had a message. He downloaded the message, whereupon three pages of questions and comments from Sy appeared on his screen.

"What if someone checks the doctor's credentials?"

"What if there's bad weather at the extraction site?"

"Why pay the crew in advance?"

Max spent the next hour or so, explaining and defending his plan, then sent the rebuttal off to Sy. While he awaited a response, his mind drifted back to a night when he got a call from Sy, completely out of the blue, asking him to come to his office on Wall Street. G.C. Waverly Investment Bank's offices were in a modern luxury high-rise just a short walk from the New York Stock Exchange. Sy didn't give a reason for the meeting, much less why he was calling it at 8 p.m. Max had assumed that the offices were closed at that time of the day.

That was far from the truth. Max soon learned that G.C. Waverly's offices were always open because somewhere on earth someone wants to buy or sell something—stocks, bonds, derivatives... anything. In addition, ever since 9/11, every building near Wall Street had beefed up their security, and Max had to pass through a security check similar to those at airports. Only after confirming his appointment did he receive a temporary badge allowing him access to a specific floor. Max was then escorted to a private elevator, which brought him to, he assumed since it had no floor designation, just a star, the top floor.

Waiting for him as he exited the elevator was a burly-looking man whose sports jacket bulged at the chest suggesting he was carrying a very large gun. He took Max through a private dining room into a lounge where Sy was seated on a leather couch smoking what smelled like a joint. The room was decorated in cream-colored, butter-soft leather chairs and couches. The Tiffany table lamps gave off a dazzling array of colors that reflected off the floor-to-ceiling windows. The room was filled with museum-quality antiques that mysteriously worked together. Knowing Sy, he had probably commissioned the best interior designers in New York to decorate his suite.

Sy took a couple long drags on his cigarette while gazing out the window at the city, then, without looking toward Max, said, "Want a hit?" Max could see that Sy was peacefully off in La-La-Land. He denied the offer whereby Sy snapped back, saying, "I get my shit from a reputable dealer in the Village," he took another drag.

"Looks like a Pall Mall or Camel, doesn't it?" he said with a slur, holding up the joint for Max to see. Brushing some ash from his white shirt, Sy said in an uncharacteristically melancholy voice, "Howie was my best friend... my only friend in the world."

Max knew that Howie and Sy had looked upon each other as brothers. Sy's last conversation with Howie was the day he shipped off from Camp Lejeune to Vietnam. Forty-five days later he learned that Howie was dead.

"His chopper was shot down over the Mekong Delta and all onboard were killed," Sy said, shaking his head.

Both men sat quietly staring out at the city until Max rose and, spotting a bar against the wall, helped himself to a couple of fingers of a single malt, neat. Max also felt the loss of Howie. Howie was Max's older cousin on his mother's side and had lived just around the corner from them. They played basketball and stickball together, and almost every Friday night they had dinner together in either his tiny apartment or Howie's.

"Help me up," Sy had commanded. "Let's go see Howie."

As Max got to his feet to help Sy, one of Sy's burly bodyguards moved between them, telling Max that it was okay, he'd help him. The guard gently lifted Sy to his feet, and with Sy in tow; they all took the elevator down to the basement garage. By the time the elevator reached the basement, the limo was waiting with its back doors open.

Without a word of instruction, the limo made its way slowly across town to the Brooklyn Bridge, where it picked up speed to enter the Brooklyn-Queens Expressway. After only a fifteen-minute ride, the limo entered the Cypress Hills National Cemetery. Max later learned that Sy had lobbied Congress to have

Howie's remains brought from Vietnam back to Brooklyn and interred in this famous Civil War cemetery.

When Sy was told initially by the Department of Veterans Affairs that the cemetery was filled, he took it upon himself to canvass the grounds to see if he could find a spot for Howie, which he did next to the 1876 grave of Sergeant John Martin, 90th Coast Artillery, 7th Cavalry at The Battle of the Little Big Horn. Sy ultimately reimbursed the Department of Veterans Affairs for all the costs associated with Howie's internment.

"Stop, stop," Sy shouted. "He's here." Max got out of the car and followed a staggering Sy down a long row of crosses until they came to a grave emblazoned with the Star of David. Shaking his head, Sy reached out to touch Howie's gravestone. Then he fell to his knees and began to cry.

"You couldn't wait for me?" he said to the gravestone. "That fuckin' war!" he shouted. Then he began ripping out weeds from around Howie's grave. After several minutes, Sy looked up and asked for help to the limo.

Once inside, he wiped his eyes with a cloth and announced, "I've got the hungry horrors. Let's get breakfast at the Coby."

The Coby Diner was a twenty-four-hour diner in Coney Island. Once again, the driver knew exactly where the diner was and how to get there as quickly as possible. In less than twenty minutes, Sy and Max were seated on stools watching a short-order cook simultaneously flip pancakes, eggs, ham, sausage, and hashbrown potatoes all while taking food orders from waitresses that spoke in diner-gibberish. Thankfully, on the way back to Max's apartment, an exhausted Sy slept. It was the first time but not the last that Max saw how weed affected Sy.

Twenty minutes later he got his response—more questions and comments. Once again Max dutifully answered Sy's questions and forwarded them back.

This time, it took Sy only seven minutes to respond in 18-point capitals: "GO."

Relieved, Max stared at his computer screen. He had just gotten the green light to conduct the most elaborate and expensive jailbreak in history. One that, if successful, would go down in the annals of crime with the likes of The Great Train Robbery of 1903, the 1981 Brink's job, and the 1990 Gardner Museum heist.

The plan was so diabolically simple that it gave Max the jitters just thinking about it. He knew that its success or failure were linked to keeping to a precise timetable. Any glitches and it would be curtains for him.

Chapter 6: Joe

Joe returned home from Atlantic City just as his daughters were jumping off their school bus.

"Hey, how about a hug?" Joe said, getting out of his car. Surprised to see their dad waiting for them, the girls sprinted to give him a big hug, their ponytails flying behind them. They felt happy and warm in his arms as he lifted them collectively off the ground. He wondered where Patty was.

"Daddy, Mom said we could get a puppy!" his ten-year-old Rosie exclaimed.

"Oh boy, you're getting to be such big girls, Daddy can no longer carry you," he gently put them down.

"I'm hungry," Caroline, his twelve-year-old, said. "Can we go to McDonald's, Dad?"

"Sure, let me change my clothes and we'll go," he said. After washing up, Joe went into his basement office and looked through the files Sam Craven had given him on Ruth Madoff's comings and goings. It seems that shortly after Bernie had copped a plea with the feds, Ruth started seeing a Ben Levine, MD, every other week. Craven had put Psychiatrist in the margin next to his name. His office was located in a brownstone, which the records indicated he owned, at 787 East 54th Street. Joe Googled his bio and found that he was a graduate of Columbia Medical School and had completed his residency at Bellevue Hospital, where he received his board certification in psychiatry. Being that his office was located on the

Upper East Side, Joe surmised that his practice focused on rich matrons suffering from, amongst other things 'schadenfreude,' a common class-conscience malady in which one derives pleasure from the misfortunes of others. Joe was certain that with his roster of clients, Doctor Levine had paid off his student loans ages ago.

"Daddy, Daddy, we're ready!" cried the kids in unison.

"Be right up," replied Joe as he printed the doctor's name and address onto a sheet of paper, folded it, and placed it in an envelope. He planned to tell Tina at Global who the recipient was in person. Then he and the kids were off to McDonalds. Halfway through their Quarter Pounders, fries, and Cokes, though, Joe received a frantic call from his sugar baby. It seemed that her sponsor took umbrage with the fact that she was shacking up with an occasional interloper. He had unceremoniously kicked her out of his condo.

"What am I to do? I don't have anywhere to go. Joe, have you got a place for me?" she asked. Upon hearing her wailing, Joe told the kids that he had to take this call and went outside of the restaurant where they could talk.

"Where are you now?" he asked.

"I'm downstairs in the lobby and, and the doorman wants me to leave." Joe thought to himself that if he were still on the force, he would have told her to put the doorman on the phone and read him the riot act. But that wouldn't help now, he had to think quickly and get her to someplace safe. Where, where, where?

"Okay, I want you to go to the Best Western Motel on 8th Ave and 51st Street. You got cab fare?" he asked.

"I've got maybe forty-fifty bucks to my name," she said.

"Good. When you get there ask for Arty, Arthur Rothstein, the manager. I'll call him and make arrangements. Stay there tonight, and I'll come get you in the morning."

"Can't you come now? I need you," she begged.

"I can't, I've got my kids with me."

When Joe called the Best Western reception desk, they told him that Mr. Rothstein was out and that they would put Ms. Baures up for the night if he gave them his credit card, which he did. Joe then called his sugar back and told her she was all set for the night and that he'd be over in the morning.

"But please, you've gotta come now I haven't got anything, he put my things in storage. You owe me, didn't I take care of you?"

"Calm down, honey, I'll be there tomorrow. For now get your sweet little ass down to the Best Western," Joe said. The thought then occurred to him that Sugar might pose a problem in the future in that she might be what is commonly referred to as "high maintenance."

When Joe finally got back to his kids, they peppered him with probing questions for which he had to improvise—well, lie a little.

"Daddy's got to help someone who's in trouble, and —" he began, when out of the blue Caroline asked, "Is this about your girlfriend?"

Where the hell did that come from? He thought.

"No, no," he tried lying his way out of it. "It's business and who told you Daddy has a girlfriend?"

"Mommy said you have a girlfriend and that's why you're not home when we go to sleep," she said sounding like her mother.

"Oh, baby, you're my girlfriends my only girlfriends," he said messing their hair.

Joe made up his mind to have a talk with Patty about her not being home when the kids got off the school bus and the shit she was dishing out about 'the girlfriend.'

It was stop-and-go traffic the next morning all the way into the city, and Joe, already aggravated, had to think of what he could do with Sugar. When he stopped at the motel's front desk to ask what room

Mary Baures was in, Mr. Rothstein came out of his office to greet Joe with apologies. He said that the kids on duty last night had run his credit card. He couldn't comp the room, but would provide a full breakfast for Joe's guest and himself. Joe reassured him that he understood and appreciated his offer.

Joe took the elevator to the fifth floor and knocked on Room 515. After a few brief moments, Mary opened the door with the chain on, saw it was Joe, and fumbled with the chain, finally allowing Joe to enter. Mary had nothing but a blanket wrapped around her, which fell to the ground as they embraced.

Oh man, he said to himself as he became consumed with lust. Undressing as quickly as he could, they embraced and began making love on the edge of the bed, then in the middle of the bed, then on the little desk against the wall, and finally, on the carpet. Spent, they lay there panting and staring at the ceiling.

It doesn't get any better she's so easy to love, he thought. If there was one thing in life that Sugar was good at it, it was hands down satisfying a man. She had all the moves, the moans, the gentle biting and scratching, the whole shebang. She was a pro.

After a long, badly needed shower, with time out for another quick joust, they dressed and hurried down to the dining room for breakfast. Mr. Rothstein had already advised the dining room staff that their breakfast was on the house, and he stopped to say hello. This was his way of thanking Joe for coming to his help years ago when he found the body of a teenage prostitute in one of their rooms. Joe and his partner had carried the body out of the hotel and then conveniently discovered it sometime later in the alley. No mention was ever given of the Best Western in their report.

"Now tell me what happened with, what's his name?" Joe asked sipping his coffee.

"His name is Jerry, Jerry Shaw," she said looking around to make sure they weren't overheard.

"Okay, what did Jerry say and do?" Joe asked.

"He said, quote, I know you're fucking around and I want you out of my place immediately," Sugar said. "He said my things would be packed up and brought to a storage locker and that the doorman would give me the key tomorrow, meaning today. That he's having the locks changed to the condo, cancelling my credit cards, my debit card, department store credit cards, and anything and everything he pays for on my behalf," she said with a shiver.

"What proof did he give you?" Joe asked.

"Oh please, he knows," she said.

"That you're fucking an ex-cop?" he said. "Do you like this guy?"

"What's not to like?" she hedged. "He's rich I mean, like, fuckin' crazy rich."

"Would he take you back?" Joe asked.

"I don't know, I've never seen him this angry. Maybe," she said hopefully.

"Okay, let's do this. We'll pick up the key to the storage locker, then your things, and then I've got an errand downtown."

It turned out that everything went as expected, without a glitch, and they finally ended up at Global on Mulberry Street where Joe picked up an envelope from Sergio Leone, most likely the people he wanted him to run through the police database. In return, he gave the receptionist Tina an envelope that contained the name and address of Ruth Madoff's psychiatrist. Joe put any thoughts out of his mind on how Sergio was planning on getting Ruth's psychiatric file. He just needed it.

Joe still had the problem of what to do with Sugar. He didn't have access to the kind of money to set her up in new digs. He decided to get her out of the City, find her somewhere cheaper to stay closer to his home. A place he could get to on short notice, the thought, and shag her if the mood was right. The thought got him excited and after aimlessly running around he found a small motel just a few miles from his home. Even better, he was able to get a walk-in, ground-floor room at the rear of the building where their comings and goings would not be noticed. He took the room for a week and paid in cash. With that out of the way, they decided to break in the king-sized Posturepedic mattress.

Chapter 7: Max

Max was elated and at the same time frightened that he might have bitten off more than he could chew. Pushing back from the table he walked over to a pair of floor-to-ceiling windows and yanked on the curtains drawstring exposing a raw mist that had engulfed the city. Below cars scurried up and down Sutton Place with headlights ablaze and wipers racing.

He braced himself against the window. "What the fuck have I done?" He walked into the kitchen and opened the refrigerator door, aimlessly gazing at its contents. It crossed his mind that this might be a case of buyer's remorse, reminiscent of his days at the advertising agency, where he created campaigns to sell products that people didn't want or need and then hoped they wouldn't return it. He decided that he had to tell Margery exactly what he was planning to do for Sy. That it was dangerous and might blow up in their faces. He had to give her the option of saying, 'No, it's all yours, baby. Keep me out of it!'

He went into the bathroom and splashed cold water on his face. Looking up at the mirror, he saw through bloodshot eyes flashbacks of the various scenarios he'd brainstormed. He had studied the prison's layout for hours on Google's Satellite Maps and saw that the prison abutted a thick forest on one side separated by a two-lane service road. On the other side of the road, there was what looked like a chain-link fence of an indeterminate height enclosing a baseball field. He contemplated attacking the prison from the woods when the prisoners were playing on the field. If they could isolate Bernie from the other inmates while he was on the field they might be able to extract him by helicopter.

Max had ultimately ruled this scenario out, fearing that a quasi-military option would result in too much bloodshed. His idea was to grab Bernie without the need for casualties on either side. That meant that the extraction had to be attempted outside the confines of the prison grounds on neutral turf. He thought that if Bernie could fake an illness, they could grab the ambulance on its way to the hospital, but this, too, was unrealistic since a quarter of a mile away from his prison was a large federal correctional hospital. Nope, their best bet was to get Bernie out of prison on some pretense where they had a modicum of control. The plan that he ultimately decided on, and which was approved by Sy, did exactly that. Naturally, being a cunning businessman, Sy wanted an idea of its success-to-failure ratio. The best that Max could guesstimate was 70% success and 30% failure.

Anxious to get the ball rolling, Max called the first two names on his list, Stan Sabin, AKA The Major, and Sally Litton, AKA His Lady, to bounce his proposal off. Max had employed these two fine actors in the past and felt confident they could pull off their roles. He asked them to meet him at The Barn, a theatrical hangout on the Lower West Side.

Max took a taxi downtown arriving at The Barn some twenty minutes earlier than the appointed time. He settled into a tight-fitting wooden booth at the back of the bar. The Barn was a classic throwback to Prohibition, its walls covered with photos of old-timey actors, celebrities of a foregone era, and nefarious Tammany Hall politicians who ran the city for their own financial gain during the turn of the century. After ordering a Guinness, Max relaxed and watched the antics of a couple men at the bar. They were arguing about a prizefight the night before between a young up-and-coming Irish lad who lost a close decision to a journeyman fighter from New Jersey.

"He stole the decision," the first man said.

"No, no, no, the fix was in," his friend said.

"But he's one of Sullivan's boys."

"So?" the other man said.

"So, Sullivan protects his boys," the first man said.

"So, he's told when to take a fall, and last night was how he paid his dues."

"Ah, come on they don't do that anymore," the first man said.

"Ah, you're still smoking that angel dust, aren't you?" the other man was saying when into the bar strode the Major and, on his arm, His Lady.

"Greetings and salutations to all," said the Major to the patrons at the bar. Each raised their drinks to salute him, and he acknowledged them with a touch of his index finger to the brim of his hat. Max rose as they approached, raising his Guinness as a greeting, and after a brief hug, they settled down with refreshments and began to discuss the reason for the impromptu meeting.

Without going into too many details Max first asked if they were available for the next few weeks. Then he told them that the mark was a prisoner at a federal penitentiary in the heart of Dixie and that they would be part of a group that would extract him from prison. At this point Sally, unable to contain herself, asked, "Is he is he someone we know like one of the producers who ran away with our money?"

"Close but no cigar," said Max with a smile. They spent the next several minutes going over the minutiae of their roles. The prison was in North Carolina, the extraction depended on precise timing, and it was fraught with danger. Their roles would be playing a medical doctor and his nurse. The setting would be a private house nestled in the woods, equipped with medical monitoring displays as in a hospital room. Their patient would be an elderly woman. Sensing that he might have scared them off, Max switched to their possible rewards.

"Okay," he began. "If we pull this off, you'll both be financially set for life."

"Exactly what do you mean, Max?" the Major asked.

"If all goes as planned, you'll receive two million dollars," Max replied. Stunned, the Major and His Lady sat there uncharacteristically speechless.

"We'll earn two million dollars?" the Major whispered.

"Yep," replied Max. The Major and His Lady pressed their backs against the solid wooden booth and looked at each other.

"You are serious, Max?" asked the Lady.

"Yep," said Max. "The money will be deposited in an offshore financial institution that you'll have complete and sole control of from anywhere in the world."

"For the first time in my life," the Major began, "I am speechless," he found his lifelong partner's hand and pressed it to his lips. "If she says yes," he looked into her eyes, "we'll break a leg for you. No, no, no both legs," he said kissing the palm of her hand.

Sally, beginning to tear up, replied, "Yes, my Lord, your faithful Lady will follow you to the ends of the earth."

"Good, I was praying you'd join with me on what will be your last and most rewarding performance," replied Max.

While the lovers silently embraced, Max thought for the first time about the mark, Bernie Madoff. He, too, had a life and love like the Major and His Lady. Bernie's wife Ruth had also been a faithful and loyal companion for all of his life. The two of them had suffered unspeakable sorrow and that Bernie's sentence was a form of cruel and unusual punishment based solely on what the prosecution felt was politically correct and would advance their own political careers. After all, the boys on Wall Street stole trillions of dollars from countless millions of investors and were they prosecuted? No, they were bailed out. They were rewarded with million-dollar bonuses and told to continue the true role of Wall Street in America: the fleecing of the unsuspected investor into larger, more complex, and grandiose scams all with the full knowledge that when the shit hit the fan, as it would again, the taxpayers would have to clean it up.

Max told them that they'd hear from him in several days and that he wanted them to have passport photos taken. Once they had the photos in hand, they were to contact him. He'd send a courier to collect them. Then, smiling at them, he raised his glass to toast the occasion saying, "God willing our final act will bring rave reviews."

Chapter 8: Joe

After spending a sleepless night thinking of what he could do regarding Sugar's predicament, Joe came up with a plan to investigate Jerry Shaw, the ex-boyfriend, and get the dirt on him. He figured the condo was relatively new and had, most likely, a state-of-the-art security system. That meant video cameras with 24/7 digital recorders, probably archived in the cloud. Now if he could get his hands on the codes to access the files, there might be compromising shots of Sugar and Jerry. Joe vaguely remembered something that Sugar once said, that 'Jerry was so horny after he had a few drinks, he liked to dry hump her in the elevator.' Man, if he could get a copy of one of their sessions, it would be golden.

He made a mental note to ask the research department at Waters if they could download the files. Then again, maybe not. They'd probably give him some shit about how it was connected to his case and if it would open them up to a lawsuit. No, no, if it were possible, it had to be on the QT and off the grid.

Sometimes Joe wondered to himself if Sugar was worth all the aggravation, but he always determined she was one in a million and that was good enough for him. Just the thought of a morning shag with Sugar was enough to start the day off right. Maybe for once, he thought, it might work out all right. With that thought in mind, he put the pedal to the metal all the way to her motel. However, when he entered her room, she was gone and so were all her belongings. Worried for her safety, he called her on her cell.

It rang a few times before she finally answered, "Joe, I'll call you right back."

Stunned, Joe sat on the edge of her bed, staring at his phone, waiting for her call.

After a few minutes, she pinged him back.

"Joe, Jerry called and said he was sorry. He said that he loved me and that my affair with you was, well, more than he could handle. It just broke him up. He was weeping on the phone," she said.

Joe sat there on the crumpled bed sheets unable to say anything.

"Joe, are you there?" she asked.

"Yeah, yeah," he said.

"Look, I told him that you and I were through, that I won't see you anymore. Do you understand?"

"Sugar, I do," he blurted out.

"No, you don't. I've got kids, a little boy and girl. They live with their father," she said.

"I didn't know," Joe said.

"That's because you never asked," she said bluntly. "Jerry's going to help me, help me have a relationship with them. They're living in Wisconsin and..." Mary began to cry. "God, I miss them so much, and this is my only chance. He's a good man, Joe, and he loves me."

"Sugar, you're one in a million. I wish you all the happiness in the world," Joe said and broke the connection. He sat for a few moments more, wiped his nose with a towel, and slowly closed the motel door. He got into his car and, with tears in his eyes, headed for his office.

Waters was busy when Joe arrived.

"What's going on?" he asked the receptionist.

"I don't know. If I told you, I'd have to kill you," she smiled. Joe realized for the first time he belonged there.

It wasn't just him, everyone at A.J. Waters was fucking crazy. Joe walked over to a glass door marked "Research: Authorized Personnel Only" and pressed the buzzer. A woman inside the room glanced up from her terminal and pressed a button on her desk allowing Joe to enter. Joe told her that he had a list of names to run, and she gave him the appropriate form to fill out. Joe sat at a nearby desk and checked off what information he needed and the case number to charge it to.

"How long will it take?" he asked as the woman perused the list of names Sergio had given him.

"What's your extension? I'll call you," she asked.

"Thanks," Joe said as he waited for her to buzz him out. While waiting for Research to run his names, Joe decided to make an unannounced visit to see his old friend, that son of a bitch Sam Craven, who had sent him to see Angelo Spatuzza in Atlantic City. Stopping at his door, he knocked softly and tried the doorknob. It was locked, so he knocked firmly. He waited and waited nothing. Just as he decided to walk away, he noticed the doorknob was slowly turning and the door was ever-so slowly opening.

"Sammy, it's me, you can open the door. I'm unarmed," Joe said. Sam opened the door, looked left and right, and told Joe to come in. Then he swiftly closed the door.

"What the hell's going on with you?" Joe asked.

"There's something going on out there this morning," Sam said conspiratorially.

"It looks busy. Is it always like this?" Joe asked.

"Not unless they're preparing a firing squad," Sam said easing himself into his chair. "It must be someone high up."

"You know who it is, don't you?" Joe said.

"I don't know. Now what do you want?" replied Sam.

"Why didn't you warn me about Spatuzza? I would have worn my black Speedo," Joe said.

"You wouldn't have gone if I told you about Angelo," Sam said.

"I don't understand what they really want," said Joe.

"Look, they're probably skimming cash from the casino, and Madoff's their fall guy. Did you meet Sergio?" Sam asked.

"Yes, is he their consigliere?" Joe asked.

"Yeah, he's the brains of the operation. They imported him from some university in Milan a few years ago, he's their new whiz kid. Supposedly a fuckin' mathematical genius they say."

"What did he ask you to do for him?" Joe asked.

"Nothing," Sam said too quickly sitting back in his chair.

"Don't bullshit me. What did he want?" Joe demanded.

"I don't know what you're talking about. Don't you have some paperclips to organize? Get the fuck out of here," Sam said, picking up his phone.

"Yeah, well, they told me that after seeing you in the steam room they learned you had no balls. How perceptive they were," Joe said heading for the door.

When he got to his cubicle, his message light was flashing. It was from the Research Department, advising him that his job was ready. After signing for the materials, he brought them back to his desk and quickly went through them. What he first noticed was the extent of each file. They contained photographs, police department records, court documents, newspaper clippings, investigator's notes, and, to his surprise, one of the men was a CI, a Confidential Informant. This is what Sergio was after, the rat in the family, a guy who would probably join a long list of missing persons earmarked as fish food for Angelo's aquarium, he thought. Joe examined the guy's rap sheet and decided that one less murderer was no loss to society, so on his way home that night, he enclosed all the files in an envelope and dropped them off at Global for delivery to Sergio.

Since it was a Friday night and the traffic to the Lincoln Tunnel was, at best, slow going, Joe had an opportunity to think about how he had singlehandedly fucked up his life. He couldn't blame the coke or the broads or the lack of opportunity. That was all bullshit. He wanted everything and didn't care who he hurt, his wife, his kids, his mistresses, anybody. It was all about him. These were things he never thought about until now. Not until his daughter asked him if he had a girlfriend. He realized that he didn't even know his own kids.

Even when Sugar told him that she's dying to see her kids and that's why she's going back to her john it didn't register. All he cared about was satisfying himself. If one broad wasn't enough, maybe two was better. He didn't have a life, he had a circus act. He was not only a juggler, he was a clown. How'd he get to be such a schmuck? Even when he was on the police force he took to hustling as part of his routine duties. These guys on his beat were begging to give him their money for protection... okay, protection from him. He used the extra cash to get high and on broads. He rationalized it, everyone's in on it, and it empowered him. When they met for drinks at Carmine's after a shift, they had swapped bullshit and lies. A NYPD cop had to be tough, and these guys had his back, he often bragged. But looking back, they all had miserable home lives. They got drunk and either beat their wives or their children or both. He was just part of a collection of drunken misfits who had a badge and carried a gun. Hooray.

As he finally made his way up and out of the tunnel, the sun was setting in the west. The sky at dusk shown pinkish red with streaks of white that looked like intersecting jet trails. A thought came to him like a revelation. Was it too late to change? Could he pretend that yesterday was a dream and that tomorrow is a new day? Could he start over with his wife, his kids, and put everything he'd done in the past? Could he pretend, assuming they let him, and wipe the slate clean? He could make it his business to be there for his family, to watch the girls grow. He would go to their school plays, watch them play soccer, see them graduate from school, go places with them, all the things a real dad does. Couldn't he?

Chapter 9: Max

Max arranged to meet Margery for dinner at a restaurant that held a great deal of meaning to them, The Bacarra, on East 46th. It was there some years ago after a magic night of lovemaking; they threw on some clothes, hopped in a cab to the Bacarra and bribed the captain into giving them the last available table. They then proceeded to wash down Lobster Thermidor with a 1994 Château Lafite Rothschild.

Arriving earlier than his reservation, Max attempted to get the same table as on that memorable night but found that an older couple had already parked there. After Margery arrived, they ordered drinks, and while perusing the menu, Margery looked up with a smile on her face.

"Well, I assume you tried to get our usual table over there, but I can see it's occupied. What's so important that you feel you've got to butter me up before telling me something?" she asked.

"That's what I love about you, you can read me like a book," he said.

"So, tell me," she asked, sitting back in her chair. Max then, as he intermittently sipped his scotch for fortitude, told Margery everything that had transpired with regards to Sy's ultimate acceptance of his plan to spring Bernie Madoff from prison.

"When you say he's funding the plan, what kind of figure did you come up with?"

"Ten million dollars up front," Max replied downing his scotch.

To that and somewhat taken aback, Margery whispered, "Ten million dollars?"

"Yep," replied Max.

"Well, that's a horse of a different color, isn't it?" she replied, taking a swig of her dry martini. "Have you looked at the menu?" she asked changing the subject.

"I understand the duck is first rate," he replied.

"No, I think I need something more substantial," she said.

"You're not thinking," he began to say when she interrupted.

"Yes, my dear, the Thermidor," she said putting down the menu.

"And the Rothschild?" he asked.

"But of course! It's all or nothing!" And that was that. From then on, Margery and Max were co-conspirators in the plot to extricate Bernie Madoff from prison.

The next day, Max advised Sy (by email) that Margery was on board and that they had begun recruiting their team. Max was confident that Sy would approve of his enlisting Margery's support since he knew she was an intelligent and resourceful individual. Some time before, Margery had been called upon to appraise several works of art for an auction house when, out of the blue, Sy arrived to bid on one of the works. Since then, Sy had enlisted her support in sourcing and appraising abstract art. Sy was a major collector of works by Pollock, Rothko, de Kooning, Miro, and Kandinsky. Coincidentally, Margery was considered an expert in abstract art, holding degrees from the Royal College of Art in London and in modern and contemporary art from the University of Edinburgh.

Max and Margery then set about dividing the many tasks that each one would be responsible for; Max was to recruit and train the team while Margery secured costumes, props, and venues. The rationale was, if they were to put their people out into the field, they had to have credibility. In other words, they had to copy a real person. That meant that if someone checked out The Major, who was playing the part of a New York doctor, they would find that he had an office in the city, a medical degree, a current license to practice medicine, and a hospital affiliation. This also necessitated finding a medical doctor who was out of town and incommunicado for the duration of the plan. In addition, it had to be someone who was the right age, had an impressive curriculum vitae, and most importantly, had no photos anywhere on the Internet. However, knowing that the charade had a time limit, Max was confident that once they found the right doctor to impersonate, the Major and His Lady could walk the walk and talk the talk.

Max then turned his attention to contacting the next prospective member of the team, Tyler Perry, AKA the Prince of Second Avenue. If he could secure his services, it would go a long way towards the success of the mission. The Prince was perfect for the part of the white-shoe attorney. Physically speaking, he was tall, thin, with pitch-black hair and dark eyes that oozed savoir faire. As part of his mystique, he was always seen with a drop-dead gorgeous woman on his arm. Since the Prince wasn't listed in the phone book, Max put out feelers hoping one of his contacts could find him. As chance would have it, within twenty-four hours, Max received a call from the Prince himself.

"Max, what's so important that you interrupt my massage?" he asked.

"Oh, dear me, did I get you in a, ah, compromising position?" Max asked.

"No, no, that comes later."

"Can you take a meeting?" Max asked.

"It depends. Is it important?" asked the Prince.

"Very," said Max.

"Is it worth my while?" asked the Prince.

"I'll make you an offer you can't refuse," Max said confidently. There followed a brief pause while the Prince digested the meaning of what Max had just said.

"When do you need me?" he asked.

"Yesterday but I'll settle for ASAP, till say two to three weeks from now for the job."

"Sounds... sounds interesting. I'll catch a flight to New York tonight and will contact you tomorrow," said the Prince.

"Excellent!" responded Max as he hung up.

The Prince called the next day and asked Max to meet him at a jewelry store on 11th Street in the West Village. When he arrived, he was escorted through a door behind a jewelry counter that led to a stairway up to a large second-floor apartment. The apartment was tastefully furnished with a white leather couch and matching side chairs, glass cocktail tables, modern floor lamps, and attractive modern artwork. Greeting him as he entered the room was a stunning young woman in a very tight black leather outfit. On second thought, Max realized her outfit probably wasn't leather—it was plastic, no, body-hugging latex! After Max realized he should have brought his blood pressure medication with him, she escorted him, making every step something to watch, through the kitchen and dining room to a door that led to the Prince's office. Seated behind a modern glass table on a luxurious desk chair made by the famous Italian racecar design firm, Pininfarina, sat the Prince wearing a black silk robe. After a warm greeting, he dismissed his lovely young creature, much to Max's dismay, and the two men got down to the nitty-gritty of the meeting. Max carefully explained the roles that the Prince would play. One would be Ruth Madoff's personal attorney, tasked with hiring a local attorney to represent her in Butner, North Carolina. Preferably a local attorney who was connected in some way to the warden where Madoff was incarcerated. The other would be a go-between in helping to secure access to a funeral home in Butner.

After the presentation, the Prince had several questions which Max tried to answer as clearly and succinctly as possible.

"When is D-Day? Do I know any of the other members of the team? Can I take my people with me? My assistant Betty Owens and private security? All expenses— by the way, what are we talking about moneywise?"

"Okay, let's start with the kickoff. At this point in time, it's after we get our ducks in a row, possibly a couple of weeks," Max began.

"Do you know any of the other members of the team?"

"Yes, do you remember the Major and His Lady? They were in on the Japanese investor fiasco four years ago," Max said as a smile came on the Prince's face.

"Yes, I remember. The mark beat up some hooker, and I had to drag that bastard kicking and screaming all over the city."

"Yeah, the Major finally gave him some knockout drops and put him on a plane to LA," said Max. "About your people, you're free to use anyone who can assist you in accomplishing the mission with the one caveat that they keep their mouths shut no matter what happens, du shayn?"

The Prince nodded that he understood.

"Now, about the money. You'll will be paid two million dollars for yourself upfront and the members of your team will be expensed by me up to $250,000," Max said. At that point, he looked at the Prince to get a sense of his reaction to the compensation package but got only a blank expression.

"Expense-wise, you've got to look and act the part. You'll buy yourself and your team the appropriate clothes to fit the role. I expect you to wear three- to five-thousand-dollar conservative suits, five-hundred- to one-thousand-dollar shoes, shirts, ties, pocket squares, stockings, the whole shebang. You must be seen entering and leaving with matching Louis Vuitton luggage. You must set up shop in a suite at the fanciest hotel in town and hold all your meetings there. You will be provided with a Lincoln limousine, and you will scrupulously avoid surveillance cameras wherever you go. We'll also establish an expense account to pay for your out-of-pocket expenses," Max said.

The Prince took the liberty, without flinching, to repeat what Max said just to be sure he heard him correctly. The Prince began:

"Number one: we start the job in two to three weeks. The job itself should be about a week.

"Number two: I have to deal with assorted riffraff.

"Number three: I need to hire and pay, from a separate expense fund, of course, a Butner attorney to represent Ruth Madoff. She'll give him power of attorney.

"Number four: you'll communicate with Ruth for me.

"Number five: Ruth will be in the care of our 'doctor,' whom we both know is the Major.

"Number six: All payments will be through a legitimate offshore account. No hanky-panky.

"And number seven: I get two mil upfront and a quarter-mil for expenses. Is that right?"

"Ya got it," replied Max. With that, the Prince pushed a button on his phone and told Miss Latex to wheel in the bar.

"We're going to memorialize our deal," he said flashing Max a brilliant white smile.

Chapter 10: Joe

After years of playing the rogue and scoundrel, being a 'family man' was somewhat awkward for Joe, a macho, macho man. All the people he knew and worked with shared a common love of guns, fast cars, big tits, beer, John Wayne movies, and all the money they could grab from the man—but not necessarily in that order. 'Tits' came first. After all these were real men, not some 'girly boys.' Joe's father made sure of that. He didn't believe in any of that bullshit.

"Men are the boss, in life, business, and in the home." Any other way, his father often said was a sign of weakness. He didn't like to, nor did he ever, show any affection to his wife or son. He had rules and obedience was rule #1, obedience to him and God. Yes, Joe's father, in his mind, was a devout Catholic, and although they didn't attend church, Joe's father had crosses and pictures of the Pope in every room of their modest house. Their only communication with the church was the weekly parish bulletin, which was delivered to their doorstep every Saturday morning. The only trips the family took were an infrequent ride to the Jersey Shore during the summer. Other than that, Joe's father went hunting and fishing by himself in the Adirondacks. Any activities he had was his business, and Joe and his mother knew better than to ask any questions. When Joe's father died, Joe didn't go to the funeral with his mother since he felt 'it was none of his business.'

Joe usually slept late on Saturdays, but this morning he couldn't. He had things he wanted to investigate, no pun intended, so he threw on his bathrobe and went down to his office and booted up his computer. After an hour or so, he'd printed out how long the trip would take, where to stay, what the amenities were, places to eat, and the sights. Hearing the kids were up and Patty preparing breakfast, Joe marched up the stairs, and with his printout in hand told everyone the good news.

"We're going on an adventure," he said to three puzzled faces. "After breakfast I want you to wash up and pack a bag for an overnight trip to the mountains —the Poconos."

"Where are we going, Daddy?" asked Rosie excitedly, nearly spilling her orange juice.

"You know the kids are supposed to see my mother today," said Patty, cracking some eggs for an omelet.

"That can wait. We need to do things as a family," Joe said.

"Since when?" Patty said sarcastically, pouring the eggs into a hot frying pan.

"If you don't want to come, I'll take the kids," he said getting himself a cup of coffee.

"Where's this place?" she asked, adding some cheese to the omelet.

"It's in the Poconos! I booked a night, tonight, at a resort. It's a cabin on a lake, with boats, miniature golf, an indoor pool, and a big breakfast included in their guesthouse," Joe said, reading from the printout.

"How far is it?" Patty asked.

"It's about an hour and a half west of here, off Route 80."

When Patty didn't respond, the girls cried out in unison, "We want to go! Mommy, please?"

"I'll let you know," she said dividing the omelet into three servings. Joe resisted the urge to shout at her but decided that he'd given her a chance to be a part of the adventure. Damn it, if she didn't want to come, if it was part of her way of hurting him, so be it. He'd take the girls and have fun.

By and by, with the packing, planning and excitement, of the impending trip, Patty eventually rolled over and silently, for the sake of the girls, went on the trip to the Poconos, a land she'd heard people speak of but never had any desire to visit. Surprisingly, the trip was the perfect elixir for bringing the family together. The resort turned out to be more than the glossy photos on their website. The cabins were roomy, clean, and well-equipped. Their cabin had two bedrooms, a kitchen, a living room with a widescreen TV, bathroom, porch, and a wood-burning fireplace. However, the one thing Joe didn't count on was that it got cold up in the mountains, which was actually a good thing since it gave them a sense of urgency in finding suitable clothing for the expedition. This was quickly solved by Patty who Googled "outdoor clothing" on her cell phone and found a Army-Navy Store on Main Street in the local town. With warm hooded sweatshirts, woolen socks, and Navy Watch caps, they were ready for the elements. Joe then Yelped "family restaurants in the area" and found a family-friendly restaurant that served fried chicken dinners within walking distance. After dinner, they stopped at a general store on the way back to their cottage and picked up a bag of marshmallows and a tin of Ghirardelli's hot cocoa.

After Joe made a roaring fire in the fireplace, the girls toasted marshmallows while sipping hot chocolate. To cap the night off, he placed the girls' mattresses on the floor near the fireplace, and as Joe and Patty relaxed on the couch watching TV the girls went quickly to sleep. The fire snapped, crackled, and popped into the wee hours of the night. When Joe and Patty finally got under the sheets, after some awkward moments, they made very quiet love so as not to be heard by the kids. The next morning at seven, they were awakened to the soft sound of a bugle. Venturing out onto the porch to investigate, they saw a little honor guard of children raising the flag by the guesthouse. It was also a touching moment to see the other guests in pajamas and robes standing on their porches in silent reverence to the unity of our people and the freedom we so easily take for granted.

A family-style breakfast was exactly what Joe and the Mancuso family received at Stillwater Lake Cottages. Tables were linked together down the middle of the room with diners seated on long rows of benches. The food was plentiful, and was served on large platters with waiters circling the tables pouring juice, coffee, milk, and tea. Another nice touch was that the setup lent an opportunity for families to get to know each other. Most, if not everyone, had a nice thing to say about the accommodations, the lake, and the family who ran the resort. As a farewell treat, guests were encouraged to take bags of chocolate chip cookies, apples, and chocolate bars from the nearby Hershey factory for their ride home.

On the trip home, Joe received a message from Tina at Global that there was a parcel waiting for him. However, when he told Patty that he had to go into the city, she looked at him disapprovingly, wondering if it was business as usual, or just another guise for a clandestine romantic meeting. Joe picked up on the vibes and tried to reassure her that it was merely a package he was picking up and that he'd be right home. Hoping that this time it was the truth, Patty called her mother and asked her if she could see her that afternoon. When Joe told her that he'd be home for dinner, Patty felt relieved and offered to pick up a pizza.

After dropping Patty and the kids off at home, Joe headed into the city to pickup his parcel at Global. Surprise was the only word to describe what he collected. The parcel was a 2'x18"x18" box that weighed about twenty pounds, which he humped down the street to his parked car. Although he was very tempted to look through the contents of the box, discretion was the better part of valor, and he waited until he could get to the privacy of his home before opening the box.

The box contained approximately fifty folders with pages upon pages of scribbled, handwritten notes, photos, newspaper clippings, and doodles. In a separate metal container were forty-two microcassettes each labeled with the dates on which they were recorded. Enclosed with the cassettes was a sealed envelope with two cassettes and a short note from Sergio. The note said, "On the May 23rd tape, I want everything you can get on Zack—his social security number, last name, aliases, addresses, family, friends, employment records, photographs, criminal records, clubs, and associations. On the Dec 7th tape I want the same information on a man named Harry (Greek)." Joe estimated that it would take him about two to three days to read through the notes since some were indecipherable, filled mostly with the doctor's psychobabble to impress his colleagues with how smart he was, how astute, how scientific, and why he could charge such exorbitant rates. However, the tapes were another matter. Joe couldn't scan the tapes in the way he could with written matter. He had to sit there and listen with pen and paper and stop, go back and listen again lest he missed something important. In total, counting the two that mentioned Zack and Harry, there were forty-four tapes. Guessing that each tape was a session and there were about forty minutes per tape... God, that meant there was 1,760 minutes to listen to. He could probably sit there, listening to five tapes a day before going out of his mind. That would be about 200 minutes per day, which meant it would take him almost nine days to get through them all. By that time, he'd need his own psychiatrist.

There had to be another way to do this and keep it in the family, so to speak. Then it hit him—why not? He'd hire his wife Patty to scan the tapes and pay her as a freelancer. She'd shown herself to be a great snoop, he thought, so why not put her talents to good use and at the same time create a mutual bond by working side by side? Shit, he thought, what a great idea! She'd jump at the opportunity to snoop on his activities, what he really did, where he really went, who he was hooking up with. She'd be champing at the bit and, best yet, get paid to do it. Yes, sir. Joe sat back in his chair. It was a win-win.

Chapter 11: Max

Once Max could see his way clear of leaving the Prince and Miss Latex, he caught a taxi home to begin the devilish work that would make the endeavor feasible. In other words, their cover story and financial arrangements. Sy had agreed to a precedent setting prepayment terms for him and his crew, so it was time to dot the I's and cross the T's. Max set up his computer to ask for Sy's guidance on how he should handle the disposition of the funds. After plugging the thumb drive into his computer's USB port, he entered the password that would open an encrypted pathway to Sy's email. After a few seconds a message appeared on his screen asking if he wished to send or receive a message. He clicked the send box, and he was once again ready to send Sy a message that only the two of them could read.

Max began his query with questions regarding which bank and/or banks he and his crew could draw their funds from. He posed the same question with regards to credit cards and cash advances. Max also asked Sy if he had a source for valid international passports and US driver's licenses. Max had many more questions he needed answers for but doubted that Sy had the resources and connections or, for that matter, the desire to be in any way connected to the plot, now that it was in motion. Max knew that he still had to find a general contractor to source and direct the areas he had no expertise in, including:

excavation and tunneling, pyrotechnics, carpentry, video, and electrical cabling. It would be easy if he could only Google it. Could you give me a quote on a secret six-foot deep by four-foot wide tunnel running, say, six feet beneath ground level and one hundred feet long? he thought to himself.

After staring at his monitor screen for several minutes, he decided that Sy probably checked his inbox only a couple of times a day, and turned his attention to finding a general contractor. There was a guy he used some time ago, a jack-of-all-trades, but he didn't know if he would take the risks associated with the plan. His name was Glen—now what was his last name, he thought—and he lived in the Park Slope section of Brooklyn. I too young to be having a senior moment, he thought to himself. Glen A, Glen B, Glen C, Glen D...

"Oh shit," he said out loud. "Glen Carson. Now, does he still live in Brooklyn?" He Googled the White Pages for his phone number. Twenty-one Glen Carsons in New York City, but none matched his age category. However, he did notice that the listings referenced spouses and siblings. Then it came back to him, Glen's wife's name was Dotty or Dorothy. This also was a dead end, though, since there were no references to a Dotty or Dorothy in the listings. That left two possibilities: Glen either moved or was dead. Then, with a stroke of genius or a good guess, he reached out to the New York State Licensing Division for the whereabouts of a Glen Carson. He was, at one time, a licensed contractor in New York, and they may have had a lead on where he might be living. Max shuttered the thought of getting any information from the Licensing Division. However, he must have hit the right person at the right time. She checked her computer and found that, although Glen had not renewed his New York State Contractor's License, the division did confirm that he was in good standing in New York State when he applied for a contractor's license in Reno, Nevada.

"Bless you, bless you," Max told the clerk and asked her name planning on sending her some flowers, but she demurred saying it was just part of her job.

Max wondered how Margery was doing and was about to call her when his computer notified him that he had a message. Once again, he had to go through the rigmarole of plugging the thumb drive into the USB port and entering his password and waiting until he received an acknowledgement that they were ready to transmit or receive. He checked the receive box, and the screen immediately displayed four pages of Sy's comments and questions. Sy began by explaining the banking process. He wrote that one of the most popular banks in Mantattan for their purpose was called, The Triple C's, whose initials stood for, Craven, Comstock, & Cummings. That The Triple C's was one of the first steps in laundering vast sums of money, as it acted as a 'feeder bank' distributing funds to a host of offshore banks. It was basically a common practice for wealthy individuals to launder vast amounts of money though these so-called feeders. Sy said that his sponsor has deposited $10 million with The Triple C's, in Max's name for disbursement to his team.

Wait... wait... what was this shit about 'his sponsor'? The phrase jumped out at Max. What is he talking about? Max always thought that Sy ran the show. "Whom am I working for?" Max said to himself. Was Sy sending him a message? Was Sy implying that he was merely a go-between in the jailbreak? Oh me oh my, we haven't even started and now Sy's gone and muddied the waters, Max thought to himself. He took a deep breath, shook his head, and went on reading Sy's instructions.

"With regards to your crew; I advise depositing their funds in The Triple C's. They have a special department (nicknamed 'The Laundromat') that will handle their funds. However, I caution you that paying people in advance has its drawbacks. Once their funds cross this threshold, into their bank account, you can't cancel the transaction...meaning you'd better be absolutely confident on their loyalty and willingness to complete the mission. In addition, the $10 million we've deposited in your account is fixed; meaning if you feel you might run over this amount, you must justify any and all additional funds...with me.

"Now with regards to your funds, here are the details; I've established an account in your name, Max Rosen at Craven, Comstock, & Cummings. Your account number is: 700826944 and I've taken the liberty of establishing a preliminary password: 4me4you4us. (Case sensitive) I suggest committing your account number to memory and changing your password at your first opportunity. I know this all might seem somewhat convoluted, but this is standard operating procedure in the world of high finance. Join the club.

"With respect to international passports, there are several sovereign nations that for a fee will issue 'Valid Passports,' one of which is the Commonwealth of Dominica in the Caribbean. We have an attorney in Dominica, a Lloyd Carmichael, who will handle the details. I'll send you by email the necessary forms. Just have your team complete them and you can return them to Lloyd with their digital passport photos. I urge you to jump on this ASAP since it usually takes two to three weeks for them to be issued.

"On the matter of valid US driver's licenses, I do not have a source, but I will make some inquires. The only other option is a 'cut-and-paste' job. For all intents and purposes, it will look real and pass muster in most instances, but if push comes to shove, the photo on the license will not match the one on file with that states registry. Further, if time were of the essence, I'd go with the cut-and-paste. <End of message.>"

Chapter 12: Joe

Joe waited until the kids were off to school to broach the subject of Patty working with him on the Madoff case.

"Do you want another cup of coffee?" he asked her as she stacked the dishwasher with breakfast plates.

"No, I think I should cut back on the caffeine, it's making my heart race."

"In that case, why don't we start drinking decaff?" Joe responded, putting his cup into the dishwasher. "Look, when you're through in here why don't we have a talk in the office?" Joe was careful not to say 'his office' or personal space but one they now would share. Whether Patty recognized his concession or not, the invitation to talk was bit of a surprise and piqued her curiosity enough for her to abruptly stop what she was doing and follow Joe down into their office.

"Take those papers off the couch and just put em on the floor," he said. He then reached under his desk and took out the metal box that held Ruth Madoff's psychiatric recordings. This was no surprise to Patty. She made it a habit to frequently go through Joe's secret hiding places looking for evidence that he was cheating on her. Likewise, Joe was aware that Patty was rifling through his things, owing to his custom of marking the position of sensitive materials with an erasable pen that left a clue when the item was moved or opened. It wasn't something he'd learned as a detective; it was merely a scene from an old war movie detailing how British MI6 caught a spy in their midst.

"You know I'm working on finding Bernie Madoff's hidden treasure," he began, "and quite frankly, although I work for a large organization, I'm really on my own."

"You mean they don't help you? Patty asked.

"Well, they do and they don't," he opened the box. "I'll give you an example," he said taking out one of the microcassettes. "This is a tape that Ruth Madoff made at her psychiatrist's office on March 23. It has two sides, side A, 30 minutes long, and side B, also 30 minutes long. From what it looks like, each tape has about forty to fifty minutes of conversation on it."

"Where'd you get those tapes?" asked Patty.

"I can't go into that, and it's best that you don't know. Okay? But what I'm trying to say is that I had to get them on my own. Do you understand?" he said.

"Oh shit, you're not going to lose this job, too?" she cried.

"Relax, relax, let's focus on what these tapes can do for us. These tapes give us a window into Ruth's inner thoughts, motives, and actions. They're a treasure trove that no one has even heard, outside of her shrink. If it helps us find the money, no one will care, and we'll be able to write our own ticket."

"So, what do you want me to do?" she asked assuming her pensive pose of folding her arms across her chest.

"I want you to start with these two tapes. On this tape," he said, handing it to Patty, "Ruth mentions someone named Zack, and on this tape," he handed another tape to Patty, "Ruth mentions someone named Harry as a 'trusted and wise advisor.' Now this is how you can help me. I'm going to hire you as my research assistant and pay you out of my expenses."

"How much can you pay me?" she asked.

"I'll get to that in a moment," he said.

"You're not going to screw me?" she replied sitting back on he couch and folding her arms across her chest.

"Not right now," he said with a wide smile. "Now there's about forty hours of conversation on these tapes," he said, tipping the box so that she could see the contents. "I want you to listen to each one and record any reference to everyone she mentions, and if she hints in any way that this or that person is a confidant, partner, associate, and/or friend of Bernie and or hers. I want you to stop the tape, and on this log," he showed her a form, "write the names, information, date, and digital position on the recorder of the conversation. This is the machine you'll be using," he pointed to a Sony digital recorder on his desk. "I'll go through it with you later. Do you think you can do this?"

"Sure, but what about the money, boss?" she teased.

"I'll have to expense you on a biweekly basis, that's how Waters accounting works. They have a form, you know, how many hours you worked on such and such a day. The hourly rate at Waters for a research assistant is $28.84 per hour, but I can kick it up by adding an additional hour or two each day."

"How much is that per week?" she asked. Joe punched in some numbers on his desk calculator and ripping off the paper printout, turned to read Patty the results.

"Assuming you worked five hours a day for five days you'd be making $721.00. However, if I boosted it by a couple of hours each day, you'd be making $1009.00. But, that being said, they will issue you a 1099 for taxes," he said.

"How much would they take out?" she asked.

"I don't know. We'll worry about that later. Meanwhile, Mrs. Lincoln, how'd you like the show so far?" he joked. Patty, pleased with what she heard, got up from the couch and slowly and sensually moved towards Joe. She extended her hand. "Now is it time to get screwed?"

Several hours later, invigorated after a matinee tryst, Joe went out to pick up something to eat while Patty dove headlong into listening to the tapes before Joe had an opportunity to instruct her on the machine's operation. Grabbing a tape, any tape, she fumbled with the eject button until a window opened and after a couple of tries, was able to insert a tape into the machine. She really didn't care what tape it was nor which side to start first, A or B, she just wanted to hear what it was like to be psychoanalyzed.

After playing with the volume lever, she heard the psychiatrist ask Ruth, "When did you learn of it?"

Then after a few seconds, Patty heard Ruth say, "He never spoke about them. His family history was always... Let's just say, he was uncomfortable speaking about his past, and after a while, I never brought up the subject."

"And this, this secret was hidden from you for over thirty years?" the psychiatrist asked. At this point without a response Patty figured that Ruth merely nodded her head in agreement.

"Patty, I got us a pizza from Romano's for dinner! Where the hell are you?" Joe shouted as he placed a large sausage pizza on the dining room table. Patty, unable to contain herself, raced up the stairs to greet Joe and tell him what she had found.

"Joe, Bernie had a secret! A secret he hid from Ruth. Come listen to it," she said heading down the stairs with Joe in hot pursuit.

"Oh Patty, I hope you didn't fuck up the tape. You should have waited," Joe said dejectedly.

"How do we rewind the tape?" Patty asked starting to press every button on the recorder.

"Wait, wait, you can erase everything if you hit the wrong button," Joe replied getting between Patty and the recorder.

"Let's see, did you start on side B? Joe asked.

"Yes, I just wanted to hear how it sounded and—"

But she was interrupted by Joe who said, "It's okay, let's rewind it and listen to the part you heard."

After rewinding and listening to what little conversation Patty heard on side B, Joe ejected the tape and reversed it to listen to the end of side A. With a few taps on the rewind button, Joe was able to jog back long enough to listen to the mysterious conversation between Ruth and her psychiatrist.

"What precipitated the conversation? In other words, what triggered his confession?" the psychiatrist asked.

"It was a old black-and-white movie on TV. A World War II movie that took place in North Africa, like Humphrey Bogart in Casablanca, but this had Marlene Dietrich and she was entertaining British troops. I remember we were sitting on the couch and Bernie wasn't watching the movie. He was fidgeting with a jammed stapler when she started singing 'Lili Marleen' to the troops."

"Exactly what did he say to you?" the psychiatrist asked.

"That's the point, he didn't say anything," she replied. "He just left the room. I found him in the upstairs bathroom leaning on the sink, staring at himself in the mirror and mumbling.

"He was saying, 'Who am I, who am I, who am I?' and when he realized I was there, watching him, he was angry at first. Then he smiled, rinsed his face with water, and began drying his face with a towel. I followed him into our bedroom and we sat on the bed. Then as we looked at each other he said, 'I don't know who I am.'

"I wasn't sure I heard him, so I asked, 'Bernie what do you mean?' I remember it as if it were yesterday, he reached out and took my hand and opening it he kissed the palm of my hand and began to cry. I tried to comfort him, but he pulled back and said he must tell me something. My first thought was that he was sick, he had a serious illness. I couldn't have imagined what he said next:

"'Ruth, I don't know who I am or where I came from.'

"I didn't understand what he was talking about. Bernie and I grew up together. I knew and liked his parents, Carol and Marty Madoff. They knew my family, we went out for dinner, socialized, everything. At that point in time, we'd been married, had two wonderful boys, started a business, made new friends, and now he tells me he doesn't know who he is. I was shocked to say the least."

"Go on," the psychiatrist encouraged.

"This is what Bernie told me," Ruth said. "Bernie began by saying...

"'This is what I remember, just bits and pieces, flashbacks and nightmares that I've lived with in silence. I remember a little girl; she held my hand tight that night they brought us to the boat. My father was arguing about something with the man on the boat. He wanted to go with us, but only the little girl and I were allowed onto the boat. When they brought us below deck they put a string around our necks with a sign. There were many children like us with signs all sitting on the floor. I don't remember the passage or where we put ashore, but a bus collected us and took us to a large hall where we were sent to families. The girl and I went to stay with a family in a nice house. I think they were called row houses. There were these two children there, a boy and a girl, but we couldn't speak with them because they didn't understand us. Then one night, the sirens went off and we ran to a tunnel with crowds of people, down the steps and around and around deep under ground with the ground shaking. When we got as far as we could go, we sat on the floor, with our backs to the wall hugging our knees. Some of the blasts showered us with bits of the ceiling covering us with this white powder. Everyone looked like ghosts. I remember to this day the taste of the powder. It tasted sour. One night, the sirens did not warn us that there was an attack and we had to run as fast as we could to the tunnel, but we got separated when a building collapsed. The next thing I knew, a passing man grabbed me up into his arms and carried me into the tunnel. After the raid, someone took me to my host family, but they didn't know what happened to the little girl. We couldn't go back to their house because the whole street was on fire. Their house and every house on their street had been destroyed, so we found shelter at a relief center. They spoke to the people at the relief center. I think some men went looking for the little girl the next day, but when they returned they shook their heads and I knew by the way they looked at each other that she was gone. Soon after that, a van collected the children from our boat, and we were taken out into the country. The van made several stops along the way, and children were dropped off with new families to stay with until there were only me and this other boy. We were both very scared, but at the next stop, a man took me to a house—a funny-looking house with a huge grass roof. I remember that in front of the house they had a big white goat. I met a man and woman who gave me a big hug and took me to a room and said, "this is your room, little man," in Yiddish. I was so excited I almost peed in my pants. I was so happy that they liked me and that I could understand what they said. They had one son, John, who was in the army, but when I asked where he was, they said that they didn't know. I liked living with the Hammonds, they were very kind. They sent me for English lessons to a woman in their town so that I might attend school. She told me to never speak German in town, that they were at war with Germany. One memory I have of my life with the Hammonds was that after dinner they'd often played records, especially a record John brought back for them. Oddly, it was in German, so I was the only one who knew the lyrics. It was 'Lili Marleen.' I lived with the Hammonds until the end of the war, until they learned that John was missing and presumed dead. The shock and sorrow of their loss was too much for the Hammonds. One day a woman from a Jewish Relief Agency came to see the Hammonds, and I was told that I was being sent to America with other foster children. It was a sad day, the day I said goodbye to the Hammonds. It was like they lost two sons in one year.

"'The trip to America was exciting and very long. First by rail to Southampton then by ship to Boston and then by rail to New York City, where buses brought us to the ballroom of the Waldorf Astoria to meet our adoptive parents. One by one we were escorted to a room to meet our new parents. Mine were Carol and Marty Madoff.'

"Bernie said that he knew the instant he met them that God had blessed him. 'They got down on their knees and hugged him with tears flowing from their eyes,' Bernie said tearing up with the thought of that special time and place."

"But what was the significance of the Marlene Dietrich movie? I don't get the connection," asked the psychiatrist.

"It was at that instant that Bernie realized that the little girl in his dreams was his long-lost sister, Lili," Ruth said sobbing.

Chapter 13: Max

Max and Margery decided that the characters in their grand scheme must be effectively incommunicado during their timetable. Moreover, these crucial elements, which could result in the ultimate success or failure of the plan, were Margery's responsibility. It was up to her to source not only the support staff and offices, but the collateral (business cards, stationery, phone lines, post office boxes, and fake photo IDs). In addition, Margery would have to build several websites to correspond with the various roles being played by the team.

An incident in her youth that brought this to the fore was at the prestigious Woldingham Boarding School in Surrey, where she was confronted by the persistent harassment of an upper classmate. The straw that ultimately broke the camel's back took place in the school's dining room when the bully drew an "A" on the back of Margery's school blazer in chalk at lunch. Margery slowly rose from her seat, removed her blazer, placed it on the back of her chair, and said to the girl, "Defend yourself." The much older and taller girl merely looked around and laughed. Margery straightened her pose and said, pointing to a spot on the parquet floor, "You will soon lie there in a heap." Then from out of nowhere, Margery struck the girl with a swift karate strike at the bridge of her nose, knocking the girl off her feet and landing her precisely where Margery said she would. The dining room erupted in cheers, seeing the bully finally get her comeuppance. Then raising her on high, they began carrying Margery on their shoulders around the dining room, singing:

"Ding Dong the witch is dead!

Which old witch?

The wicked witch.

Ding Dong, the wicked witch is dead."

At first the school considered expelling Margery, but after Margery's father, a prominent MP, offered to pay for the girl's reconstructive surgery, the school relented. They also wanted to avoid any bad publicity associated with being known as a school that tolerated hazing.

With Margery busy looking for office space on Park Avenue, Max contacted Margo Adler Casting to put out feelers for a Bernie Madoff look-alike. He told Margo that he was making a documentary on Madoff, and for a, realistic touch, he wanted to cast an actor who had a strong physical resemblance to Bernie Madoff. Max told her that in lieu of headshots, he wanted DVDs of each candidate. Margo agreed to the conditions and emailed Max a standard casting contract. The contract stipulated that Adler would screen candidates and produce a thirty-second DVD of each one for Max's consideration. That upon receipt of a signed contract and a $4,500.00 retainer she would advertise the listing, screen candidates, and produce DVD's. In addition, as an incentive, if one of her candidates were chosen for the role, she would receive an additional $2,000.00 bump. Max signed the contract and sent a copy and check by courier to Margo with a little note thanking her for her assistance and urging her to get him some good candidates ASAP.

With that out of the way, Max once again turned his attention to contacting Glen Carson in Reno as a possible general contractor. Once again, the Internet Yellow Pages held the answer.

"Glen, how the hell are you?" Max exclaimed when he finally picked up.

"Who's this?" asked Glen.

"A guy from your distant past," Max responded.

"Where do I know you from?" inquired Glen.

"We go back a long time," Max said.

"You sound like someone I knew in a previous life. Why are you calling me after all this time? Do I owe you money?" said Glen now amused. Then after a few seconds, "How are you, Max?"

"Busy," Max replied. "I could use your help on a job back east."

"What kind of job?" asked Glen.

"A big, big job."

"When you say big, do you mean size or time-wise?" asked Glen.

"Short time, short size," said Max.

"Tell me about it."

"Can't. Gotta show you," said Max.

"What's in it for me?" asked Glen.

"Big money," said Max.

"How big?"

"That big!" replied Max.

"When?" asked Glen.

"Now," said Max.

The men exchanged cell phone numbers and email addresses, and Glen said that he'd try to extricate himself from some of the jobs he was working on.

"Try. It's worth it."

Relieved that he was on his way towards rounding out his crew, Max called Margery to see if she could meet him for a bite.

"Where, honey?" She asked.

"Let's meet at P.J. Clarke's on Third Avenue, say, in an hour?"

"P.J. Clarke's in an hour, got it," she replied.

When Max arrived at the restaurant, some guy at the bar was bending her ear about how important he was and that she had to have dinner with him.

Seeing she was in distress, Max gently extricated Margery from the boring idiot and led her to the dining room where they could relax and compare notes. After ordering cocktails, Margery took out a small steno pad and went down the list describing the pros and cons of the various offices she'd inspected on Park Ave. It reminded Max of the "Three Bears", too small, too noisy, too dark, too high, till she showed him a lease agreement for an office at 197 Park Ave, which was 'just right' and available yesterday!

"Wonderful!" replied Max raising his glass and downing the last few drops of his scotch and soda.

"It has an attractive reception center that controls the entrance to several internal offices," she said.

"How are we coming with the doctor?" he asked.

"We have several names that we can use, but I'd like to do another search to confirm their retirement," she said.

"Retirement?" Max asked.

"Yeah, it's much safer to use a retired doctor, and honestly, most of the doctors I've looked at on Park Avenue? They're retired and living in and around Palm Beach."

"They probably keep their offices on Park Avenue as a business expense," Max said nodding his head. "What about the attorney?"

"Oh, I forgot to mention it yesterday. We've got one for the Prince. His name is Todd Steele, and he's at his villa in the South of France for the next eight months," she said proudly raising her glass and finishing her Cosmo. "By the way, what name are we using for the film company and other endeavors?"

"I've used the name the Alpha Group on our contract with Margo Adler Casting," Max replied. "Remind me, I think we should also use the Alpha Group on our New York bank account."

Margery nodded with agreement and picked up her menu to peruse what looked appetizing. "What are you having?" she asked.

"The veal scaloppini is to die for," Max avowed.

"Well, that settles that," she said folding her menu and placing it on the table.

After what was a memorable dinner at Clarke's, Margery and Max ordered drinks while listening to Broadway hits played by a gray-haired gentleman impeccably dressed in a black tux. What made Clarke's an outstanding venue was the freedom entertainers felt about strolling over to the piano and singing for an appreciative audience. There was nothing more New York than an intimate piano bar.

Chapter 14: Joe

"Don't tell anyone what you've heard on the tapes," Joe cautioned Patty.

"Don't worry, I'll never tell anyone," Patty said.

"Look, I'm going to put them in the safe with my guns." Joe opened the closet door, then pushed some clothes to one side, exposing a wall safe. Squinting at the small keypad he punched in the combination.

"I'm going to put them in here for safekeeping," he said putting the tapes in the safe.

"You'll give me the combination, right?" asked Patty.

"Yeah, it's, or was, my badge number: 395119," Joe said closing the safe. "Remember, after you're done listening to the tapes, put everything back in the safe, capische?"

"Si," responded Patty with a smile. For the first time in a long while she felt that she and Joe had connected as partners.

Joe then called the research department at Waters and asked them to get the FBI files on all Madoff's employees, with their bios, years of employment, home addresses, and telephone numbers. He was told that they couldn't start on it until he submitted a request for information.

"You know the drill," they said. "Because we have to bill someone for the research costs, right?"

They advised him that the form was online and that as soon as they received it, it would be assigned to a research assistant.

"How long will it take?" asked Joe.

"Don't know, but if it's all online, you're probably looking at three to four hours," she said.

Joe filled out the form and requested that the materials be sent to him by email. He then took out Bernie Madoff's folder and began reviewing his file, looking for any references to his adoption, but couldn't find any. Usually there was a section devoted to one's early life, but in his case, it said that he was the only son of Jewish parents, Carol and Marty Madoff of Brooklyn, New York. That he graduated from Tilden High School and worked his way through the University of Miami as a clerk at a brokerage company. Upon graduation he moved back to New York, got a brokerage license, and with the help of some startup money from his parents, launched his own investment company. His firm grew by attracting investments from family and friends and by using a sophisticated computer program to process quotes. Madoff's computer programs were the forerunners of the NASDAQ stock exchange.

"With all that shit going for him, why did he try to screw people? He could have ripped them off legitimately as a stockbroker," Joe said to himself.

About two hours later, he received a text message from Waters that his RFI had been sent to him via email. However, when he scrolled through the materials, he was amazed by the depth of the report. It was not only the bios of Bernie's twenty-seven or so employees, but newspaper articles, video clips, trial transcripts, credit and financial statements, and investigative summaries of interviews of the subject's friends and associates. All in all, aside from the video, it was several hundred pages long—much too long for his pipsqueak bubble-jet printer. Joe called the research assistant, thanked her for compiling the information, and requested a printout of the report.

She in turn told Joe that he had to send her an addendum to his RFI, which he promised to do.

When Joe hung up, he couldn't help saying to himself, "How can you get anything done when they fuckin' bury you in paperwork?"

But he needed it. Like that line in Annie Hall about the guy who thought he was a chicken and his family couldn't bring themselves to have him committed because, well, because they needed the eggs!

So, Joe sat back and began perusing the materials on his little monitor looking for anything on someone named Zack. After a few keystrokes the program brought him to a file, some thirty-six pages long, on a Zack Titus. Skimming through Zack's early years, Joe noticed a comment from a social worker who mentioned that Zack was a truant and probably 'homeschooled,' which was not unusual at that point in parts of Tennessee. Further along, he came upon some 1099 tax receipts from a variety of software companies in and around New York. It looked like Zack jumped around for three years until he became an employee of something called the Madoff Consulting, LLC, where he was paid a salary of $75,000 per year plus, strangely, his room and board. In addition, on a separate filing, Madoff Consulting also paid all of Zack's, city, state, and federal income taxes. The rest was the customary blah, blah, blah, until Joe came upon an interview that one Sue Lipson, an ex-Madoff employee, gave to the New York Post after Zack's apparent suicide. She said, "He was one of the most sensitive human being she'd ever met. That in his own rights, he was a genius, like an Einstein, a problem-solver. He might have had difficulty communicating because his mind was wired differently, but we all loved him and will miss him terribly."

Checking the date of Zack's suicide, Joe realized it was just four days before Madoff confessed to his crimes. Did Madoff tell Zack that the jig was up and that drove him to commit suicide? It had all been seemingly swept under the rug with the issuance of a one-line statement by his own NYPD.

It said, "Zack Titus of New York City committed suicide by walking off the 48th Street platform into the path of an oncoming train." End of Quote.

"Really, guys, was that all it was?" Joe said to his monitor screen. After reading several accounts of who Zack really was, Joe had a picture of an early savant child who had an unusual gift for computer science. He was a man whose language was displayed as a computer code. Madoff had realized Zack's gift and took him under his wing by taking care of his creature comforts as if he was his own child. Zack in turn had rewarded Madoff by creating intuitive programs that literally revolutionized the game of stock trading, and it was his revolutionary computer programs that later became the basis of the NASDAQ stock exchange. This had propelled Madoff into the role as chairman of NASDAQ. However, after digesting everything there was in the reports on Zack, Joe came to the conclusion that there was no there there. Madoff, for whatever reason, wouldn't have used Zack to knowingly divert investor funds to himself, which he did, but not in this manner. Just to be sure, he called over to his friend Mo at his old division to give him the lowdown on the case. After exchanging a few pleasantries, Mo read him some of the investigating officer's findings:

"Let's see, Zack Titus, 1172 West End Avenue, NYC. apparent suicide, 48th Street subway station, northbound train, remains released to Richardson Funeral Home, 27 Bay Ridge Parkway, Queens, New York, for cremation at the bequest of a Bernard Madoff."

"Does it say anything about Zack's family or belongings?" Joe asked.

"Nadda," replied Mo. "Hope it was of some help, though."

"Thanks, buddy, it was." Joe hung up.

He wondered if this tragic, desperate act pushed Madoff over the cliff and into the hands of the Justice Department. Maybe he just couldn't live with himself knowing he caused the death of a frightened boy that he cared for like a son.

Feeling suffocated in his office, Joe decided to take a ride over to Zack's apartment on West End Avenue. When he arrived at the address he found a plaque above the letterboxes referring all inquiries to a May Management Company with a telephone number. Joe surmised that, by the look of the building and its address, there probably was a super in residence. After pushing several buzzers, sure enough, there was 'Herbbie the Super.' After assuring Herbbie that he wasn't from the Health Department, Joe showed Herbbie a photo of Madoff. He learned that he was there after Zack's death and took away several boxes of computer hardware and electronics. He was sure it was Madoff since he paid him fifty bucks just to help put the stuff in the trunk of his car.

"And it was just computer stuff?" Joe asked.

"Yeah, like I said, I put 'em in the trunk of his Black 600."

"Say what—600?" Joe asked, confused.

"Haven't you ever seen a Black Mercedes 600?" Herbbie said.

"Okay, yeah, I've seen them," Joe said. The question now was, what did Zack have on his computer, and moreover, what did Madoff do with it? The thought, ever so remote did come to mind: was the missing link to Madoff's hidden treasure on Zack's hard drive? And if so, where was it now?

On the way back to New Jersey, Joe turned his attention to Ruth Madoff's mention of an important financial consultant called, 'nother car the Greek,' so he called Patty and asked her if she had found any additional references on other tapes so far. She told Joe that she hadn't heard anything so far and wanted to know when he'd be home. Joe told her of his visit to Zack's apartment and what the super told him about

Madoff's removal of Zack's computer. Then, to reassure her, he said that he was on the George Washington Bridge heading home. Joe smiled as he put his cell phone back into its holder, thinking that it was refreshing and much easier to be honest with Patty. He was never good at lying; he often forgot what he told her and eventually he'd contradict his stories and there'd be a row, but in the back of his mind, he wondered if he could stay clean and forget about Sugar.

Chapter 15: Max

With several irons in the fire, Max was anxious to roll out the program and required, at this point in time, Sy's assistance with transportation. It was obvious that the members of the crew had to avoid any and all means of transportation where CCTV cameras were in use, especially airports where there was intensified security. Max and Sy had briefly touched on the matter at an earlier time, with Sy mentioning he'd arrange the use of an aircraft in G.C. Waverly's fleet. This was wonderful but somewhat vague. Max felt that now was the time to nail down the details, so he sent Sy a cryptic encoded message:

"We are ready to deploy. Send instructions for use of aircraft ASAP." Luckily, Sy must have been sitting at his computer because the reply came back in short notice.

"Your aircraft is a Lear 60 with the number 9J551 on its rear fin. It is parked at Hangar 27, Teterboro Airport, NJ. The Lear 60 specs are as follows: seats eight passengers and two crew, cruises at 550 mph, max altitude is 41,000 feet, with a range of 2,975 miles, and requires 5,000' of runway for takeoff. Your cost is $2,500 per hour, wheels up to wheels down, that being said; all booking must come from my office. Now, when do you need the plane, how many passengers, what is your destination, and when is your return?"

Max sent Sy the following message: "Request Lear tomorrow, July 2, 10AM, six (6) passengers, departing Teterboro, destination Raleigh-Durham, NC. Return Open."

"Roger, out." Seeing that Sy terminated the connection, Max sat back and felt a little chill in his extremities. "I guess it's show time," he said, picking up the phone to call Margery.

"Have you spoken to the Prince?" she asked when she picked up.

"No, I'll give him a call," replied Max.

"I'd better call the Washington Hotel and reserve the Presidential Suite for tomorrow night," she said.

"Yeah, if you have any trouble" Max started to say when Margery interrupted him.

"No, I've spoken to them. They're holding the suite for us."

"Excellent, do you have the burners?" he asked.

"I've got a dozen prepaid cell-phones," she replied.

"We'll probably need a dozen more. I don't want any possibility of the feds tracing their calls. I'm going to instruct them to use their phones for communicating with each other and with us only. If a mark needs to get a hold of them, they're to leave a message at our office. If there's a breach, they're to destroy their phone."

Max then called the Prince and advised him when to meet at Teterboro Airport and that he'd arrange for a Lincoln Limousine to be at his disposal when they landed in Raleigh.

The next morning Max and Margery got an early start, hoping to beat the traffic on the George Washington Bridge to New Jersey, but due to an accident on Riverside Drive leading to the bridge, the best their driver could do was race around side streets in an effort to gain access to the bridge's little-used upper deck. All in all, with the hurry up and wait, they reached Hangar 27, just ten minutes late only to be greeted by the Prince, standing on the top step of the Lear.

He was dressed to the nines in a pair of white Tommy Bahama slacks, a powder-blue polo shirt, and navy blazer, holding a cup of coffee in his hand. He inquired of Max, "Say, old chap, do you have a boarding pass?"

Once the driver stowed Max and Margery's luggage on board, Max introduced he Prince, Betty (AKA Miss Latex), Marco (a sturdy, no-nonsense bodyguard), and Jerry (Prince's aide-de-camp) to Margery. He checked the time on his cell phone and, picking up a handset at his seat, Max told the captain that all were onboard and ready for takeoff.

A few minutes later, the passengers felt a jolt. The aircraft was connected to a pushback tug, which moved the Lear out of its hangar onto an access road to the runway. Soon after, the aircraft started taxiing towards a line of aircraft awaiting their turn for takeoff. Once on the main runway, the captain increased the RPM on both engines until they began to shake and whine. When both were in perfect sync, the Lear was ready for takeoff. At that point, the first officer released the brakes and, like a sprinter, the Lear sprang off its starting blocks and began racing down the runway at 100... 200... 300 mph and then, suddenly, with its nose skyward, the Lear jumped off the runway and soared like an arrow upward into the clouds, banking ever so slightly to the southeast on its way to the Great Smoky Mountains of North Carolina.

The captain came on the intercom a few minutes later and told his passengers that it was safe to move around, about the food and refreshments in the galley, the communications systems, Internet access codes, and restrooms. He also told them that the radar indicated that it should be smooth sailing and that if anything changes, he'd advise them. Upon hearing the good news, Max asked the Prince to join Margery and him for a coffee in the galley. The Prince declined the invitation for coffee and after rummaging through the refrigerator took out a large bottle of Saratoga Springs sparkling water. Gathering around a small, round table, Max handed folders to the Prince and Margery. They contained a timetable of tasks that each was assigned to accomplish. The first issue was security, in that, everyone must be careful of what they say to, "outsiders," he reminded them that people by their very nature, are inquisitive, especially of strangers.

"Stay away from any and all places that are monitored by CCTV cameras," Max said.

He also told The Prince to have all his meals in his suite, saying, "After all royalty demands privacy." Max handed him a box that contained eight cell phones for his team's use, with the caveat that the cell phones were for the sole purpose of communicating with Max, Margery, and his crew.

"If you want someone to contact you by phone, give them your business card," Max said handing the Prince another box, this containing business cards and stationery for his new alias: Todd Steele, Esquire, 107 Park Avenue, New York, NY. "We have you covered back in New York—Park Avenue office, receptionist, secretary, answering service—the whole shebang. In addition, here are American Express and VISA credit cards with your name on them: Todd Steele, Esquire. Your reservation at the Washington Hotel is under that name.

"Are you following me?" Max asked as The Prince inspected his new business cards.

"Yes, and I like the font you used. What is it called?" the Prince inquired.

"I'm not sure, what is it, Margery?" Max said looking over at Margery.

"It's Snell Roundhand," she said.

"Okay, moving right along. Have Betty check in at the front desk and give them your American Express card. Have the porters bring your Louis Vuitton luggage to the Presidential Suite. Porters usually try to engage in small talk. Where are you from, how long will you be staying with us, and so on, thinking that by breaking the ice they'll get a big tip. No small talk, period.

"Further, a man of your stature never tips. He has his driver take care of those matters. A C-note is customary at the Washington Hotel.

"Tomorrow I'll be casing a couple of funeral homes with crematoriums in Butner. From my research, they both look good, but just to be sure, I want to see them for myself before I call upon you to negotiate the use of the building," Max said looking at the Prince who was now preoccupied, inspecting his stationery. "In the interim, I need you to focus on finding a local attorney who is on a first-name basis with the warden at Butner Penitentiary. Try canvassing church membership, fraternal orders, country clubs, charities, and familial relationships for someone who can approach the warden as a representative of Ruth Madoff.

"Have you got any questions?" he asked. With no hands raised, Max looked directly at the Prince and in a soft voice said. "I know that what I'm asking you to do is dangerous. We're all walking a tightrope. Keep your eye on the prize and you'll never have to worry about where the next trick will come from."

Chapter 16: Joe

The files on Madoff's former employees was so comprehensive that Joe had a hard time trying to focus on why he ordered them. Sometimes too much is a bad thing, he thought. Who in a small operation like Madoff's would know Harry the Greek? In a cursory read, using his computer's search function, there were no hits on 'Harry the Greek' or any substantive combination of the words. However, the file on Natalie Shoar, Bernie's office manager, was intriguing. She was with Bernie for sixteen years and ran the secret seventeenth-floor operation—the nexus of the Ponzi scheme. From what Joe read, Natalie was a cooperating witness for the prosecution and, in lieu of jail time, received a sentence of four years' probation. In fact, except for some perfunctory information, there was very little in her file. It was clear to Joe that her interviews with state and federal prosecutors were absent by design, which brought up a red flag. What did she know? What were the feds hiding? Joe copied down her last known address and decided to give her an unannounced visit.

The trip from his Midtown office to her address in Queens took about forty-five minutes. She lived on the first floor of a two-family house on a quiet, dead-end street. Looking around as he got out of his car, he noticed a couple of children's bicycles chained to a street light in front of the house. He went up a short flight of steps and rang her buzzer. He could clearly hear it ringing from his vantage point, and when he got no answer, he rang the buzzer of the family on the second floor.

Once again, there was no reply on the house's intercom—until he heard a voice from a woman hanging out of a window above him say, "What do you want, mister?"

Joe looked up and saw a woman in her late thirties, maybe forties, wearing a bathrobe. "I'm looking for Natalie," Joe told her.

"Who are you?" she said in her best Queens tang.

"I've got something for her," Joe said politely.

"What do you got?" she replied.

"It's personal," Joe said.

"Bullshit," she said and closed her window. Joe tried to get her again by ringing her doorbell, but she ignored his attempt to continue his questioning her. Joe went back to his car and rang his office.

"Give me the record room, please." Joe gave the clerk the address and apartment numbers and requested both phone numbers. Within a few moments, the clerk got back to him with the names and phone numbers of the occupants of that address. Joe first tried Natalie's number, and when there was no answer, he called the tootsie in the floor above. When she answered, Joe was apologetic, telling her that he was a cop and was looking for Natalie. Nothing serious, just a few matters to clear up, when unexpectedly the buzzer rang letting Joe into the building.

"Up here," she said from the floor above. When Joe got to her floor, he was met by a vollabuster, honey-colored blond, wearing a skimpy black robe exposing the rack to end all racks. They looked at each other and almost instinctively, like two wild animals, embraced and began making mad passionate love in the doorway, on the kitchen floor and the living room couch. Later, they split a beer, smoked a couple of joints, and did it all over again, this time on her luxurious Sleep Number adjustable bed. She told Joe that Natalie hadn't been home in over a year and that she had said something about visiting her sister upstate. As Joe was preparing to leave his newfound squeeze, whose name was Mona; she told him that her kids were in school on weekdays from eight-thirty to three-thirty. He smiled and gave her a long kiss goodbye, promising to call.

Back in the car and in need of a shower and a change of clothes, Max stopped at Macy's and bought a dress shirt and underwear. Stopping briefly at the 14th Street "Y," he showered and changed. Disposing of the evidence in a trash bin, Joe headed for his office to check out the lead on Natalie. Once in his cubbyhole, Joe checked his messages and played back several from Sergio demanding updates on "a matter they had discussed." Sergio, obviously unaccustomed to subordinates not fawning over his every word, was telling Joe that he was upping the ante, that he'd better do what he said or else. Knowing Sergio, it was no veiled threat. Joe figuring that it was better to confront him rather than blowing him off, so he picked up the phone and called him. He was told that Sergio was in a meeting and that he would be advised of his call. Joe was relieved that he had momentarily dodged a bullet, both literally and figuratively, and he turned his attention to finding Natalie Shoar. Her file gave him neither a clue to her sister's address nor to any other living family members. It was as if the feds had scrubbed her file as a condition of her cooperation. However, there was a reference in the file that the judge sentenced Natalie to four years' probation.

Technically speaking, depending on the severity of the crime, she would have to see her parole officer either once or twice a month. Add to that the heavy load each parole officer carries, and she could be mailing it in from God knows where. On an off chance, Joe Googled the White Pages for every Shoar in New York state. That, too, came up dry based on age and sex.

Joe realized that his legal options were little or none, and decided to broach the question of finding Natalie with Eisenstaedt's help. With her file under his arm, he marched into Eisenstaedt's office. Surprisingly he found that his boss had a new secretary who acted like she was the gatekeeper to the Fuhrer.

Looking down her nose, she inquired, "And who are jew?"

"Did she say what I heard her say or was it her accent?" Joe murmured to himself, smiling down at her.

"I'm Joe Mancuso, fräulein," he said.

Not amused by Joe's remark, she inquired, "Do you have an appointment?"

"No, I have an important matter to discuss with Mr. Eisenstaedt," he said.

"And what is it in reference to?" she asked.

"That's none of your fuckin' business," Joe said in disgust.

The secretary grabbed her phone and told Eisenstaedt that she had to see him immediately on a sensitive matter. She then got up, leered at Joe, and entered Eisenstaedt's office. A few long seconds later she returned and, with her head down, told Joe that Mr. Eisenstaedt would see him.

"What did you say to her?" said Eisenstaedt shaking his head.

"She's a piece of work with an attitude," Joe replied.

"You can't say things like that here. You're not at a precinct in the Bronx. There's all types of laws against employee harassment, especially towards women in the workplace. Okay, she may have an attitude, but I'll handle it—not you. Do you understand my drift?" Eisenstaedt said. "Now what's so important that you have to rough up my new temp?"

"I've got to find an ex-employee of Madoff. She's off the grid. She was on probation and hasn't been at her apartment in Queens for almost a year according to a neighbor," said Joe.

"Who is she and why do you want to find her?" Eisenstaedt asked.

"Her name is Natalie Shoar. She was Madoff's office manager for sixteen years. I received a tip from an anonymous source that she may have information on an international consultant who was referred to as 'Harry the Greek' by Madoff. I also learned from that same source that Natalie may be with her sister in upstate New York. It also looks like the feds have put a blanket over Natalie to protect her from retribution. In any event, I'd like to know if her parole officer knows where she is."

"Hum," said Eisenstaedt nodding his head. "Queens, that means her parole officer works out of the federal building in Brooklyn. Offhand, I don't know anyone who knows anyone who knows anyone in Brooklyn, but I'll make some calls—with one caveat."

"What?" asked Joe.

"On your way out, you see Miss Ratner and apologize for your remarks. You hear me?" he said, standing and extending his hand. They shook hands, and Eisenstaedt told Joe to leave Natalie's file with him. Joe left with a serious face, stopped at Miss Ratner's desk and humbly expressed his apologies for his inexcusable remarks. Then, with his tail between his legs, he pigeon-walked out of her office.

About forty-five minutes later, Miss Ratner called, asking him to come to her office to pick up Natalie Shoar's file. He did not know if Eisenstaedt had any luck with the parole office in Brooklyn. Not wishing to get on the wrong foot with Miss Ratner again, Joe knocked first, waited a moment, and entered her office. There was Ratner all smiles holding Natalie's file in her hand.

"Any message from Mr. Eisenstaedt?" he asked thinking it was all a futile gesture.

"Look inside," she said handing him the file.

Joe opened the file and saw attached to the cover sheet a yellow Post-It note: Natalie Shoar, 4450 State Road 17, Kiamesha Lake, New York. Elated Joe didn't know what to say; he just stood there nodding his head and then began waving the file above his head as he left her office.

The first thing Joe did when he got back to his cubicle was Google Natalie Shoar's address to see where she was living. The driving directions indicated it was ninety-three miles from his office, and the satellite images showed what looked like a small farmhouse with a barn on Route 17. Owing to the rural nature of the setting, the vehicle in the driveway was the ubiquitous pickup truck. Seeing it was only two hours from the office and happened to be geographically desirable on the Jersey side of the George Washington Bridge, Joe decided now was better than later. He called Patty to tell her he'd be late tonight. He explained to her that he was able to finagle the address of Bernie's office manager with the help of Eisenstaedt and was on his way to Kiamesha Lake in upstate New York.

"How far is it?" Patty asked.

"Not far at all, it's near Monticello," he said.

"The Borsch Belt Monticello?" she asked.

"Yes, just a few miles north of Monticello, but unfortunately it's nothing like it used to be. Kiamesha Lake was the home of the Concord Hotel back in the sixties."

"I know, I think my parents went to a wedding at the Concord," she said softly.

"Do me a favor, check your notes if Ruth ever mentioned Bernie's office manager Natalie Shoar. I'm hoping she knows who Harry the Greek is, and better yet, where I can find him."

However, just as he was closing his desk lamp and locking his file cabinet, his cell phone rang. The caller ID said it was from the Majestic Hotel, meaning Sergio. He'd been ducking Sergio's calls for the past several days and felt he couldn't string him along any longer.

"Mancuso here," he said.

"Please hold," a young lady said.

After a moment, Sergio came on the line. "Mr. Mancuso, I do not relish being put off when I call for updates on my case," he said hesitant to say anything that might be recorded.

"Please forgive me, Signore Leone, but I've been pursuing several of the leads we recently discussed, and I was preparing to present our findings to you at our next meeting," Joe said minding his P's and Q's.

"That's fine, bring it with you tomorrow," Sergio said slamming his phone down. Joe sat back in his desk chair and realized that dealing with Sergio was like stepping in shit. You can clean your shoe, but you can never get rid of the smell. He also realized that there was more going on at the Majestic Hotel and Casino than he had guessed, something like faking investment losses as a way of covering up skimming cash from the casino.

Chapter 17: Max

The flight from Teterboro Airport to Raleigh-Durham was just as the pilot had predicted, smooth as silk. Once on the tarmac the pilot taxied to Hangar 14A, a temporary bay designated for corporate aircraft. Parked outside the hangar were the vehicles Margery had arranged for the Prince and his team, a Lincoln limousine and two nondescript white Honda Accords for her and Max. With the arrangements out of the way, the Prince and his crew took off in their Lincoln limousine, heading for the Washington Hotel. Max and Margery watched the Lincoln race towards a security checkpoint leading out to the highway hoping that Prince's driver would be more prudent when travelling in North Carolina.

"It's stupid mistakes like that that can fuck up the plan," Max said in disgust.

"You'll have to say something to the Prince about his driver," Margery said.

"I know," he said shaking his head.

Margery and Max sat together in one of the Hondas to compare notes. Margery's mission was to secure three houses: one for Ruth and her crew, the second for the construction crew, and the third for Max and herself. They had to bypass motels because the local police made it a part of their routine surveillance to check motel parking lots for transients driving rental cars by copying down their license plates and putting them through their database. Moreover, in a rural town like Butner, North Carolina, rental cars parked several nights at a motel would likely set off bells and whistles.

Max's task was to reconnoiter prospective funeral homes that had crematoriums. He had a general idea of their layouts, but he had to make sure. To that end, he'd prepared a list of the pros and cons of each site. First, the crematorium must be somewhat isolated with no adjacent buildings overlooking the grounds. Second, it must have a parking area or vacant lot where an escape tunnel could be dug. Third, the room in which the cremation was conducted must be able to be sealed off from witnesses. Only when he'd found a home that fit all three criteria would he ask the Prince to use his negotiating skills to close the deal. Max had previously seen the Prince in action and was confident that if anyone could pull it off, the Prince could. He'd cast a spell over the proceedings, and after working his magic they'd be eating out of his hand, begging for them to take the place on their own terms. After all he was not reputed to be the son of the Russian mystic Svengali for nothing.

Like Max, Margery had done her homework and had several houses to inspect. Each house also had specific requirements: being furnished with four-plus bedrooms, two or more bathrooms, central air, with shades/curtains/blinds, Internet service, and above all, they must be secluded, set back from the road, hidden from prying eyes by a combination of trees, walls, shrubs, privacy fences, and the like. In addition to a road leading to the house, it would also be advantageous if it had another leaving in a different direction.

Using a Multiple Listing Service, she had selected a different real estate company for each of the three houses she'd found. It would be very suspicious to lease three houses in a small town like Butner. The first house on her list was for Ruth Madoff, her bodyguard Otto, his son Levi, the Major (AKA Patrick Houghton, MD) and His Lady (Nurse Ida). Margery had also ordered Ruth's bedroom furniture and medical equipment to mimic a hospital intensive care suite. It had an adjustable hospital bed with rails and a sliding tray, an IV stand with fluids hanging from hooks, oxygen tanks with a digital regulator for a nasal cannula, EKG, blood pressure and pulse monitors housed in a console preprogramed to simulate Ruth's vital signs as well as a medical cabinet with vials of injectables and disposable syringes, gloves, and supplies. Her arrangement with a medical supply company in Raleigh would hold her order in their warehouse until she called. Then they would then be given an address in Butner to deliver the order and make the installation.

Margery met the first broker, Mary Anne, parked next to a mailbox off State Road 312 in Butner to inspect a house for Ruth. After a brief how-do-you-do, Margery followed the broker down a narrow gravel road to a large colonial-style house. When she got out of her car, she looked around to see if the house was hidden from the road, which was a major concern in the selection of a house. Mentally she gave it an okay. The broker showed her around, ticking off the house's many features, and led her out the back door to see the fenced-in yard. "In case you had a dog," Mary Anne said. Satisfied that the house would work, Margery startled the broker by saying she'd take it.

Flabbergasted, the broker didn't know what to say and began fumbling with her papers until Margery suggested they sit down and sign the lease. All in all, it had taken less than forty minutes to get the house lock, stock, and barrel. As soon as the broker left, Margery got on the phone and called the next broker, Paul, and hoped that the next house would be as easy. Paul was a sweet, roly-poly guy with a gift of gab who had probably, according to his repertory, sold hundreds of homes. The first house didn't pass the "hidden" requirement, and Margery, with a little urging, told Paul to show her the next house on her list. The second house was so-so and, because it may have to accommodate two crews at once, a little cramped. However, the third house, like the three little pigs, was just right. It was hidden down a long, dirt road. It was a massive, two-story log cabin on a sixteen-acre lot. The furnishings were hand carved. It had a great room, surrounded by bedrooms and bathrooms and a dining room large enough for King Arthur's court.

"I'll take it," Margery told Paul and signed the lease agreement. Paul was so happy that as he handed her the keys, he bowed like a southern gentleman. Watching Paul's car disappear down the driveway, Margery called Max to tell him the good news. "Did you find a place for us?" he inquired.

"Not yet. It's the next house on the list," she said.

"Well, I hope you find something or we'll be sleeping in the woods tonight," he said.

"Don't worry, if push gets to shove, I've got the keys to two houses to choose from."

"Great," he said, "and by the way, the funeral home and crematorium on Reagan Road is perfect for our plans. I'm just going to see the last one to rule it out. I'll call you later to arrange a meeting place."

"Roger and out," she said

"Very funny, ten-four," he said.

"Love you," she said.

"Love you, too," he said.

The last broker, Bonnie Graham, was late getting to their appointment on Rosewood Lane to show Margery the house. She explained that she was at a house inspection and the buyer was looking for any excuse to back out of the Purchase and Sale Agreement. She told Margery that it was a classic case of buyer's remorse. Bonnie said that the buyer told her she didn't want to buy the house because "it didn't smell good."

When Bonnie asked her what it was supposed to smell like, she replied, "Like they just baked a loaf of bread," whereupon both women agreed that it was a good reason not to buy the house.

Bonnie then showed Margery the house. Margery liked what she saw and signed a lease. Now, Max and Margery had three houses in Butner to choose from. Being that the one on Rosewood Lane was going to be their residence, Margery got the bags and some groceries she'd picked up out of her car and began making the bed and filling the dresser with their clothes. With perfect timing, Max called and told Margery that he had ruled out the last site.

They decided that Max should pick up something for dinner, either pizza or Chinese. "Which one?" he asked.

"Surprise me," she said.

It was pizza that night. Max couldn't find a Chinese restaurant on Yelp within thirty miles of their location, whereas there were four pizza places within a mile of their house. However, by the time Max got to the pizzeria, Margery discovered that, as it was getting dark, the house she had just rented did not have electricity. Luckily, she was able to reach Max while he was waiting for his pizza to come out of the oven.

"Max, where are you?" she asked.

"I'll be at the house in ten minutes," he said.

"Wait, before you come here there's something I've got to tell you," she said.

"What's up?" He asked.

"Well, you know the house I just rented for us? I did so in a hurry," she explained.

"Yeah, anything wrong?" he asked.

"A minor detail, the power is turned off," she said.

"Honey, did you check the circuit breakers?" he asked sympathetically.

"Hold on, I'll check," she said scurrying around the house looking for the fuse box. Entering the garage she saw the fuse box next to the water heater. She opened it and threw the 200-amp circuit breaker and voila, it was show time.

"You were right, you can come home now," she said.

"Does the house have a working fireplace?" he asked.

"Yes, a pretty white one in the living room. I think it works since it has burn marks," she said.

"Good, there's a hardware store across the street. I'll see if they have some of those prefab logs," he said.

"Why, do you feel romantic?" she asked

"I'm always romantic when I'm with you," he said.

"In that case I should have brought my Victoria Secret nighty," she purred.

"Be right there," he said as he grabbed his pizza and headed out the door.

When Max arrived at their new Butner abode, he was quite impressed by the layout and most of all seeing Margery sprawled on the couch in a satin negligee. She was stunning, he thought.

"What do you want for your first course: the pizza or me?" he asked, in his best Cary Grant imitation, opening the box for her to see a sausage pizza with extra cheese.

"Oh too tempting, big boy." After due consideration she said, "Just leave the pizza and get into something comfortable."

"Where did you put our clothes?" he asked putting the pizza down on the coffee table.

"Upstairs in the master bedroom, behind the mayonnaise," she joked.

With the alluring image of Margery waiting for him on the couch, Max ran up the stairs, found his robe hanging in the closet and hurried back to the living room to see her on the floor gazing up at a blank TV screen with the remote clicker in one hand and a large slice of sausage pizza in the other.

"Well, I guess you've chosen the pizza over me," he said sitting down beside her and picking up a slice of pizza.

"How do you put this thing on?" she pleaded pushing all the buttons on the TV clicker.

"Your guess is as good as mine," he said.

"Did you at least get a bottle of Chianti to go with the pizza? she asked.

"They don't sell fine wine at Vinny's Pizza Emporium," he said through a mouthful.

"Barbarians," she said scooping up a small nibble of sausage from one of the slices in the box.

"Hey, that's a no-no where I come from," he said.

"Ya think?" she replied, imitating his Brooklyn accent.

Max sat back watching Margery finagle the clicker, thinking how lucky he is. He had the undying love of a woman who was and would ever be a free spirit in tune with the world, the good and the bad, ever willing to explore her passions with a deep reservoir of love and kindness. Deep down he hoped that this new, dangerous endeavor would not put her in harm's way. He knew that whether or not they were successful, life would never be the same for them.

Chapter 18: Joe

Joe left his office in a hurry, hoping to miss the rush-hour crowd heading off the island of Manhattan. So far, so good, he thought making all the lights on Eighth Avenue heading uptown. Maybe they've finally figured out how to synchronize the traffic lights like most of the major cities in the world—no, that would be asking too much of a city of eight million people that's run by a bunch of clowns. However, this doubting Thomas cruised over the George Washington Bridge in record time and was on the well-travelled Route 17 headed to what many New Yorkers considered The 'Land of Oz,' the Catskills. Back in the 1960s and 70s the Catskills were the land of sprawling hotels with Olympic-sized pools, golf courses, massive dining rooms that fed hundreds of guests per seating, "all-you-can-eat" breakfasts, lunches, and dinners, and best of all, an extension of the 'Great White Way.' The finest talent that Broadway had to offer played the Catskills, notably at the Saturday night shows, which were extravaganzas: singers, dancers, and capping the night off, the comedians who had their audiences rolling in the aisles and pissing in their pants.

As Joe entered Kiamesha Springs and approached the house, he noticed an old blue Pontiac in the driveway and pulled in next to it. Glancing at a photo of Natalie on the seat next to him he wondered how much she might have changed in the twenty or so years since the photo was taken. However, the woman who opened the door to him had not changed one iota. Yes, her black curly hair had turned gray in some places, but her brown eyes and olive-skinned complexion, framed in houndstooth eyeglasses, were a dead giveaway that she was the elusive Natalie Shoar.

"Natalie, I'm Joe Mancuso, and I'd like to talk with you," he said.

"What do you want?" she asked suspiciously, looking over his shoulder to see if there were others with him.

Taking out his ID, he said, "I'm a private investigator and I need some information."

"Look, I don't know why you're here and I don't have anything to tell you, so goodbye," she said starting to close the door.

Joe reached up and held the door open. "Natalie, I've dragged my ass up from New York City and I'm not going to leave until we talk."

"Get out of here or I'll call the cops," she threatened, trying to shut the door.

"Go ahead. I'll tell them some shit about you that they'll run you out of town for. Now stop playing with me. I'm not here to harm you, I just want some information on Zack," he said.

The very mention of Zack's name changed everything in her demeanor. Her face went from a scowl to one of somber reflection.

"We can't talk here. Wait, I'll get my car keys," she said, retreating into the kitchen to get them.

"Follow me," she said as she returned, closing the door behind her.

"Where are we going?" Joe asked as she got into her Pontiac.

"There's a little park down there with picnic tables," she said pointing down the road. "Follow me."

After a mile or two, Natalie pulled into a gravel parking lot. Adjacent to the lot, in a wooded area, were picnic tables and barbeque pits. Natalie got out of her car and began walking through the picnic area with Joe a few steps behind her. Joe sensed that Natalie wanted to be as far off the road as possible to avoid being seen with a stranger. Sitting opposite each other at a picnic table, Natalie asked, "What do you want to know about Zack?"

Natalie turned out to be a fount of information about Zack, who Bernie recognized as a gift from heaven. She didn't know how Zack came to work at their fledgling brokerage, but his genius opened up a whole new method of buying and selling securities. She said that Bernie treated Zack as if he were his son. There was nothing he wouldn't do to help him lead a safe, comfortable life in a city that could be very cruel to a boy who had trouble coping with reality. She said Bernie personally canvassed the area for a suitable apartment within walking distance of their office and rented it for Zack. Then he had the apartment furnished, stocked it with easy-to-prepare meals, took him to Macy's for clothes, and gave him a generous weekly allowance. On holidays he took Zack home with him to be part of his family. Sitting back with tears filling her eyes, she said that she believed it was love, pure and simple love, given and received, that gave Zack the inspiration to create, out of thin air, the most revolutionary method of trading securities the world had ever seen. His method cast aside the inefficient "specialist system" that had been prevalent for over a century, with an electronic trading model that, as the NASDAQ, became the standard for markets worldwide.

Now that Joe had effectively broken the ice and Natalie had overcome her doubts about speaking to him, he introduced another character he needed information on.

"Natalie, what can you tell me about Harry the Greek?" he asked. Natalie seemed confused by the question and using her hands, palms up, she shook her head.

"Did Bernie ever mention someone called Harry the Greek?"

"No, I've never heard Bernie or anyone in the office ever mention that name," she said.

"He might have been a financial adviser or a banker," he said.

"Beats me. Who told you Bernie knew him?" she asked.

"His name came up as someone who may have helped Bernie find clients. You know, high rollers," he speculated.

Natalie smiled at the thought of Bernie needing clients. "In the beginning maybe, but once the word got out that he was guaranteeing ten percent or more on investments, he didn't need any side action," she said proudly. Before Joe could ask another question, she continued in the same vein. "They were coming to him with bags and bags of cash, pleading—no, begging—to get into our exclusive investment club."

Not wishing to belabor the point, Joe switched to Bernie's wife. "When you were working for Bernie, was Ruth working there, too?"

"Yes and no, in the beginning she helped out with the kids on the sixth floor, the brokerage division. That's not to say she didn't come up to the seventeenth floor to see Bernie," she said beginning to look around.

"Maybe this Greek guy was an investor," Joe said.

"Honestly I don't know anything about this guy Harry," Natalie said, then looking at the sky above, she smiled as if she remembered something and said, "The oranges, those boxes of oranges we got during the winter from Florida."

"What do you mean?" Joe asked.

"Someone he knew sent him oranges from Florida, these big freakin' boxes. There were so many, we used to take bags of them home."

"Really?" Joe said, pretending to follow along but not understanding its significance.

"Yeah, and as I remember, they were from some Greek guy he knew," she said.

"Do you remember where in Florida they came from?" he asked sitting forward on his seat.

"No, you order them from some grower and he ships them to you with a card from the sender," she said.

"Did you ever look at the card?" he asked.

"No, by the time I got my cut of the oranges, there were only a few left," she said, starting to get antsy. "Look, I've got to go now; my sister will be home soon looking for me." She got up and headed for the parking lot.

"Wait, one more question," he said coming up alongside of her.

"Bernie never mentioned who the sender was, other than he was Greek?"

"No, he didn't," she said. As they reached their cars she turned and said with a smile, "Look for him where the Greeks go."

Satisfied that he had been able to get a modicum of information from Natalie on his first attempt, Joe turned his attention to following up on the lead that Harry might be somewhere in Florida. With a two-hour trip home ahead of him, he called his office and asked for the research department. Then after going through the customary mishmash of identifying himself and the case file, they finally assigned a research assistant to field his questions.

"Good evening, Joe, I'm Nancy Ramos, how can I help you?" she asked.

"Nancy, where do all the Greeks call home in Florida?" he asked.

"Gimme a second, I'll check," she said. A few seconds later she said, "That was easy. A place called Tarpon Springs."

"Really?" he said. "How did you get the town so fast?"

"It has the largest Greek population in the United States, that's how," she said.

"Interesting, where's the nearest Waters office to Tarpon Springs?"

"I thought you'd ask that question. Waters has a office in Tampa only thirty miles from Tarpon Springs."

"One more thing, I'm looking for a man whose first name is Harry that may live in Tarpon Springs. How would I go about finding him?" he asked.

"Can you give me more information on him? His age or marital status, number of children or occupation? How long he's lived there, or his income, things like that?" she asked.

"Yes and no, and this is just guesswork on my part. He's probably over sixty years old. Don't know if he has any family. I think he has a banking or finance background," he said.

"That's something at least," she said.

"Well, can you compile a list of every Harry in Tarpon Springs over sixty who might fit this vague description?"

"Sure, but I'll have to compare several lists. You know there are 23,484 Greek people in Tarpon Springs. And that doesn't include snowbirds."

"Shit, I didn't think of that," he said.

"Look, can I reach you on this number if I have anything?" she asked.

"Yep, it's my cell phone," he said and broke the connection just as an incoming call came from Patty.

"How'd it go?" she asked.

"Well, she was noncommittal until I got her in a chokehold, then she spilled the beans," he said sounding serious.

"No, cut the bullshit, what did she say?"

"At first, she was very reluctant, out of fear of the feds and the investors, or anyone looking to get even with the people who stole their life's savings," he said.

"Did she know who Harry the Greek was?" she asked.

"No, but she did give me a possible, with a small "P" lead, that he lived in Florida. Most likely Tarpon Springs, which is supposedly the nearest thing to a Greek elephant graveyard in the United States," he said.

"So, is it a dead end?"

"I've got Waters working on it and should know something by tomorrow. Meanwhile, I should be home in a couple of hours, should I get something to go?" he asked.

"I've already fed the kids. Do you want me to order a pizza from Gino's?"

"Yeah, I'll call you when I'm about fifteen minutes from home."

"Drive careful," she said and hung up.

Chapter 19: Max

After a restless night, Margery and Max awoke with the hungry horrors, and while Margery went downstairs to put on a pot of coffee, Max took a shower. Then, the roles were reversed with Max starting breakfast: orange juice, bacon, eggs, and toasted English muffins while Margery took a well-deserved, leisurely shower. Returning to the kitchen with a towel wrapped around her head, she joined Max in wolfing down every morsel of food on their plates. Satiated, they took their coffee cups out onto their deck and began the process of outlining their plans.

Once settled on the deck, Margery took out her steno pad and started listing the who, what, when, and where for each member of their team. The Prince and his team were at the Washington Hotel in Butner. Their job was twofold: first, to secure complete control of the funeral home and crematorium for a period of thirty days, and second, to hire a local attorney who was on a first-name basis with the warden. The Major and His Lady were in New York City, where they were gathering the props—a seven-by-ten-foot blue cloth with a white Star of David embroidered on it, an elaborately carved wooden podium, yarmulkes, shawls, and a Torah for the video production at Studio 4U on West 23rd Street. The Major was also coaching Bernie's 'look-alike' on his lines and stagecraft. He was also to take him to Barney's on Seventh Ave. to purchase his costume (a black suit, white shirt, black clip-on tie, black socks, and black loafers, the identical outfit Bernie would wear at Ruth's service). The Lear would then take the Major and His Lady to rendezvous with Margery in Butner in anticipation of Ruth's arrival. Max had spoken with Glen, the general contractor, and was arranging for the Lear to collect them and the pyrotechnics engineers in Reno, and bring them to Butner to inspect the site. Max has requested that Sy give Ruth the signal to leave New York by car for the house in Butner where the Major and his Lady would be waiting.

Just hearing Margery's recitation of the list gave Max the shudders. It would be like juggling a half-dozen eggs: if they dropped one it would be impossible to put it back together again.

"Is that all there is?" Max said half jokingly.

"Oh no, that's just page one, the preamble. Do you want me to recite page two, the rollout?" she said.

"No, save that for later, let's get the hospital suite set up at Ruth's house."

Margery called the medical supply company and requested they deliver her order between one and two that afternoon. They said that the earliest they could send their truck out with her order was four, which she reluctantly agreed to.

"Not bad for a last-minute request," Max said.

"You're right. I was pushing it," Margery said. "When can we expect to see Ruth Madoff?"

"If they can slip out of the city without the feds in hot pursuit, they should be here in a couple of days," Max said.

"I assume they'll stop along the way?" Margery asked.

"Probably halfway, Maryland or Virginia," Max speculated.

"Anyway, Sy will advise us when she's thirty minutes out."

"When is the Prince seeing the owners of the funeral home?"

"I don't know. I don't want to pressure him, and, more importantly, I don't want him to think I'm micromanaging his job."

"You might be right, my dear," Margery said in her best Southern drawl.

After Max and Margery finished checking with their office in New York, fielding questions from their staff, they headed for the house they'd rented for Ruth and her people. Since this was the first time Max had seen the house, Margery showed him the room she'd chosen to install Ruth in. The room that would become Ruth's medical suite was a first-floor fifteen-by-twenty-foot bedroom with an adjoining bathroom. Margery and Max removed the furniture in the room that was not needed and stored it in the basement. Then, with time to kill before the delivery of Ruth's equipment, they drove to the local supermarket to stock the house with provisions. Max and Margery decided to divide and conquer; each armed with their own shopping cart they proceeded to fill their carts with what they thought would be the bare necessities for Ruth, her bodyguard Otto, his son Levi, the Major and His Lady. Meeting at a checkout cashier, each perused the other's cart with an eye for duplications and omissions. However, once in their car they realized that they hadn't checked to see if the house had enough dinnerware, anything that one might require to prepare and serve a meal for five people. Googling on their way out of the parking lot, Margery found to her surprise a Crate and Barrel only ten minutes away. This time instead of separating into competing scavenging hunts, they teamed up and literally raced around the store, throwing in their cart a box set of silverware, dinnerware, and glassware. Since time was of the essence, they raced to the house to find that the medical supply truck waiting for them. Leaving their packages in their car they greeted the deliverymen and showed them where to place each piece of furniture and equipment. After which, they had them test the electronics and run simulations of blood pressure, pulse, the EKG, and oxygen levels. With everything running to their satisfaction, Max gave each man a C-note for their help.

After unpacking their car, they found that a "furnished house in Butner" came with most of the items they had purchased at Crate and Barrel but were pleased that they had at least covered all the contingencies. Exhausted, Margery put on a pot of coffee as they sat in the living room trying to catch their breath before driving back to their house.

"It's as good as it gets," Margery said sipping her coffee.

"Do you remember how to run the cardiovascular simulation?" Max asked.

"Yeah, it's a no-brainer. Each monitor has its own test function, and unless you've worked in the ER, you'd never know the difference," she said.

"In other words, it'll pass the sniff test," he asked.

"They can sniff all they want, but they'll never know it was just a fake," she said.

On their way back to their house Max broached the subject that had been bothering him since his last communiqué from Sy. "I'm trying to think of who the sponsor might be, and the only one that makes any sense is Ruth," he said.

"That might be reasonable if she had the money," Margery replied.

"She may not have the money on hand, but she may know where it is," Max said.

"Or she may not know where the money is, but Bernie does and she needs his help to get it."

"On the other hand, let's assume Bernie and Ruth can't get their hands on ten million dollars—then who? And if they had that amount of money, why should they risk everything to break Bernie out of prison?

Family, friends, business associates, an investor seeking revenge? I don't know and that troubles me."

"Look, we've agreed to a dangerous mission and have been paid the money in advance. I don't think it's asking too much to know the identity of the sponsor," Margery said.

"You're right, but Sy might come back saying that we've accepted the job on a 'need-to-know basis' and knowing the identity of the sponsor is not part of the assignment. In other words, we don't need to know who it is to accomplish our mission," Max said as they arrived at their house.

"That's true, but the thought that we may be delivering Bernie into the hands of an assassin troubles me," Margery said as she exited the car.

"You're right, I never thought of it that way, but how can we be certain without knowing the identity of the sponsor?" Max said, using his cell phone as a light to illuminate the front door lock. "Do you have the key, Margery?"

"Yep, wait a second," she said, opening the door. They went around the house putting on the lights and opening some of the windows to let a cool breeze in. Max instinctively opened the refrigerator door to see if there were any snacks worth taking out.

"Do you want some cheese and crackers?" he called out to Margery as she checked her email on the computer.

"Max, I need your thumb drive decoder. You have a message from Sy," she said. Max sat down beside Margery and inserted the thumb drive in the side of the laptop and entered his password to retrieve Sy's message. Max glanced at the message and read it out loud.

"Ruth Madoff, Otto Klein, and Levi Klein en route to Butner by car. ETA Thursday, will update with 30-minute window. Stan Sabin (AKA The Major) and Sally Lipton (AKA His Lady) ETA Raleigh Airport, Hangar 14A, Wednesday 1500 hours."

Max acknowledged receipt of Sy's message, hoping that Ruth would not use any of her credit cards or cell phones during their journey. He exited the secure email setting and made a note for Margery to collect the Major and His Lady at the airport at three tomorrow. He then called the Prince for an update on the crematorium situation. The Prince told Max that the current owners inherited the business last year and that it had had a spotty record with many complaints according to the Better Business Bureau. He said that he'd invited the owners for dinner with him at his hotel and that he anticipated that they would be interested in the deal.

Max told the Prince that Ruth Madoff and her party would be arriving in a couple of days. He wanted him to be available to discuss how to handle any visitors to Ruth's house, the most important of which was the local attorney that was to represent Ruth in her request for Bernie to attend her funeral. The Prince said he had a good prospect for the job, a guy who cuddled up to the warden at he Butner Country Club. He expected to interview him shortly. Max advised the Prince that he would be returning to New York to tape the cremation scene with Bernie's look-alike and that he'd like to have unrestricted access to the crematorium when he got back to show his general contractor what he wanted done. The Prince said he should be able to finalize arrangements by then. Max thought to himself as he hung up that he hoped it wasn't wishful thinking on the Prince's part that they would have access to the crematorium so quickly, but if anyone could pull the rabbit out of his hat, it was the Prince.

Chapter 20: Joe

At seven forty-five the next morning, Joe was awoken by a phone call from the research department at Waters. "Is this Joe Mancuso?" said a bright, cheerful voice.

"Yep," said Joe getting out of bed and heading for the kitchen with the phone.

"We have narrowed your request for information to three male prospects who fit your description in Tarpon Springs, Florida," she said.

"Gimme their ages and occupations?" Joe said popping a K-Cup into the Keurig coffeemaker.

"The first one is a Harry Proferes, seventy-one, Chicago bank president, clean as a whistle. The second one is a Harry Papandreou, eighty-three, savings and loan officer, mixed up in the subprime mortgage scandal; he pled guilty and received three years' probation. The third one is a Harry Sarandopolis, seventy-seven, financial consultant with an eight-page CV," she said.

"Tell me more about, I can't pronounce his name, the third one."

"Sarandopolis is a graduate of the London School of Economics and received his Ph.D. from the Harvard Business School. He was a professor of economics at the Harvard Business School for twelve years and later joined Marshall, Cartwright, and Dwyer as a partner in charge of international monetary affairs. He retired three years ago," she said.

"Have you got an address?" Joe said searching for cream in the fridge.

"Yes and no, his address is listed as Slip 4 at TSM," she said.

"Email me what you have on the third one," he said and hung up frustrated there was no cream. Hearing the ruckus, Patty joined him in the kitchen.

"Who was that?" Patty asked looking through the box of K-Cups for her French Vanilla coffee pod.

"Who drinks the fuckin' cream?" Joe said smelling the container of milk.

"The milk's okay, I bought it yesterday," she said.

"That was Waters, I think they found Harry the Greek," he said tasting his coffee.

"Did you check the date on it?" Joe started to complain when Patty interrupted saying, "Stop being a prima donna."

"Okay," he said and headed down to the office.

"What are you going to do?" she asked, following him down the stairs, cradling her coffee. Joe's first thought was to check the flights from Newark to Tampa, but on second thought, why not have Patty do it?

"Get me a non-stop flight from Newark to Tampa today," he instructed Patty. Excited that she was given a modicum of responsibility, Patty dutifully complied while Joe printed his email from Waters. While his little bubble-jet spit out page after page on 'the third one' Joe had requested, he perused the report.

"There's a non-stop from Newark to Tampa at one forty-five today," she said.

"Book it, Danno," he said, engrossed in the report.

"When do you want to come home?" she asked.

"Leave it open. It depends. I think he's the one, but maybe he's not, so, we'll keep the return open," he said.

Hearing the kids in the kitchen, Patty said, "It's all set up. Enter your company credit card and print your ticket." She headed up the stairs to start breakfast for the kids.

During the two-hour flight from Newark to Tampa, Joe studied the report on Harry Sarandopolis looking for clues to any possible involvement he may have had with Bernie L. Madoff Investment Securities. It couldn't have been at Harvard, so it must have been while he was with Marshall, Cartwright, and Dwyer, but international monetary affairs—what's that have to do with Bernie? The report didn't say anything vaguely suspicious about Sarandopolis' duties at Marshall. According to his CV he was an academic bigwig, nothing more.

After collecting a rental car at the airport Joe set his GPS for the Tarpon Springs Marina and settled back listening to The Chairmen of the Board, the crooner with the perfect pitch, sing the melodies of the fifties and sixties. Oh, those were some great times back then, he thought. The Jersey Shore was rife with music, food, and beautiful babes. Joe took a deep breath, and for an instant, he could smell the fryolators cooking zeppoli and see a young girl asking if he wanted confectionary sugar sprinkled on top. He could taste the rawness of the fried dough and the sweetness of the powdered sugar, and all in all what he needed now was an ice-cold beer. Instead, he tried his best to accompany Sinatra in "Fly Me to the Moon."

A turn here and a turn there and voila, he was in the parking lot of the Tarpon Springs Marina. As he got out of his car he was hit with the combination of a blazing sun mixed with the smells of low tide. From his vantage point looking down at the sprawling marina he realized it wasn't some fancy-schmancy club for parking yachts. Yeah, there were some big ones, but the mood and décor was more like he'd seen in Key West. Putting on his sunglasses, he scanned the marina looking for an office where he could ask about Slip 4. He stopped when he saw a man standing on a huge, white yacht docked to the outer part of one of the slips. The man was giving orders to a group of men loading provisions onto the ship.

"That's gotta be Harry," he said to himself. Going down a weathered flight of wooden stairs, Joe made his way up and down the maze of slips until he came to a pathway to the yacht. Stacked by the yacht were cases of wine, canned goods, spring water, and some boxes just marked 'Deliver to TSM Slip 4.' Well, if anything, Joe thought, it's Harry's ship.

Coming back on deck, the man looked down at Joe and said, "Come on, hand me the wine."

Dumbfounded Joe could only reach down, lift a case of wine, and hand it to Harry.

"Good, bring the water on board with you," Harry said as he disappeared down the steps into the galley. Doing what he was told, Joe lifted the case of water and made his way up the gangplank onto the deck. Peering down into the galley he saw Harry looking up at him.

"What are you waiting for? Bring it down," Harry said. Joe eased his way down the stairs and placed the case of water on top of a case of Cape Cod potato chips.

"Not there, you'll crush the chips," Harry said pointing to a spot where he wanted Joe to drop the water. "Now, who the hell are you?" he asked when Joe had done so. "I know most of the people down here and I've never seen you around."

Joe reached into his back pocket and took out his wallet and showed Harry his photo ID. Harry took the wallet and looked at the photo of Joe saying, "This is a recent photo of you. You're new to the game, aren't you?"

"You should have been a detective instead of a college professor," Joe said.

"Well, Mr. Mancuso, what do you want with an old salt like me?" Harry asked.

"Is there someplace we can talk?" Joe asked.

"Oh, this sounds serious. Do I need my attorney?" Harry said with a smile.

"No, just a conversation amongst friends," Joe said.

"Excellent, in that case let's get a drink," Harry suggested. Joe followed him down a passageway to the bow of the ship into an air-conditioned lounge.

"Make yourself comfortable. What do you drink? Beer, wine, whiskey?" Harry said, holding a bottle of scotch.

Noticing that Harry was holding a bottle of Glenfiddich single malt, Joe said, "Scotch on the rocks."

"Good man, there's nothing like a smooth single malt to break the ice," said Harry. After both men had a sip of the rare elixir, Harry came to the point. "Where are you based?" he asked.

"Sounds like you've heard of Waters," Joe said.

"I know of them by reputation only," Harry said.

"I'm out of the Manhattan office."

"Is it government business that brings you here today?" Harry said, taking a slow sip.

"No, I'm working on the recovery of the ill-gotten gains of Bernie Madoff," Joe said also taking a sip.

Harry sat back and smiled at Joe. "And how did you find me?"

"It was the oranges," Joe said.

Harry looked at the ceiling and began to laugh. "Really, the oranges?" he said in disbelief.

"Yep, those oranges brought me here," Joe said with a smile.

"They don't sell them anymore! A handful of growers control the market today, and they make more money extracting the juice," Harry said.

At that point as Joe and Harry were savoring their scotch in came a young beautiful girl.

"Papou, they want to test the"—upon seeing Joe, she said hi, then continued without missing a beat —"bow thrusters."

"Lisa, this is Mr. Mancuso. He's a private eye," Harry said half jokingly.

"Really, like Inspector Hercule Poirot?"

"Sort of. Without the moustache, of course," Joe replied.

Amused, Lisa continued along the same vein, "Has there been a murder?"

"Not yet," replied Harry struggling to get out of his chair. "Let me see to our engineer. Lisa, take care of Joe until I get back inspecting the beast below decks," he said, finishing his drink.

"So, do you have a gun?" she asked Joe when Harry had left.

"No, my weapon of choice is my irresistible charm," Joe said taking a slow sip of his drink.

Lisa seemed fascinated by this stranger and didn't know how to react. She began aimlessly walking around the lounge picking up things and then putting them down.

Joe noticed that her movement had a grace to it and asked, "Where did you study ballet?"

"How did you know I was a dancer?" Lisa asked.

"I'm a detective. I detect," Joe said with a smile.

"I danced in college," she said pouring herself a lemonade and plopping on the sofa.

"And Harry is?" Joe asked.

"My grandfather, don't you see the resemblance?"

"Of course, it was his beard that threw me off," he said as Harry returned.

"Has she told you all of our secrets?" Harry asked.

"No she clammed up as soon as you left," Joe said, sharing a smile with Lisa.

"Well I'm happy to know that she hasn't told you about the treasure map," Harry said glancing at both of them.

"Papou, that's our secret! I'd never tell," she said seriously.

"Good, did I ever tell you that you're my best granddaughter?" Harry asked Lisa.

"A thousand times. He says that because I'm his only granddaughter," she said to the amusement of both men.

"Well, we have work to do before we set sail on the morn," Harry said. Joe rose from his chair figuring that the interview was over. But then Harry approached, extending his hand and saying, "We're throwing a party for a few guests tonight. Join us and we can continue our discussion, say, eight o'clock?"

"Count on it," Joe said.

The men shook hands and Harry asked Lisa to escort Joe off the ship.

Chapter 21: Max

"Voila," said the Prince at eight o'clock the next morning.

"Is that you, Prince?" murmured Max cradling his phone while sliding out of bed.

"We've got the barbeque pit all to ourselves and they're packing up as we speak. Should be able to pick up the keys this afternoon."

"Great," said Max, telling Margery the good news.

"The deal was a six-month lease with an option to buy, and they grabbed it. They can't wait to get out from under, no pun intended, the business of 'cooking people.' Their words, not mine," the Prince said.

"Let me update you on some of the comings and goings," Max said. "Now, thanks to you, we've got the crematorium, I'll arrange to get our contractor out to look it over. Also, Margery is collecting the Major and His Lady today and bringing them to their house in Butner. Lastly, Ruth Madoff is en route by car to Butner. Her ETA is some time tomorrow. Is there anything you need?"

"No, not at this time. We should have a local yokel attorney to act on our behalf with the warden soon."

"Excellent," Max said breaking the connection and turning to face Margery. "I don't know how he does it but, he should be known as the Wizard of Second Ave."

While Max was putting a few things in his suitcase Margery was composing a note to send Sy regarding their flight plans. With the Major and His Lady en route to Raleigh, she wanted to advise him that Max would be returning to Teterboro on the Lear. In addition, she wanted to arrange for the Lear to collect six passengers at the Reno-Tahoe International Airport, then stop to pick up Max at Teterboro, then fly them all to Raleigh. She was hoping that Sy could make the arrangements on the fly, so to speak, and work around their constantly changing schedules. Showing Max what she had come up with, Max said that, on short notice, her schedule was the best they could come up with, especially since it was getting to the short strokes. Margery inserted the thumb drive, entered the password, crossed her fingers, and sent the coded message to Sy.

During their ride to the airport, Margery and Max discussed the forthcoming mock crematorium taping using their Madoff look-alike.

"He's a spitting image of Bernie," Max said.

"Did the Major rehearse what he's supposed to do with the Torah?" Margery asked.

"Yes, the Major should have instructed him what to do and say. The one saving grace is that although he'll be speaking his lines, there won't be any audio to worry about. We'll advise the guards there's no audio. In fact most surveillance setups lack an audio component."

"What about the smoke and fire, will that be real?" Margery asked.

"As real as we can make it. I've hired one of the best smoke-and-mirror guys on Broadway to stage that sequence, which we'll use to show Glen's pyro guy what to copy at the crematorium." Max turned into the security entrance to the private plane hangars. "Luckily, they just wave you through," he said, in light of the lax airport security, "which will be important for our getaway."

For some unknown reason, 1500 hours was a busy time at Hangar 14A with several corporate jets parked in the taxiway.

"I hope there won't be a delay getting our Lear to the hangar," said Margery.

"Don't worry, we can pick them up at an adjacent hangar if need be," Max said finding a parking space that overlooked the main runway. It was considerably busy at the airport that afternoon. It seemed that there was only a matter of seconds between those planes landing and those taking off. Max told Margery that without complicated algorithms, air traffic controllers wouldn't be able to handle the demands of today's airline traffic.

"I still don't like it. It puts too much pressure on pilots and controllers," she said as she caught a glance of what resembled their Lear landing.

It was their plane, and within a few minutes it was taxiing towards Hangar 14A, when, to their surprise, a jet that was idling on an access road began to move out of the way allowing their Lear to approach the hangar. Once the Lear came to a stop and the engines were idling, the cabin door opened and the stairway descended to the ground. First off the plane was the Major followed closely by His Lady. As Margery hurried to meet their new arrivals, Max was digging out his suitcase from the trunk of the car.

"Quite a brilliant plane," said the Major to Margery as he greeted her with a kiss.

"A pleasant flight, I hope?" Margery said as Max joined them, suitcase in hand.

"She flies like a Spitfire, an RAF fighter plane. What an experience!" he exclaimed. As Margery led their guests to her car, Max went on board to speak with the pilots. He told them that he'd requested permission to fly back to Teterboro Airport with them, but they hadn't heard from Sy. The pilot sent a message to Sy asking for permission to take Max to Teterboro and said he could wait forty-five minutes before he had to leave.

Max returned to Margery and explained his predicament. Luckily, when Max returned to the Lear, the pilot said he'd gotten an okay and that Max had a message from Sy. Max called Margery and told her to bring the Major and His Lady to Ruth's house and that he'd contact her when he got to New York. With all the formalities out of the way, the pilot retracted the stairs, locked the cabin door and proceeded to the runway for takeoff. Max whipped out his laptop, inserted his thumb drive, and retrieved Sy's message. To begin with, Sy's demeanor was different from his usual all-business staccato. It seemed that Max's requests were taken as orders and that didn't go over well with Sy. Sy told him that his flight schedules were "problematic and apt to draw attention to the use of a $2,500 per hour asset."

Sy then drew upon a familiar colloquialism to make his point saying, "Use your fuckin' head next time," and okayed the use of the Lear with the caveat to space its use with an eye on how others might view the use of a "$24 MILLION DOLLAR CORPORATE AIRCRAFT!"

Needless to say, Max got the point. He decided to be more careful in the future on the use of the Lear, realizing that Sy's neck was also in the noose.

The ride from the airport to Ruth's house had an air of tension. The Major and His Lady seemed troubled but couldn't get what was bothering them out. The chipper, upbeat rhetoric of the Major was now uncharacteristically short, with long pauses and aimless looks out of the window.

"What's wrong?" Margery finally asked.

The Major and His Lady glanced at each other before she broke the silence by softly saying, "We're suffering from stage fright. We don't know where to go after our performance is over."

"I understand," Margery said, "but you have to think of it as your escape, too. I'm sure you've often thought of what and where you'd like to enjoy your sunset hours but ruled it out because it was beyond your means. Well, now you'll have the money to go almost anywhere."

"That's the point, we love Manhattan. All our friends are there, but once our faces are plastered on every TV in the world, all we can do is dig a hole and jump in," she said filling up with tears.

"Easy, my love," said the Major hugging her and drying her tears.

"Granted the metropolis is off limits but there are literally hundreds of places to hang your hat if you're careful and use some stage magic," Margery said.

"What type of magic do you have in mind?" asked the Major.

"The magic of the theater! The application of makeup and costume. You can create a new persona, a new identity, a new appearance that would fool any Inspector Javert. Your credo for over fifty years has been that the world is a stage. Well, tomorrow is Act One."

It took a few moments for what she said to sink in, but from that point on, the Major and His Lady acted as if they had a new lease on life. They turned their attention to the roles they were commissioned to play, or, as they referred to it, The Great Escape.

Once at their new house, Margery showed them their living quarters and where their performance would be staged. To her delight, the two old pros began rearranging things so that the set conveyed a message.

"It's all in the lighting," the Major said. "The scene is somber, where death is an uninvited guest. We must therefore transform this antiseptic scene," he pointed to the array of monitoring instrumentation, "into one of quiet reflection."

"How do we accomplish this reflection?" Margery asked skeptically.

"We do this by introducing the artifacts of her life as a wife, mother, a Jewish mother. Surround her with photographs, doilies, religious memorabilia, small potted plants, cakes and candies, and of course, darken the room with shades because light is our enemy," said the Major with a theatrical wave of his hand.

His Lady added, "Throw away the medical gowns. She should be wearing a fine silk bathrobe and sipping tea from fine English China."

"Excellent, my dear," exclaimed the Major.

"Furthermore, she, Ruth, is the lady of the house, and our acting must follow the formal rules one uses to address a lady. Respect for her station, her needs and desires, and that her commands must be fulfilled. The mark, this local attorney, must get the impression that his role is to convey Ruth's requests to the warden as if he were her subject. He must obey her will at all costs. She's a queen, and he's her subject," said the Major proudly.

"Do you think we're putting it on too thick with the queen stuff?" Margery asked with a smile.

"I want him to be subservient, not the other way around. Yes, it is a slippery slope, but he must do it our way. Once we start taking orders from a good ol' boy, we'll lose control. He'll get suspicious. We must keep him on a short leash," replied The Major. "All agreed? Now let's talk about dinner. I do hope you've stocked the wine cellar with some fine French wines."

Chapter 22: Joe

Joe checked into a motel near the marina recommended by Lisa and immediately called Patty to tell her to get him a return-trip reservation the next day, preferably around noon.

"You found Harry?" she exclaimed.

"In the flesh."

"What's he like?" Patty asked.

"Well he's about seventy-seven, five-foot-ten, a hairy motherfucker, built like a weightlifter, and has a profile of a Greek god, like the ones you see in museums...with a broken nose."

"Does he know where Bernie's hideaway is?"

"I can't tell. He lives on a yacht, a big one, and they're leaving for a voyage tomorrow," Joe said.

"Where's he going?"

"Didn't ask."

"So that's it?" she said dejectedly.

"I've got one last shot. He's having some friends over tonight, a sort of farewell party, and he's invited me," Joe said.

"What do you think?" she asked.

"I think he either knows or has an good idea of what Bernie did with the money," he said.

"Meaning?"

"Look, he's a crafty son of a bitch and he doesn't know me from Adam. On top of that he's a fuckin' brilliant man. He probably wrote the user's manual on money laundering," he said.

"Is he playing you?"

"I don't know. If he was, he didn't need to invite me over tonight. He could have just cut the line," Joe said.

After a few moments of silence, she said, "Well, good luck tonight."

"Thanks, and get me a reservation," he said, closing with, "Love you."

If this was Harry's idea of having a few friends over, Joe thought, looking at the queue to get on board his ship, what would he call 500 guests? A little get-together? There must have been sixty or seventy people already on board, and it was early. Joe realized that the possibility of having a private conversation with Harry was iffy at best. The one consolation was that he found Lisa in the crowd, and she greeted him with a smile and a hug. Oh, god, he said to himself getting a whiff of her youthful aroma, if I was only twenty years younger—no, maybe thirty years younger.

"Where's Harry?" Joe asked.

"Someplace holding court probably," she laughed.

"Then where's the bar?"

"It's just beer and wine tonight," she said taking his hand and snaking through the crowd to a makeshift bar in the stern. A young seaman, dressed in a white Greek Naval uniform, was dolling out beers and pouring wine.

"Marco, two Mary Rose Reds," Lisa said to the young bartender.

"What's a Mary Rose?" asked Joe.

"It's a beer and the national drink of Crete. Try it," she said handing him a mug.

"Strong," he said taking a sip.

"It's the resin. You have to acquire a taste for it," Lisa said.

"If you say so," Joe said taking a long drag.

"Harry has it shipped from Crete. It's his home," she said proudly.

"Then I'd better like it, eh?" Joe said, smiling at Lisa. "How far is it from here to Crete?"

"Just under nine thousand kilometers," she said.

"That's what in miles?" he asked.

"About six thousand. Roughly, depending on sea conditions, a two- to three-week journey," she said looking up at the starry night.

"Has he made the crossing before?" Joe asked.

"Several times, but but this, this is his last crossing," she said dejectedly.

"Why the finality?" Joe asked.

"Because he's going home. He says it's where he belongs. It's been the home of the Sarandopolis family for hundreds, maybe thousands, of years."

"You'll miss him?" Joe asked.

"He's been the father I've never known," she said filling up with tears.

"I'm sorry," Joe said.

From out of nowhere, Harry came through the crowd to comfort Lisa. "Tears at my party? No, no, only joyful laughter allowed!" he said gathering his granddaughter in a bear hug.

"Oh, Papou, I don't want you to go," she said burying her head in his chest.

"Se agapo, prinkipissa. I love you, my princess, and Papou will always be with you," he said. "Now make yourself useful and help Mrs. Soros with the hors d'oeuvres." he told Lisa, kissing her on both cheeks.

"Let's finish our conversation," he said to Joe, leading him up a flight of stairs to the bridge. "Make yourself at home." He opened a drawer underneath a radar console and took out a bottle of twenty-five-year-old Lagavulin and two tumblers.

"We'll drink these neat. I can't go on deck cause I fear I'll never get back," he said pouring three fingers of scotch into each tumbler.

"Now, where did we leave off our conversation?" Harry said settling into his captain's chair.

"I believe we were discussing the oranges," Joe said with a smile.

Harry chuckled at the thought of being found because he sent Bernie Madoff some oranges years ago. "Tell me, what will be your fate if you can't find Bernie's gold?" he asked swirling his scotch counterclockwise.

"I'll probably be drawn and quartered in front of Waters staff to serve as an example," Joe said.

"An example of what?" Harry asked savoring the smoky taste of the scotch.

"An example of my ineptitude," Joe replied.

"But I hear you were a high-profile New York City detective," Harry said.

"You've done your homework, I see."

"No, in my line of work, it's called due diligence," Harry said with a smile.

"Did you help Bernie squirrel away some valuable chestnuts?" Joe asked.

"Personally no, but we may have discussed a well-travelled roadmap used by literally thousands of individuals looking for a safe place to shelter from a storm." Harry said.

"A natural storm or a shitstorm?"

"At that point in time, the federales were looking for rustlers involved in insider trading, not reputable wealth management companies like Bernie ran."

"What do you mean by a well-travelled roadmap?" Joe asked sitting at the edge of his chair.

"My boy, it's all in black and white for anyone to read. In November 2000, years before Bernie admitted to defrauding his investors, there was an article published entitled, 'Trillion-Dollar Hideaway,' where the author outlined how and where the super-rich hide their money," Harry said.

Joe knew the clock was running down on how much time he had left with Harry before he'd excuse himself to attend to his guests.

"As you remember, how did your conversation with Bernie go?" Joe asked.

"I think I gave him a brief tutorial from the article. It's also one I used at Harvard to give my students a sense of history. As the author related in his article, at the turn of the century, American mobsters began buying up legitimate businesses in order to explain the origins of their ill-gotten loot. Popular businesses were laundries and car washes, hence the birth of the term money laundering. I told Bernie that today the practice of hiding money has reached epidemic proportions. It's estimated that between 50 and 100 trillion dollars are hidden in off-shore banks."

"Okay, imagine I'm a billionaire and I want to make my money disappear. How would I go about it?" said Joe.

"First you'd visit a bank like the UIC...the United Interbank Consortium...which has a office in Manhattan. All told, they've helped over forty thousand clients launder their assets. The one caveat is that, in order to discourage the riffraff, you must plop down at least one million dollars to open an account. The UIC will then assign you a 'relationship manager' who will handle all your financial transactions to ensure secrecy. From then on, everything is digitized into zeros and ones. No names, no addresses, nothing, absolutely nothing that connects you to your assets. Your relationship manager will ask you to come up with a code name and account transaction password. From then on, you will be referred to as a 'confidential client' and deposits and withdrawals will be executed by the use of your password. Do you follow me so far?" Harry asked.

"And this is common knowledge, and it's okay with the feds?" Joe asked.

"Joe, you've been around, you know there's two different worlds, one for the super rich and another for everyone else," Harry said getting up to refill his drink. "A little more?" Harry asked.

"Thanks, I think I need it," Joe replied. "Well, what happens to the money?"

"Oh, that's the rub, since it's digital—no, wait, let me give you an example. Imagine your money is a small metal ball in a pinball machine. You pull the lever and a spring sends the ball flying around bouncing here and there. Just that instead of vanishing into a hole in the machine, your ball endlessly bounces around. You see, when the feds go to find your money, it's not there, it's constantly moving, it's untraceable. It's magic," Harry said with a smile.

"You mean everyone knows what's going on and can't do anything about it?" Joe said.

"Exactly. They're the original 'Three Monkeys.'"

Joe took a few moments trying to process the scope of what Harry had just told him. "So, it's hopeless to think I can find Madoff's Treasure?" he said dejectedly.

"It's an exercise in futility, son, there's probably over 100 trillion dollars bouncing around out there, and no one can do shit about it," Harry said.

"Then why did you bother with Bernie in the first place if this was common knowledge?" Joe asked.

"What interested me had nothing to do with Bernie and his Ponzi scheme, it was his financial formulas. They were unworldly. Not since Einstein's theory of relativity had I seen someone apply quantum mechanics to the financial industry. You have no idea how revolutionary those formulas are," Harry said clenching his fist.

"Bernie Madoff had financial formulas? What are you talking about?"

"From what he told me, he had a boy, a savant, a genius, who saw mathematical formulas in his mind that linked the stock market and what is euphemistically called the 'shadow banking system,'" Harry said.

"You lost me, what's the shadow banking system?" Joe asked

"Oh god, I may have opened a can of worms. Anyway that pinball machine is in some ways a shadow banking system. Totally secret, totally unregulated, for high-stakes players who want some additional action, investing in hedge funds, credit default swaps, and other mysterious financial products," Harry said, really not wanting to go into further detail.

By then Joe was so confused that he couldn't think of another legitimate question.

"I'm sorry if I rambled along, but if we could get our hands on that boy's work, we could transform the world's investment/banking system overnight," Harry said with a twinkle in his eye.

"I think the boy you're talking about was Zack, and he's dead."

"I know, someone told me of his suicide," Harry said. "What do you know about Zack?"

"His name came up in my investigation. I went to his place of residence and interviewed his landlord, that's all," Joe said. After a few seconds, Joe stood up and started walking around. He looked at the ships controls and out at the harbor, then turned and approaching Harry stopped and said, "After Zack died, Bernie showed up and removed his computers, discs, and paperwork from his apartment."

Now very interested, Harry said, "Do you know what he did with Zack's materials?"

"What the landlord said was that he helped Bernie carry the stuff down to his car."

"Is there anywhere you can think of that Bernie may have brought Zack's stuff?" Harry asked getting up.

"Is it valuable?" Joe asked.

"Valuable? It's worth a king's ransom! Fifty billion—maybe more if it was auctioned off.

"I've gotta get back to my guests. If you want my advice, forget about Bernie's alleged treasure and find Zack's computers," Harry said scribbling down his cell number on a napkin and pressing it into Joe's hand.

Chapter 23: Max

Max's alarm clock went off at five the next morning giving him a couple of hours to collect himself. It felt good to be back in his condo. There was always a big difference to Max when it came to traveling on the road and the unpredictability of hotel mattresses. The king-sized bed that Max and Margery shared was actually two adjustable twin beds pressed together. His side had some type of memory foam that, once you got comfortable in it, was always the same. That may not have been true, but Max believed the write-ups. After showering, he dressed in his costume for the shoot: a black suit, starched white shirt, black tie, and black shoes and socks. In addition, Max had a small makeup case that contained a scruffy black beard to play the role of a rabbi. He briefly perused the refrigerator but found slim pickings and decided to grab a bagel with a smear and a dark roast coffee to go. With breakfast in hand and his bag of magic tricks, Max flagged a cab and told the driver to take him to Studio 4U on 488 West 23rd. The studio was housed on the ground floor of a converted movie theater that previously played X-rated films. Max pushed a button below a speaker box and identified himself, saying he was there to see Rex.

"Oh, it's Rex you'd like to see. Mr. Max, I'll tell him you're here," said an old salt. Max smiled to himself thinking that because the studio was adjacent to the waterfront, the cast and characters on the Lower West Side still thought of themselves as a seafaring lot.

The buzzer buzzed and a voice that Max recognized as Rex said, "Come on in." Rex was a seventy-something ex-boxer, auto dealer of foreign car parts that mysteriously ended up in his chop shop, and a member of other assorted rackets. In other words, he was a typical New Yorker.

"Is the set still up?" Max asked.

"Haven't touched it. It's exactly as the Major left it."

"Good, I want to go over some things before we shoot."

"Come on over to Studio B and you can tell me what we need," Said Rex. He led the way zigzagging around cables, klieg light stands and assorted props to Studio B, a thirty-by-fifty-foot studio with a twenty-foot ceiling. There he saw a stand holding his powder blue backdrop with the Star of David embroidered on it and the ornate podium in front of it. On the podium was a Torah rolled up in its protective sleeve, a couple of white yarmulkes, and a couple of white shawls. Rex said that the cameraman was on his way and that they could start without him. Likewise, Max advised Rex that his actor was scheduled to be on set at seven-fifteen.

"Great, what do you need?" Rex asked.

Max began with the set layout. "The podium should be centered and six feet in front of the backdrop. Place a fifty-watt spot on the floor behind the podium aimed up at the Star of David. You know, between the two actors who will be speaking from the podium. Now this is the important part. Set the video camera seven feet off the ground, and twenty-five from the podium with a twenty-degree angle off center, stage right. Have you got that so far?"

"So far, so good," Rex said as the cameraman entered the studio carrying a large coffee mug. Rex briefly introduced Max and then from memory related word for word what Max had told him. Max told them that he wanted to shoot and edit until they got twelve minutes of useable video. Max also confirmed that Rex knew how to handle the smoke machine, which would be used to end the shoot. Rex reassured Max that he was an old hand in burning down places of business. Rex's attitude was that anything was possible for the right price. Since he was getting two thousand dollars an hour for the time, as far as he was concerned, they could shoot, edit, and burn the place down until the cows came home.

At precisely seven-fifteen, Brian Gorman, the look-alike, arrived in his costume. Max asked Rex where the makeup room was, and he and Brian went off to prepare for the shoot while Rex and Steve set the scene as they were instructed. They could tell that Max was versed in video production by the way he gave them precise directions. This was true; Max had spent many years shooting videos at the ad agency.

Once in the makeup room, Max saw that Brian was nervous and full of questions. Max reassured him that this segment was just one of many parts of the story. He should think of it as a jigsaw puzzle; by the end, it would all fall into place. Although Max's answer was somewhat convoluted, Brian felt better about his role and ceased asking questions. Max said to himself that sometimes the 'mushroom technique' works: keep them in the dark, sprinkle them with a little bullshit, and hope that something grows. It was also the only sensible way of dealing with someone you're conning.

So, with his beard held tightly to his face with spirit gum, Max led Brian back to Studio B. It seemed at first glance that Rex and the cameraman had arranged everything as he directed. Max helped Brian with his shawl and yarmulke, thinking to himself that this fuckin' guy was the spitting image of Bernie Madoff. Max removed the Torah from its protective sleeve and opened it up on the podium.

Rex advised him that when he was ready they'd begin shooting when Max realized he had forgotten something important. The crematorium had fluorescent lighting, which was 4000 degrees Kelvin, practically daylight. Unfazed, Rex went to the lighting board and shut the klieg lights and switched on a fluorescent bank of lights. After taking some readings with a light meter at the podium, Rex told Max that it was now 'daylight, baby,' and they began several hours of shooting followed by many more hours in editing before attempting to burn the place down. The smoke scene went off without a hitch, much to the surprise of everyone there, especially Rex. After six and a half hours, Max had twelve minutes of useable video. He wrote out a check for fifteen thou to Rex— thirteen grand for six and a half hours plus a two-thousand-dollar bonus— and a $2,500 check to Brian for his only part in the movie.

Max was so pleased with himself that he didn't bother to remove his beard and travelled back to his apartment with it on much to the consternation of his doorman and elevator operator. However, he was brought back to reality when he realized that he needed a special lotion to remove the notoriously strong spirit gum. Thankfully he found a site on the Internet that recommended rubbing alcohol as an alternate to spirit gum remover, and after several applications, he was able to peel the beard off. Excited and relieved that the video was accomplished, Max called Margery to tell her the good news. Likewise, Margery also had good news. The Prince had signed up a local attorney to represent Ruth and was asking when he could bring the attorney to meet her. Also Glen was heading to Teterboro tomorrow on the Lear to collect him for their trip to Butner.

"What time do I have to be at Teterboro tomorrow?" Max asked.

"Glen said that if they get a good tailwind, they should arrive at 1400 hours EST."

"Did he say how many people he's bringing with him?"

"Yes, it's Glen and four of his people. Two from the pyrotechnics firm," she said.

"Excellent, there'll be enough seats for all of us then," Max said.

"What did you think, you'd have to sit in the lavatory going down to Butner?"

"Very funny, my dear. As usual, you've thought of everything."

"That's why you have to keep me," she said.

"Nah, I only keep you because I love you," he said.

"I love you too," she said.

Max spent the rest of the evening mentally reviewing the timetable for what Margery referred to as 'the Great Escape.' Looking for something to write on to memorialize his thoughts, he went into the office he shared with Margery to find one of her steno pads. In any event, it could be used as talking points during the flight to Butner with Glen. He began to write:

The Great Escape
1. Erect privacy fence to shield work being done at site
2. Dig tunnel from behind fence to under rear of building
3. Dig opening to tunnel and erect shed on top of opening
4. Cut hole in floor to tunnel and hide entrance to match floor
5. Mount and test video to mimic twelve-minute recording
6. Test live video feed and automatic transfer to recording
7. Install pyro equipment to go off at eleven-minute mark in tape
8. Conduct mock escape from crematorium to shed and car

Max imagined a walk-through from the time the entourage, including guards, the state police and

Madoff, arrived at the funeral home until they whisked Madoff away in their getaway car. The way he saw it, an undetermined group of prison guards and police would arrive with Madoff in leg irons and handcuffs. Prior to bringing Madoff into the building a couple of guards would do an inspection and then give the okay to bring Madoff in. The police would then interview the rabbi (Max) and staff. (Max made a note that he had to hire a coupled of local boys to act as production assistants for the service.) Most likely everyone would be searched for weapons, cameras, anything suspicious. The rabbi would brief the police on what would transpire during the ceremony and cremation. The rabbi would then show them Ruth Madoff's casket, a plain pine box held together with wooden dowels, and the Star of David branded to its lid. He would point out the podium for the service and the video camera, which would display the service in real time to a viewing room outside the crematory chamber.

One of the production assistants would bring one or more of the police into the crematorium control room to view the service live on a small monitor. When Max signaled him by raising his hand, the production assistant would push a red button on the control board that would automatically deliver the casket into the furnace. If Prince's attorney had done his homework, the guards would have removed Madoff's handcuffs and maybe his leg irons. In addition, the attorney must also have previously received the okay from the warden, based on Federal Prison Rule 433-21, which stated that the inmate can be viewed by video during special circumstances and have the religious service in private.

Madoff would be dressed in the exact same outfit the look-alike wore for the recording and stand exactly where Max the rabbi told him to stand. The rabbi would shut and lock the reinforced door and begin the religious service with Madoff at his side. With no audio, they would pretend to be reading passages from the Torah for exactly five minutes, at which time the recorder would seamlessly cease the live video feed and begin the twelve-minute video recording shot at Studio 4U. That would be Max' cue to open the trapdoor and, with the aid of Otto waiting for them in the tunnel, descend a few steps into the tunnel. If Madoff was still in leg irons or some type of monitoring device, Otto would cut them off. Madoff would then strip naked from his clothes and shoes, in case a bug was surreptitiously placed in them, and don an athletic jumpsuit. With portable LED lanterns every eight feet the men would race down the tunnel to a set of stairs under the shed. Once inside the shed, Otto would remove a panel in the privacy fence and lead Max and Madoff down a wooded path to the waiting getaway cars. One car would take Madoff, Otto, and Levi to the Raleigh Airport where the real Ruth Madoff would be waiting for them in the Lear. The other car, driven by Margery, would depart with Max to their house where they would ditch it and take another car recently purchased locally for cash. The other members of the team would have already been flown back to either Teterboro or Reno.

During the last thirty seconds of the videotape, smoke would engulf the room followed by flames to seemingly blind the video feed. When the police attempt to rescue Madoff and the rabbi from the crematorium room, they'd find the door locked and burning hot to the touch. Smoke and flames would then engulf the entire building, as an audio recording screamed, "FIRE. FIRE. LEAVE THE BUILDING IMEDIATELY."

Helpless to extinguish the blaze, the only thing the police and guards could do is race out of the building and watch the crematorium burn to the ground.

Chapter 24: Joe

Just as Joe was about to board his morning flight from Tampa to Newark, he received a text message to call Waters for an important message. With only minutes to spare before they closed his gate, Joe punched in the phone number to Waters and retrieved his message. It said, "At 10:04 a.m. Ruth Madoff's Black Mercedes Benz 600, New York State license plate number RG42HK, exited the Sutton Place Garage at 488 East 59th Street, New York. We are tracking and will update you."

Interesting, thought Joe, where can the old bird be going?

When he landed at Newark, the first thing he did was check on the status of Ruth's Benz and got the following update: "The subject's car made one stop of forty-four minutes at 189 Clauson Street in Brooklyn, a second stop of thirty-nine minutes at 1000 Third Avenue in Manhattan, and then entered the New Jersey Turnpike at 2:54 p.m. heading south at 65 miles per hour."

It struck Joe: after all these years of not using her car, what motivated her to use it now? Although, maybe someone had borrowed the car or, like thousands of other cars in Manhattan, it had been stolen. Who'd miss it anyway? It had been idle for years, and a used Benz 600 was worth seventy-five or maybe eighty thousand. But why the brief stops? Was the perp showing it to prospective buyers? Joe headed for his office juggling several possible scenarios as to the sudden use of Ruth's car. However, when he reached his office and was briefed on the progress of the car, he learned that the car had been driven away by a young man with the proper paperwork. He couldn't put his finger on it, but something was definitely up.

A young man drove the Benz 600 away. Could that be Levi, Otto's son? Joe opened the Bernie Madoff file and checked on the address in Brooklyn. Whammo, that was Levi's residence. "Okay," Joe said to himself, "Levi picked up the car, drove it to his apartment, stayed forty-four minutes, and then drove to 1000 Third Avenue in Manhattan." After a brief check of Google Maps, he found that bingo, that was good old Bloomingdale's. Something's definitely up, he thought. Kids don't go to Bloomie's unless they're waiting for someone who's shopping at Bloomie's. Another Bingo: Bloomie's was Ruth Madoff's candy store.

Joe decided that it was time to make a visit to Levi's place in Brooklyn, but before scrambling to get there, he decided that it was time to do it legally—sort of. Out of his bag of tricks he whipped a rubber stamp with the Seal of the State of New York. After a brief search of New York State forms, he was able to complete an official-looking search warrant for Levi Klein, 189 Clauson Street, Brooklyn, New York, for 'All materials pertaining to an ongoing investigation.' After signing a fictitious judge's name, he unceremoniously spit on the stamp and affixed the great seal of 'the State of New York' to the warrant.

When Joe got to Levi's apartment complex, he saw that it was a group of four-story row houses with air conditioners protruding from each apartment. It looked neat and tidy in contrast to the graffiti-marred buildings across the street. Joe found a phone number for the janitor and, in his best cop talk, told the man that he was there to execute a search warrant for a Levi Klein in Building 189. The janitor told him he'd be down with a passkey. When the janitor arrived Joe noticed he had a large scar on his forehead. Most likely an ill-advised dispute with a mugger, Joe thought.

"What do you want?" the janitor said, invading Joe's space.

Joe took a step back, grabbed the unsuspecting janitor by the throat, and quietly said, "I'll ask the questions and you do what I want, understand?"

The janitor shook his head like a ragdoll and led Joe to Levi's apartment without muttering another word. Joe told the janitor to wait outside while he inspected the apartment for evidence. He quickly looked around the studio apartment—a typical crash pad for a twentyish kid. Clothes lay on the floor, grocery bags were still on the counter, notes were on the fridge, but in the trash can, Joe found several receipts for clothes, women's clothes from upscale boutiques in Soho. On the desk, Joe saw the rectangular shape of a laptop computer in the dust next to an HP printer. He went through Levi's dresser but didn't find anything of interest. Why would he come back here? Joe thought. Either to get something or to drop something off or both. "Okay, let's be a detective again," Joe said to himself. "If he was to drop something off, it's not here. Or is it?" Joe opened the door to see the frightened face of the janitor staring at him.

"What's your name?" Joe asked.

"Victor," replied the janitor.

"Where do the tenants store their stuff?" Joe asked getting a few inches from Victor's face.

"In the basement near the, near the laundry room," the janitor stuttered moving away from Joe.

"Show me," Joe said as the janitor locked Levi's door.

Joe followed the janitor down two flights of stairs, through the laundry room to a long room with plywood compartments, each with their own lock and apartment numbers stenciled to their doors. When they got to Levi's compartment, Joe told the janitor to open it, but was told that each tenant affixed their own lock.

Joe once again got face to face with the janitor and told him to,

"Get me a fuckin' hammer, pronto."

The janitor, taking Joes words as a command, hurried away and returned with not only with a hammer but also a crowbar. Joe was able to break the lock open with a couple swift blows on the crowbar. What he saw inside the dark recesses of Levi's compartment blew his mind. There sat Zack's two desktop computers, a box of portable hard drives, and a carton filled with Zack's notes.

"Grab those cartons and follow me," Joe said picking up the two desktop computers under each arm and wondering why he didn't tell the janitor to carry the heavy computers. Once they deposited the contents of Zack's materials in the trunk of Joe's car, Joe offered the janitor a word of advice.

"Next time an officer of the court asks you to do something, you do it, understand?" The frightened janitor humbly shook his head. Joe thought that by speaking fear, a language the janitor would understand, he'd keep his mouth shut regarding what had transpired that day.

With what Harry the Greek said about the value of Zack's materials in mind, Joe called a couple of geeks he'd done business with in the Bronx and told them he wanted them to download computer files from a couple of desktop computers and eight portable hard drives. They said that they could do it for a price and that he should bring ten terabyte-portable hard drives and lots of cash. Joe stopped at a branch of his bank in Brooklyn and withdrew two thousand dollars in cash. Then he asked his iPhone for directions to the nearest Office Max on the way to the Bronx. After purchasing several hundred dollars' worth of hard drives, Joe took the Cross Island Parkway to the geeks' residence, a converted two-story garage. They opened the bay doors so that he could drive in. Joe knew that leaving a car on the street in the Bronx was an invitation to the locals to strip it for parts. Greeting him as he got out of his car were Hans and Mel. Mel was a dead ringer for Mr. T, with the chains, earrings, and body piercings

"Help me with the shit in the trunk," Joe said carrying one of the desktop computers.

They marched single file up a flight of metal stairs to what Hans and Mel referred to as 'The Laboratory.' It looked to Joe as if they'd spiffed it up since the last time he'd been there. They now had professional nineteen-inch racks filled with scopes, oscillators, audio and video duplicators, the whole shebang.

"What do you need, copper?" growled Mel in his best imitation of Jimmy Cagney.

"Okay, first out of the box, I'm a PI now," said Joe.

"Since when have you gone straight?" asked Hans examining one of the desktops.

"Just a little while," admitted Joe.

"Wait a second, kemosabe, do you know what this is?" Hans pointed to the computer he was inspecting.

"It's a desktop," Joe started to say when Hans interrupted him.

"Oh no, grasshopper, this is a fuckin' Cray supercomputer."

"What's that mean?" asked Joe confused.

"It means that all bets are off," said Mel.

"Can you copy the files, yes or no?" exclaimed Joe.

"Let me just preface the answer by saying, this is the same computer they use at NASA to send men into outer space," said Hans.

"Where did you get this hardware?" asked Mel.

"I assure you that it's not hot, it's part of a case I'm working on. It's strictly legit!" Joe said trying to reassure them.

"Look it may have a password that we can't bypass or it may have restricted software that can't be copied to a 'normal system.' In other words, it maybe too fuckin' complicated for us," said Mel.

"Well, if anyone can copy these files, it's you," Joe said stroking their egos.

"I'll tell you what we can do. Leave it with us tonight and we'll see what we can do, okay?" Hans said.

"I'd appreciate whatever you can do. Now where can I sleep?" asked Joe.

"You want to stay here?" asked Mel incredulously.

"We're in it together, right?" said Joe eyeing a ratty-looking couch in the corner of the room.

"Make yourself at home. Mi casa es su casa. We'll just add room and board to the tab," said Hans.

Chapter 25: Max

Max had a recurring thought all night that kept him from a peaceful sleep. How fast would a flight from Reno be if it was being pushed by the jet stream, and how high does a plane have to fly to take advantage of the jet stream? He knew that the Lear flies at the same speed as a commercial jet, 500 miles per hour, and that the Lear could cruise as high as 40,000 feet, so they should be on a par. Conflicted, he got out of bed to check and opened Travelocity to see if he booked a nonstop flight from Reno to New York, what would the flight times be? He found that Reno to New York was five hours and eighteen minutes, and to his surprise, the return trip from New York to Reno was six hours and twenty minutes, an hour longer. That meant that Glen's plane might arrive early, so he decided to get to Teterboro early just in case. After packing an overnight bag he retrieved his car from the garage and made his way via the George Washington Bridge to New Jersey en route to the Teterboro Airport knowing full well that New Jersey was the retro diner capital of the world with at least a dozen great chrome and neon palaces to grab breakfast.

Complimenting himself on his good judgment, Max watched the Lear taxiing to the hangar thirty minutes early. After boarding and saying hello to the passengers, Max took a seat next to Glen.

"You sure travel in style," Glen said.

"Nothing but the best for you," said Max.

They laughed like it was old times.

"Tell me, do you still play chess?" Glen asked opening a can of Sprite.

"No, I haven't played since you beat me, what was it, nine, maybe ten years ago?"

"We used to have some very interesting matches, didn't we?"

"Yeah, they lasted for days as I remember," replied Max.

"So tell me, who's paying for all this?" Glen looked around at the Lear.

"That's a good question, but I'm not at liberty to discuss who or what they are," said Max.

"You mean that there may be a group who are paying to get Madoff out of prison?" Glen said.

"Honestly can't say," said Max.

"Can't or won't?" Glen said, finishing his Sprite.

"Both," said Max. "Forgive me for not asking you earlier, but how is Barbara?" he said to the subject.

"Busy growing her cosmetic business. She's on a mission to put Mary Kaye out of business in Nevada," Glen said.

"Keeps her busy, eh?" said Max.

The two men chitchatted for the rest of the flight about business, sports, and families until the pilot put on the 'fasten seatbelts' sign and advised his passengers that they were on their final approach to the Raleigh International Airport. After a textbook landing, the Lear taxied to a temporary hangar set aside for aircraft to park and discharge passengers. Max told Glen that he wanted to show him and the pyro team the crematorium while Margery ferried his crew to their house in a eight-passenger Chevy Suburban. As they got off the plane Margery was there, as lovely as ever, with a hug and smile for Max and Glen. She gave Max the keys to their Honda, and the keys she'd recently received from the Prince to the crematorium.

"The kids are hungry, I've been told. After you drop them at the house, pick up enough food to feed an army and I'll meet you at the house in a couple of hours," Max said.

"A regiment or a battalion, sir?" she quipped. Max flushed watching her corral the men towards the waiting Suburban. "Okay, men, double-time! Throw the bags in the back!"

Thankfully when they arrived at the funeral home there was no one on site to interrupt their inspection of the building and grounds. Max walked through what was to happen the day of the "Great Escape."

After their walk-through, the pyro men made their way into the attic to see where they could place the generators that would flood the rooms with smoke and the optimal places to position the flamethrowers that would ultimately consume the building in fire. Meanwhile Max and Glen were measuring the distance from the rear of the building to where the shed would be placed.

"Everything seems cut and dry except for the tunnel," Max said.

"What do you mean?" asked Glen.

"Well, what kind of tunneling machine do we need to bore a hole some fifty-five feet under the parking lot?"

"What do you mean, boring machine? We're not talking about building a subway tunnel," Glen said with a smile.

"But how do you cut a hole underneath a parking lot without some type of machine?" Max looked confused.

"Look, it's really very easy," Glen said. "First we or some contractor will erect a seven-foot privacy fence around the parking lot and continue it to the street. Then we use a backhoe to dig a trench, say, six feet down by say four feet wide. You follow me, amigo?"

"Sí," said Max shaking his head.

"Then we place four-by-six-by-half-inch steel plates on top of the trench, cover the entire lot with some top soil, and finish it off with four inches of ¾"crushed stone. Cut a hole in the floor of the crematorium giving us access to the tunnel and likewise from the shed to the tunnel... Bada-bing, bada-boom!" Glen said clapping his hands. "Really, it's that easy? I spent countless days looking on the Internet for just the right tunnel-boring machine and all we have to do is dig a trench? How fuckin' stupid can I be?" Max said happily.

"That's why they pay me the big bucks," Glen said as the pyro team joined them in the parking lot.

"How's it look from your end?" Max asked.

"The attic is wide open with access to all the air ducts for the smoke machines. We can also disengage the sprinkler system and the alarm systems from the attic. Our estimate is that eleven flamethrowers mounted in the walls and ceiling will do the job in short order. Everything, the smoke and flames, will be completely programmable and synchronized with the videotape player. On cue from the videotape the smoke machines will pump clouds of smoke, essentially blinding everyone in the building followed by an explosion of flames from every direction. We're giving the guards enough time, ninety seconds, to realize the danger and flee the building."

"Good. If we're finished here let's lock up and get to the house to discuss what you need material-wise," Max said.

On the short drive to the house Max checked in with Margery.

"Your timing is perfect, the boys are helping me unload the Suburban as we speak. How'd it go at the crematorium?"

"Better than expected. Wait until I tell you about the tunnel," he said. "Need anything?"

"No, we bought out the supermarket," she said.

"Did you leave anything for the residents of Butner?" Max asked.

"No, we didn't leave any food or prisoners either," she said.

Max wanted to say, 'Poor choice of words,' but thought it might sound ominous coming on the heels of an enterprise fraught with danger.

Luckily the boys, as Margery called them, were experienced cooks and welcomed the opportunity to help prepare their own meals. What resulted was essentially a cauldron of Tex-Mex cuisine with rice and beans all rolled up into a taco shell. Thankfully for the gringos the hot sauce was optional. After dinner, Max, Margery, Glen, and the pyro men discussed what equipment and materials they required to complete their mission while the boys were happy to watch TV in the den. Although Max and Margery were onlookers, they brought a different perspective to the task: one of support, logistics, and research. The pyrotechnic engineers said that they required specific equipment and supplies to create smoke and fire on command, equipment that couldn't be legally shipped in the customary manner using Federal Express or UPS. In addition, they wouldn't be able to source the supplies locally due to the hazardous nature of the materials, especially since special federal licenses were necessary to procure them. This meant that they had to take the equipment and supplies from their own inventory in Las Vegas, then ship it over land to Butner. It would take about thirty-eight hours, which made it an easy decision to order the equipment and supplies immediately and have in put in one of their vans for delivery as soon as possible. Glen reiterated his suggestion that they order a seven-foot high privacy fence instead of a six-foot fence from a local contractor.

"The higher, the better fence-wise. That way, we don't have to reinvent the wheel. We can have a local contractor erect a fence to our specifications, giving us time to work inside the building installing the video, trapdoors, and the like."

"What will you need for the tunnel?" Max asked him.

"We'll have to rent a backhoe, pickup truck, Bobcat, and buy odds and ends from Home Depot. My one quest will be sourcing the steel plates to cover the tunnel. I've got to see who's got fourteen four-by-six steel plates. By my calculations, each plate weighs 480 pounds, which is over 6,720 pounds of steel we need delivered to the site."

"Do we need half-inch steel?" asked Margery.

"I'm not exactly sure of the expected weight load we'll need, but the difference between half-inch and three-eighths is five pounds per square foot. In other words, a half-inch plate weighs 480 pounds and a three-eighths weighs 450," Glen said.

With an agreement to score half-inch steel Max opened his laptop to show them the twelve-minute video he produced in New York with Madoff's look-alike.

"First I want you to notice that the camera angle from the back wall to the podium is slightly from the right. It's actually twenty-degrees from left of center to the right. So, when we switch from real time to recorded time, it must be the same. In addition, the size of the subjects, Madoff and I, must also be the same. The distance from the camera lens to the subjects was specifically shot to match the room at the crematorium, twenty-four feet seven inches with a lens stop of F 4.0. The camera was also white-balanced to match the florescent lighting in the crematorium at 4,000 degrees Kelvin. Now notice that at the eleven-minute mark we look up as smoke begins to pour into the room. By that time we'll be in our getaway cars and heading away in different directions. Do you have any questions?" Max asked after his presentation.

"Who's going to link the video recording to the pyro?" Glen asked.

"That's our responsibility," one of the pyro men said. "We'll use one of the tracks on the tape to trigger first the smoke and then the flames."

"It's no different than the fireworks we do," said the other. "They're also programmed off a tape."

Satisfied and tired from the long day, some of the crew went to bed while others stayed up to watch Law and Order reruns on television.

Chapter 26: Joe

Thankfully before Joe put his head down to sleep on the ratty couch, he called Patty, ostensibly to check on the kids. "By the way, I won't be home tonight," he said, which didn't go over well with the ever-suspicious Patty. She'd heard that excuse too many times before, and although their relationship was on the mend, old wounds had a way of bleeding from time to time. Joe sensed by way of Patty's irritability that he had to say something to justify his current situation, but he didn't want to tell her the extent of the find he'd just made. For his own fuckin' reasons, He pushed back psychologically. The old 'who does she think she's talking to' questions poured into his mind, the way he used to handle her irritating questions when he was still pushing powder up his nose or in his mouth on through his hair or rolling on the floor with it. "STOP," he said to himself "don't go there." Joe calmed down ,and without going into too many details, he explained where he was and why he couldn't leave the materials unguarded. Sensing that there was a bit of simpatico between them, Joe put his head down to get some ZZZ's.

Although he thought that he'd just put his head down for a few seconds, it was actually several hours later when Mel cried, "Eureka!" at the top of his lungs, followed by Hans and Mel giving each other high-fives. Now fully awake and confused, Joe sat up and asked where the bathroom was.

"We did it, we did it!" Mel said walking over to Joe with a smile on his face from one side of the room to the other.

"Great, now where's the bathroom?" Joe pleaded.

"Over there." Hans said pointing to a green door that said, 'Enter at Your Own Risk.' Unperturbed Joe entered and after draining his dragon, he splashed some ice-cold water on his face and joined the festive geeks at a large worktable where one of the Cray desktops was dismantled with cables running from it to some mysterious-looking jury-rigged devices.

"Why did you take it apart?" Joe asked.

"Mostly out of curiosity," Hans confessed.

"It's like nothing we've ever seen in one box. A Xeon CPU and, this is the best part, a secret Tesla P100 PCIe GPU," said Mel.

"Tell me you're able to copy the files?" Joe murmured.

"Yes, we've started dumping the files from this machine," he pointed to the dismantled Cray on the workbench, "onto one of your Terabyte portables," Mel said with a proud smile.

"How long will it take you?" Joe started to ask.

Mel raised his hand and said, "A couple of hours at the most."

"In that case, I'll send out for some chow."

When the last hard drive was safely wrapped in its own metal foil envelope, Joe took out a roll of hundred-dollar bills and asked, "What do you need?"

Mel looked at Hans and after some mental calculations said, "Twelve hundred will do it."

Joe peeled off twelve hundred-dollar bills, and on top of that, sweetened the pot by adding an additional four hundred dollars.

"Thanks for the bump, Joe, but what are you going to do with the files now?" asked Mel.

"I don't want to be coy with you, but it's really confidential. The files don't belong to me," Joe said as sincerely as a bullshit artist can say.

"You know, how do I put it, they're like nothing I've ever seen. It's like the marriage of calculus and computer code, but way out there. I think the author invented his own mathematical symbols," Hans said waving both hands above his head.

"I don't know what they are either, and if I one day find out, I'll let you know, but really guys, I appreciate what you've done and don't have to remind you that it's confidential, yes?" Joe said.

"Oh, our lips are sealed," Mel said.

"Good then, because you know, I like you and, well, I don't want to see you floating face down in the Hudson River, capische?" Joe said with a smile.

Once out of the geeks' place of business Joe headed for his safety deposit box at Mayflower Savings Bank in Morristown, New Jersey. He's had that box forever, and over the years he's stashed money, jewelry, cop memorabilia, various IDs, pills, and bags of white powder. Today he was adding eight very valuable computer hard drives. Hungry and dizzy he stopped at a diner to collect his thoughts and call Harry the Greek. After ordering a bowl of beef stew, he called the number Harry gave him.

"Harry, this is Joe. Can you speak?" Joe asked.

"Not right now. Can I get you on this number?" Harry said.

"Yes, call me we have to talk," Joe said.

Harry called back just as the waitress brought over the check to tell Joe that his trip to Crete would have to be postponed. It seemed that while coming around a reef several miles south of Key West, his drive-shaft began vibrating to the point he had to declare a mayday for assistance from the US Coast Guard. He said that his ship was currently under tow and should arrive in Miami in twelve hours. Max told Harry that he'd retrieved Zack's computers, hard drives, and notes and wanted to meet with him to discuss how they might ascertain the value of the materials. Harry told Joe that he should secure the materials in a safe, well-ventilated place until he could join him in New York.

"When can I expect to see you?" Joe asked.

"If all goes well, within twenty-four hours. As soon as I arrange for a dry dock in Miami, I'll be on the next plane to New York."

"Let me know and I'll pick you up at the airport," Joe said.

"Excellent and you must tell me how you tracked down Zack's computers so quickly."

"Will do," said Joe.

Joe kept running Harry's instructions over in his mind: a safe, well-ventilated place. Exactly what did he mean? Wasn't that a bit much, he thought, since the damned computers had been in the trunk of Bernie's car for years? When he got home, he just locked his car and went into his house as if there weren't a billion dollars' worth of computer formulas in the trunk of his car.

Patty, happy and surprised to see Joe, ran over to give him a hug until she got a whiff of his clothes.

"What is that smell? Take that shit off and throw your clothes away," she said.

"I know they're a bit ripe, but that's all they had to sleep on," he said removing his shirt.

"Go into the bathroom and shower. The kids are home. I'll get you your bathrobe. Don't put your clothes in the hamper; we'll never be able to get the smell out of them," she ordered.

"Good, we'll burn 'em later," he said half-jokingly.

'Oh, there's no place like home,' he thought as he let the hot spray wash the dirt and grime from his body. Oh God, it felt so good. he could spend all day here under the waterfall.

"Daddy, I have to use the bathroom," cried his little one.

"Daddy will be right out," replied Joe remembering that all good things must come to an end.

After dinner with the kids in their room either doing homework, or watching their TV, Patty began Joe's interrogation.

"So you had to see these geeks because you found some computers and you wanted them to do what?"

Joe got up from the table and looked for something sweet to nibble on in the fridge. "Yes, I recovered a couple of computers associated with the Madoff case and needed someone to interpret what was on them," he said.

"Couldn't your office do the same thing?" she asked taking her prosecutorial pose by folding her arms across her chest.

Not finding anything to satisfy his sugar rush, Joe turned and said, "I could have but—and this is between you and me. You must not mention what I have to anyone, do you understand?"

"What are you talking about?" she said.

"There are things, formulas on the computers that are, let's say very valuable, and at this point in time no one knows about them," he said.

"How valuable?" she asked. He could see the dollar signs flashing in her eyes.

"I don't know," he replied.

"Then what are you going to do with them?" she asked.

"We're bringing them to an expert to examine. He'll tell us what's on them and what they're worth," he said.

"You're confusing me. Who's the we?"

"Harry the Greek. He's flying to New York," he said with a small burn simmering inside him.

"Harry the fuckin' Greek! What have you gotten into now?" She said exasperated.

"Okay, I can't talk to you now. We're both upset, and I see I can't trust you with any more information, so let's leave it as is for now," he said going down to his office to check his email.

"Don't walk away from me," she demanded following him down the stairs.

"Look," he said turning his chair to face her. "I'm doing this for us, and the less you know, the safer you'll be."

"Now I'm really worried. What's going on?" she asked sitting on the edge of her desk chair.

"I've got to go into the office in a little while and speak to my boss, so right now is not a good time for a chitchat." He was trying to get back at his messages when he exploded saying, "Listen and get this through your fuckin' head. I've got a madman looking for answers that I can't give him, and he won't take no for an answer, so sweetie, let me deal with one thing at a time, capische?"

"Why didn't you just say that? What do you want me to do?" she said in all sincerity.

"This is what you can do if the shit hits the fan. Pack some bags for you and the kids and put them in the trunk of your car. I'll call you with instructions if you have to get out of town until it cools off. In any event, if I tell you to run, immediately take the kids and drive to that hospital, the one with the three-story parking garage. It's the one I showed you how to lose a tail in. You know go in the main entrance, get a ticket then drive to the other side of the garage and exit onto the street. If anyone was following you, they wouldn't enter the garage they'd look for the exit, but by the time they got around the block to the exit, you'd be gone. Just remember that before you leave the house, Google directions from the garage to those cottages in the Poconos where we stayed. Make sure you take enough cash out of the safe and don't use any of your credit cards. Leave your cell phone in the safe and take a couple of burners to call me. Their cell phone numbers are taped to the phones," he said.

"It's that serious?" she asked.

"Yes, but if we play our cards right, we may get out of this okay," he said to reassure her.

Chapter 27: Max

The next morning, the Prince called as Margery and Max were just sitting down for breakfast. He wanted to have a meeting with Ruth Madoff before he brought the attorney he'd hired to represent her over for a chat.

"What's this guy's name?" Max asked.

"Prescott G. Andrews," the Prince said.

"What's his connection with Warden Cummings?" Margery asked.

"Tight as a G-string. Their wives sing together in their church choir."

"Good, very good. I'll let you know as soon as she arrives what's the best time for a meeting," Max said.

"When do you expect her?" the Prince asked.

"Some time today. We're waiting for a call to meet her at her house in Butner," Max said.

However, as fate would have it, moments later Max received an email from Sy, which said, "Ruth ETA Butner 9:30AM today."

"Holy shit, when it rains it pours," Max exclaimed. "Ruth's only thirty minutes away. Finish your coffee, we've got to meet them at her house."

"I'll call the Major to give them a heads-up that Ruth will be there soon," Margery said.

After racing around in order to get there on time, Ruth hit a bit of highway construction and didn't arrive until some two hours later. Meanwhile, the Major and

His Lady made some tea and warmed up some scones to nosh on while waiting. Max found it amusing to see that the Major had gotten into his role by carrying his stethoscope in the pocket of his jacket.

When Ruth's Mercedes finally arrived, everyone helped unload it. After brief introductions, Otto told Max that Ruth was exhausted and needed to lie down for a while.

"We understand," Max told Otto.

"How do I contact you?" Otto asked.

"You haven't used your cell phones recently, have you?" Max asked Otto.

"No, they're in our apartment," Otto said. "If they check, we're still at home. We're using some pay-as-you-go prepaid cell phones." He showed Max his phone.

"Good, but use these," Max said pointing to several cell phones he'd brought.

"No problem," Otto said.

"Okay, you'll call me when Ruth's feeling up for a meeting. We've programmed your phones with our cell numbers. Hit #1 and you'll get me, #2 and you'll get Margery, and #3 you'll get the Prince."

"Who's this Prince?" Otto asked.

"He's an invaluable member of our team and a jack of all trades. He's acting as Ruth's attorney here in Butner. He'll also be the go between for you and a local attorney we've hired to represent Ruth with the warden at the penitentiary," Max said.

With the small talk over, Otto went to see how Ruth was doing as Max and Margery briefly spoke with the Major.

"You'll call me if they need anything," Max told him.

"She's so small and delicate, isn't she?" the Major said.

"She's been through a lot," Max said.

"We'll take good care of her," the Major said putting his arm around His Lady.

"Thanks, doc," Max said as he and Margery took their leave.

In the car, Max called the Prince to tell him that Ruth might be in a position to take a meeting in a day or two.

"Can't see her any sooner?" he asked.

"No, she's wasted after the trip. I'll let you know."

Next on their to-do list was checking on the progress at the crematorium. When they got there, they found two of Glen's crew walking around the parking lot drinking Dunkin Donuts coffee from paper cups.

"Where is everybody?" Max asked.

"Oh, Glen's gone to rent a pickup and then see a fence company," one of them said.

"What about the pyro boys, Maurice and Dominic, I think?" Max asked.

"They've gone, too," the other one said nodding his head.

"Oh, and someone came by and asked what we were doing here," said one of the boys.

"What did he want, this guy?" asked Max.

"I don't know, but he acted as if he owned the place," said the other one. Max looked at Margery with concern and asked the boys exactly what they told this guy.

"Told him he had to check with our boss," one of the boys said.

"What did he say? What were his exact words?" asked Margery.

"He said it was news to him and he'd be back," the boys said.

"Okay, no problem, just that we don't want anyone talking to this guy or anybody, except us. Understand?" Max said.

The boys nodded their heads in agreement.

"One other thing, did this man say who he was? Did he give you his name?" Max asked getting out his phone.

"Nope, he was just angry."

Max walked out of earshot of the boys and called Glen. "Glen, Max, we've got a situation. Someone showed up at the crematorium after you left and wanted to know what we were doing."

"Who is he?" Glen asked.

"I don't know, but you'd better get back here."

"Right, I'll be there in about fifteen minutes."

"I'll be waiting for you."

Max walked over to speak with Margery in private.

"What's going on?" she asked.

"I don't know. I've got to speak to the Prince and I'm afraid to leave in case this guy comes back," Max said.

"What do you think this guy wants?" Margery asked.

"We're so close, and now there's this fuckin' Murphy's Law to deal with," Max said in frustration.

"Honey, if anyone can make it all go away..," Margery began.

"...the Prince of Second Avenue can," Max said, finishing her thought. He hugged her.

Glen pulled up just then and jumped out of his car. "Has the guy been back?"

"No, but we have to keep him away from here," Max said.

"I've lined up a company to put up the fence. Do you want me to hold back until—"

Max held up his hand and said, "No, the fence shouldn't be postponed. It doesn't require any permits, and it will hide all the work we have to do outside the building."

"Did the guy give any indication when he'd be back?" asked Glen.

"No, and that's the problem. I'll call the Prince to see if he has any idea who the guy is and get him down here. Till we know what we're dealing with, stick to the modifications in the building and the privacy fence."

"Yeah, the boys should be back from Home Depot soon. We can work on mounting the camera and run the cables while Maurice and Dominic work in the attic," Glen said.

Max called the Prince and advised him of their predicament. He told him to come to the crematorium as soon as possible. The Prince told Max to sit tight and not speak with anyone until he got there, which sounded like the advice a real attorney would say.

Approximately thirty minutes later, a weather-battered maroon Buick pulled into the parking lot. Two elderly men got out and moseyed over to Max and Glen.

"Who's the boss?" one of them barked.

"I'm the foreman. Who are you?" Max said.

"I own this place, and I want to know what you're doing on my property," the man said just as a long, sleek limo pulled into the lot alongside them. The driver exited, dressed in his black uniform, and went around to open the rear door for the Prince. He made one of his classic appearances while his assistant, Miss Latex, remained in the air-conditioned comfort of the limo.

The Prince was dressed in an immaculately tailored navy suit from Savile Row. Walking over to Max and Glen, he asked them, "What's going on, boys?"

"I'll tell you what's going on, mister. They's on my property and I want 'em off. You understand me, boy?" the man said.

"What's your name?" the Prince said pointing at the man.

"My name is Cecil Moody, and that's my brother Edgar," he said with a dismissive wave of his thumb.

"Tell me what legal right you have to this property when we have the sole rights to it by virtue of our contract with the owners?" the Prince said.

This was news to Cecil. "When did he do that?" he cried. "And how could he when he owes us money?"

"What's your relationship, if any, to the owner?" the Prince asked.

At this point Edgar interceded. "He's our nephew and we loaned him some money."

"I understand now, but tell me, how much was the loan? Did he put the property in the loan as collateral?" the Prince asked.

"That's none of your damned business," Cecil said to the chagrin of his brother.

"Well, boys, we can either do it the hard way—we'll get the sheriff down here to cart you off for trespassing—or the easy way, sit down and resolve the situation like gentlemen," the Prince said.

"I'm not doing any business with the likes of you," said Cecil.

Edgar interceded again. "Be quiet for a moment, Cecil, and let's hear what the man has to say."

"That's better, but first, what was the amount of the loan?" asked the Prince.

Sensing Cecil was about to make an ass of himself, Edgar quickly said, "Twenty-four thousand dollars in total."

"Okay, this is what I propose," the Prince said as cool as a cucumber. "We meet tomorrow at the Butner Trust Company on Willow Street at one. You bring with you a cancelled check or checks in the amount of twenty-four thousand dollars payable to your nephew, and we'll pay off the note.

"You'll also agree to certain usual and customary terms regarding the property and the discharge of your nephew's indebtedness for the loan. Do you understand what I've said?"

The two old men shared a look of amazement. "What if we don't have copies of the checks?" Edgar said quietly.

"Well, how did you pay him?" the Prince asked.

Edgar noticed that Cecil was becoming agitated and said, "We gave him three checks this year to help him pay some bills. One check was to Butner Heating for a new furnace, another was to the IRS for back taxes, fees, and penalties, and the other to settle a lawsuit. They amounted to about twenty-four thousand dollars."

"Well, you put together what receipts you've got and show up at the bank tomorrow at one, and we'll cut you a check you can cash on the spot," the Prince said as he approached both men. "If it's a deal, I want your word as gentlemen that you agree to my terms and conditions. My word is my bond." He shook each man's extended hand.

After the men wobbled back to their car, Max approached the Prince to congratulate him.

"How sweet that was," said Margery giving the Prince a hug.

"Do you think they'll show up?" asked Glen.

"They've got everything to lose and nothing to gain if they don't," the Prince said with his signature brilliant smile.

Chapter 28: Joe

Thankfully the traffic from his house to the office that morning was light to nonexistent. Maybe it was a good omen, he thought. However, when he sat down at his desk to check his messages he noticed a three-by-three yellow Post-It note stuck to his monitor. It said in all caps, "SEE ME," and was signed "E."

"I guess the shit's hit the fan," Joe said to himself as he fixed his tie and headed for Eisenstaedt's office.

"Where have you been?" Eisenstaedt's ever-inquisitive receptionist asked. "Wait right there, and I'll tell him you're here," she commanded pointing to a spot on the carpet.

The first words out of the distraught Eisenstaedt's mouth were, "Shut down the Madoff case."

Both men looked at each other knowing that the first one who opened his mouth was the loser. Finally, in order to break the loggerhead and knowing full well that Joe knew how the game was played, Eisenstaedt said, "The feds are all over Sergio."

Noticeably relieved Joe took a deep breath and asked, "What did he do now?"

For the next several minutes Eisenstaedt related what he had learned from his confidant at the FBI. "It seems they flipped one of Sergio's boys and made him a CI. This guy began feeding them info on Sergio's operations: laundering money, prostitution, shaking down businessmen in Atlantic City, several unsolved murders, and, get this, skimming from his casino. In other words, the usual mob bullshit. Somehow Sergio found out that the guy was a confidential informant and had him killed. Now, this is the embarrassing part, with all this info and a twenty-four-hour surveillance they fucked up his arrest."

"You mean he got away?" Joe asked.

"Picture this, a company that shreds paper for businesses is backing down an alley to the loading ramp of the Majestic Hotel. The truck's intercepted by two FBI agents, fearing that Sergio's about to shred some of his files, who tell the truck driver to come back tomorrow. Brilliant, right?" Eisenstaedt said.

"The truck's owned by the mob?" said Joe.

"Exactly. Alcohol, linens, laundry, foodstuffs, and waste management are part and parcel of organized crime in New Jersey. The driver immediately calls his office, and guess what? By the time they were able to have a judge sign an arrest warrant..." Eisenstaedt said.

"...Sergio gave them the slip," Joe concluded.

Eisenstaedt nodded. "He probably had an exit strategy planned the day he arrived in Atlantic City."

"What are we going to tell the clients?" Joe asked.

"I've checked with accounting, and it seems we have an out. They're over sixty days behind on their payments, which gives us the right to close their file."

"What do you need from me?" Joe asked.

"I want you to prepare a summary of your findings, you know, after exhausting all avenues, both here and abroad, it is our finding that Bernard Madoff has not left any clues as to the alleged whereabouts of investors funds," Eisenstaedt said, as Joe scribbled down some notes. "Let me have something from you before you leave tonight with the file and all the work notes that pertain to the case. Oh, in addition, I've decided to reassign you to the white-collar crimes division," Eisenstaedt said. "Just like you wanted."

With Sergio in the wind, Joe rushed back to his desk to call Patty. "Patty, it's me, remember what we spoke about yesterday?" he said quickly.

"Remember what?" Patty asked.

"You know, about taking a trip with the girls?" he prompted.

"Oh yeah, what's up?"

"Now's the time to go! Right now," Joe emphasized.

"But the kids," Patty started to say but Joe cut her short.

"Get the hell out of the house now."

"Okay, when will I hear from you?" she asked, fear entering her voice.

"I'll call one of the burners tonight. Now remember what I said about losing a tail? Do it," he reiterated.

Joe then grabbed all the files he'd accumulated and put them in a box marked with the case number. He made sure that none of them spoke about Zack, Harry, Natalie, or that hubba-hubba broad in Queens. Putting the finishing touches on his findings he brought everything over to Eisenstaedt's office and left it with his ever-curious secretary. Joe was also concerned about what to do about letting people he didn't know review Zack's computer files. If they were as valuable as Harry said, what was his recourse if someone copied them? He needed some legal advice, so he took out his iPhone and scanned his directory of contacts looking for someone.

Yes, Phyllis Barmash... I wonder what she's up to after so many years? Is she still at the DA's office? So, he called the only number he had for her, her cell. After several rings, her recording came on, and he left her a brief message to call him about a legal matter. Hungry—no, famished, Joe walked over to a Lebanese restaurant and ordered a gyro from the counterman then found a seat next to the window. It always amazed him how, regardless of the day or night, Manhattan was like a sea of people that came at you in waves. Maybe it had to do with the traffic lights. They'd freeze people at stoplights, then as they changed from stop to go, a wave of humanity rushed to cross the streets. It was while in one of his nostalgic moments that his cell phone buzzed.

"Is that you, Serpico?" a woman's voice said.

"Phyllis, are you still fighting crime for God and country?" Joe asked.

"No, I've taken the path less travelled and now have a house in the burbs with a white picket fence, a brood of young'uns, and a chocolate Lab called Henry," she said.

"Me too... that is without Henry," he said.

"So, are you still pounding a beat?" she asked.

"No, the NYPD and I parted ways, and I'm now a private eye," he said.

"Like Sam Spade in The Maltese Falcon?" she joked.

"Yeah, and don't play it again, Sam," he said in his best Bogart imitation.

"Well, stranger, what can I do for you?"

"I need some legal advice, and I immediately thought of you."

"Oh, what trouble are you in now? An angry husband?" she asked sounding concerned.

"No, nothing like that. Can you spare a few moments?" he asked.

"For you, my dear, I'm all ears," she said.

"Well, I was working on a case where an investment company stole millions of dollars from investors and may have stashed it in an offshore bank," he said.

"Oh, how unusual," she said sarcastically.

"Well, in the course of my investigation I found a trove of software that a deceased employee of the company, which is no longer in business, created and that might be very valuable," he said.

"Wow, that was a mouthful. Who told you the software might be valuable?"

"A consultant who has seen a portion of the software and had it authenticated by experts," he said.

"What do you want to do with the software?" she asked.

"I want to find out what it's worth," he said.

"Can't the consultant tell you?"

"I'm in the process of doing just that, but it means we might have to leave the materials with these so-called experts. I'm afraid that they might scoop them up for themselves. Do you know what I mean?"

"Sort of, let me ask you. Who owns the software?"

"No one. As far as I'm concerned, it's finder's keepers," he said.

"Really, don't you think it belongs to the defunct investment company?" she said.

"What if the director is in the slammer?" he said.

"In that case a judge would probably award the software, if it's actually worth anything, to the investors and creditors. Also, who is the 'we' in, 'we might have to leave them?'"

"The consultant," he said.

"Is he your partner?" she asked.

"Sort of, if you put it like that, yes," he said.

"Okay, so let me rephrase your situation. You've got some software from a deceased individual who worked for a crook. A consultant to said crook told you that the software was valuable, according to someone you don't know. Did I get that right?" she asked.

"If you put it like that, yes," he repeated.

"Well, my dear Sam Spade, private eye, you're in what we call a conundrum. Based on what you've told me, there are no safeguards since you don't have any legal right to the software. There are too many people in line who have a legal stake in the proceeds. Therefore, I cannot in clear conscience advise you what to do under these conditions," she said very distinctly.

"Phyllis, I understand perfectly what you've said, and I appreciate your wise and learned comments. I won't belabor the—"

"Wait, wait," she interrupted. "What I said to you was from one friend to another. I'll always be in your corner, just be careful," she said breaking the connection without saying goodbye.

Joe sat there for a few moments, holding his phone to his ear, with the image of a young girl with curly blonde hair walking beside him at the water's edge one summer's day at Rockaway Beach. Joe shook off the moment and, taking the phone from his ear, called Harry.

"Joe, it must be déjà vu. I was just about to call you," Harry said.

"When are you coming north?" Joe asked.

"That's what I was calling about, I'm on the three o'clock flight to Newark," Harry said.

"What's the carrier, and what time do you arrive?"

"Delta, with a ETA of 6:34 p.m.," Harry said.

"Good, I'll be outside the Delta arrivals in a black Ford Taurus," Joe said.

"You got everything with you?" Harry asked.

"Yep, when can we see your guy?" Joe asked.

"I told him I'd call when we were on our way. It's only forty miles from Newark, less than an hour."

"Looking forward to seeing you," Joe said.

"Likewise," Harry said.

Joe walked over to Waters garage and after checking his trunk, drove to a self-service copy shop to transfer Zack's paperwork to a disc. With the deed done, Joe felt better knowing that he had a copy of all of Zack's work. The final step would be to secure the disc in his safety deposit box, which he did. Now he could meet these so-called professionals with full peace of mind.

Chapter 29: Max

Max arrived at the Butner Trust Company to find the Prince's limo parked in the spot reserved for the branch manager. Beside it, in a visitor's spot, was the Moodys' maroon Buick. Not seeing Prince or the Moodys in the lobby, Max asked the receptionist where the meeting was being held. The receptionist dropped what she was doing, sprang to her feet, and marched double-time up a flight of stairs to a conference room. After briefly tapping on the door, she opened it for Max who saw at the head of a long, mahogany table the Prince with the Moodys seated to his left. In the center of the table was a round silver tray with coffee service for four.

"Good morning, Max. Help yourself to some coffee. It's quite good, tastes like it has some chicory in it," the Prince said.

"Good morning," Max said to the Prince and the Moodys, who were busy signing some papers. Max sat in the chair to the Prince's right as if to say to others that Max was his right-hand man. Max loved the way the Prince played his part; he seemed to know instinctively the nuances for every situation and effortlessly moved people around like chess pieces on a board.

"We're memorializing the final arrangements before issuing the check to the Moodys," the Prince said, sliding another paper in front of the brothers for them to sign.

"Excellent, gentlemen, we're now ready to present you with a check made payable to Cecil and Edgar Moody in the amount of twenty-four thousand dollars," he said.

The Moodys were so happy that Max feared they might have peed in their pants. The Prince rose with check in hand and strode over to a telephone on a side table and asked for the manager to please come to the conference room. Within a matter of seconds, the bank manager entered and stood at attention by the Prince's side while he motioned for the Moodys to come forward to receive their check.

After handing them the check, he shook their hands with them and directed the bank manager to, "Take these gentlemen to a teller. They wish to make a withdrawal." What happened next was truly inexplicable. If Max hadn't seen it for himself, he wouldn't have believed it, but the Moodys bowed and backed out of the room, as one would when leaving the presence of a monarch.

"You can now proceed with the renovations at the crematorium without any further interference," the Prince said.

"You continue to amaze me," Max said as he shook his hand.

"I've heard from Prescott that he's got an appointment tomorrow with Warden Cummings. If all goes according to plan I should hear back from him shortly after the meeting," the Prince said.

Max walked the Prince down to his limo. As his chauffeur opened the door the Prince paused to look back at Max and engulf him in his smile. He then turned, entered the limo, and was gone. It was at that moment that Max understood the spell the Prince could cast on people. He was an enigma, a mythical figure from another time and place, one that could perform miracles.

Back at the crematorium the fence contractor was running stakes into the ground every eight feet around the perimeter of the site where the privacy wall would be erected.

Entering the building, Max saw that the camera was up and that podium and backdrop had been delivered from New York. Glen came over to say hello and show Max a space-age device he'd purchased to accurately measure the angle from the podium to the camera. The device once placed in the center of the podium shone one red laser beam at a ninety-degree angle to the back wall and another red laser beam at a twenty-degree angle to the camera lens.

"That's amazing. Back at the studio in New York we had to use a protractor and a flashlight. I hope we came close to the accuracy you've got with that gizmo," Max said.

"We'll test it by superimposition with the videotape when we do a dry run with you and a Bernie stand-in," Glen said.

"What about the trench?" Max asked.

"We're picking up the backhoe and bobcat tomorrow."

"Have you been able to source the steel plates?"

"Not locally, they don't have many steel mills in the Carolinas, but we'll find some," Glen said confidently. "How did it go with the old geezers?"

"Signed, sealed, delivered. We can do whatever we want with the place without worrying about the Moodys."

Margery called later that afternoon to tell Max that the Major had called asking if they could stop over to brief Ruth on the status of the plan. "It sounded like she's getting anxious about where we are and needs some handholding, some reassurance that all is well."

"Can you tell them that we'll be over at five with dinner?" Max said.

"Good idea, pick me up at four," she said.

When Otto greeted Max and Margery at the house they had rented for Ruth, he was like a different person. Their first impression of him had been formed in the scramble to unload the car, fixing a place for Ruth to relax, getting some of the communication preliminaries out of the way, and assuring him that they were on call if they needed anything.

However, the thought that Otto was formally a trained assassin for Mossad lingered in Max's mind. He imagined that somewhere in the house, Otto had probably secreted a weapon. Some type of 9mm semiautomatic, Max thought. His imagination was based solely on James Bond movies where 007 dispatched the bad guys through cunning and stealth. In that case, Otto didn't fit the profile. The baldheaded man who greeted them at the door wore a festive, self-assured smile, khaki chinos, sandals, and a white, long-sleeved shirt open at the neck with sleeves rolled up. However, his handshake gave no doubt that he could crush Max's fingers if he wished.

"Come. Ruth wants to see you. And this must be the lovely Margery I've heard about," he said extending his hand to her as well.

Seated on a faux red velvet Chanel armchair was Ruth Madoff. It seemed that the Major and His Lady had set the stage precisely as they desired, making Ruth the center of attention.

"Good afternoon, Mrs. Madoff," Max said. He approached to shake her hand, which she graciously extended with a smile.

"The pleasure is mine," she said.

"And may I introduce my partner, Margery," Max said thinking that the meeting had started off on a high note. Everyone was soon going to break out into "Kumbaya." However, Ruth was anxious to get down to serious matters. After everyone had found a comfortable place to nest she asked about the timetable.

"When do you plan to get Bernie out?" Ruth asked.

Max looking directly at her and said, "It is our hope that within the next eight days we will be able to reunite you with your husband."

Hearing that word, 'reunite,' took Ruth's breath away. Max noticed that she clenched her fists and leaned forward in her chair.

"Can you give us an idea of how you plan to do that?" Otto interjected.

"Yes, but I'm not sure how much of the plan you know," Max said.

"Pretend we know nothing," Otto quickly shot back.

"Good, then I won't be boring you with details you already know." So, Max outlined the various phases the plan took. After his presentation he fielded a few questions from Ruth and Otto.

"What role will I play in the escape?" Otto asked.

"Forgive me for not mentioning your important part in the escape.

"While Levi," he nodded to the boy, who was preoccupied with something on his iPad, "waits in your getaway car, you'll be in the tunnel assisting Bernie, helping him down into it, removing his shackles and ankle monitor if he's wearing one, removing his clothes in case they're bugged, and helping into a jumpsuit, then guiding him to the exit in the shed and down the hill to the getaway car."

"And my part?" Ruth asked.

"You'll be taken to a private Learjet, which will be waiting for you and the arrival of Bernie, Otto, and Levi at the Raleigh Airport. In any event, rest assured we will rehearse the escape on site when we're ready," Max said feeling that they understood the complexity of the endeavor and that there was a good chance of pulling it off. He also made it clear that there was always the unknown factor that could come into play and that it might end up a failure. With that out of the way they all scurried into the dining room to feast on Southern cuisine: ribs, fried chicken, French fries, greens, and grits. Max noticed that as the meal came to a close, Ruth seemed to be having difficulty staying awake and decided to take his leave.

During the ride home, Margery broached the subject that had been bothering Max. Was Ruth the sponsor?

"As far as I can tell by their demeanor, I mean both Ruth and Otto, she's not the sponsor," Margery said.

"I agree. If she was the sponsor she would have known that we were about a week away from launch by virtue of the fact that Sy would have told her," Max said.

"So, who then?" Margery asked.

"Either a benevolent benefactor or an investor bent on punishing Madoff for his crimes," Max said.

"Time will tell," Margery said as they dove off into the darkness of a country road.

Chapter 30: Joe

After Joe had waved off several attempts by a New Jersey State Trooper to move his car, Harry came out of the Delta arrivals bay and jumped into his car.

"How's the boat?" Joe asked weaving his way out of the airport.

"She'll be laid up for some time in dry dock till they get a new cutlass bearing and replace the shaft," Harry said.

"Sounds expensive."

"You know what they say: 'If you have to ask the price...'" Harry said.

"Yeah, that's so true," Joe said trying to keep the conversation going. "Did you call your guy?"

"Way ahead of you. Sent him a text as soon as we landed and told him we should be there in about an hour or so," Harry said.

"If you got the address I'll put it in my GPS."

"Excellent. I've got it on this slip of paper," Harry said, handing him the address. Joe glanced at it and noticed that it had a building name and room number.

"It's not at his home?" Joe said, handing the paper back to Harry.

"What's the problem? That's where he works," said Harry.

"We gotta talk," Joe said. He quickly turned into a gas station and parking by the air pump.

"What's bothering you, Joe?" Harry said.

"I'll tell you what's bothering me. I'm concerned that this guy may copy the data and kiss us off saying that it's worthless. That's what's bothering me."

"But I've known this man for many years. He's an authority in a very technical field of computer science, and—"

"That's all well and good. but if it's worth as much as you say it might be, all bets are off."

"What do you mean by that?" Harry said, getting frustrated. "Don't you want to know what the formulas are? Their real value?"

"I do, but don't be naïve. We just can't give it to him without any safeguards," Joe said.

"Then what do you suggest?" Harry asked.

"First, you and I have to have an understanding. If it's worth millions or billions or whatever you and I have to agree on a split."

"What do you suggest?" Harry said.

"We'll be partners, fifty-fifty," Joe said extending his hand.

"Fifty-fifty. Agreed," Harry said shaking Joe's hand.

"Next, I don't know this guy from Adam. You do. If you're willing to vouch for him I'm okay with it as long as he follows our rules. He can review the materials, but he's prohibited from making any copies. In addition, one of us must monitor what he's doing twenty-four seven."

"I don't know if he'll go for it under those conditions," Harry started, "but—"

Once again, Joe jumped in to say, "Tell him if he can help sell the formulas we'll cut him in on the action."

Harry thought about it for a while and then turned to Joe. "I think he might go for it, so let's get going."

Joe pulled out of the gas station and onto the highway heading to Princeton. By the time they got to the university's computer science building, classes had just ended, and literally hundreds of students were scurrying to their next class or off to the student union for a snack. Joe wondered what his life would have been like if he could have afforded to go to college instead of joining the Marines. It was impossible, his father was a selfish SOB and any thought of an education for his son wasn't even discussed. His only option was to join the Marines and make a life for himself. Unfortunately, after four years, the only field the Marines had prepared him for was law enforcement. To make matters worse, the highest paid jobs for a patrolman at that time were in Manhattan, where it was impossible to live due to the high cost of housing.

"You okay?" asked Harry.

"Yeah, let's see him first before we start humping the stuff into the building," Joe said.

Professor George Holmes was on the second floor of the in Room 221, which Harry pointed out as a reference to Sherlock Holmes.

"You mean they gave him the room because of his name?" Joe asked.

"At Princeton, nothing is done by happenstance. I believe it was a form of respect or admiration," Harry said, leading Joe into Dr. Holmes' office. The office was clearly a haven for books, academic journals, term papers, and binders, interspersed with overstuffed dark leather chairs and in one corner a fully stocked wine bar. It seemed to Joe that the good doctor enjoyed his grape juice.

"It's a pleasure to see you again, George," Harry said as Holmes rose from behind his desk, fumbling with his spectacles.

"This must be your associate, ah..." Holmes started to say, but clearly forgot Joe's name.

"Joe Mancuso," Harry said. The men shook hands, then, following Holmes' example, took a seat.

"You brought the materials?" he asked. Harry jumped in to say yes, and for the next few minutes Harry and Holmes made small talk. Joe was anxious to get a word in. He told Holmes in no uncertain manner the terms of the evaluation as he saw it. As they had anticipated, Holmes took umbrage to this.

"What do you mean twenty-four seven surveillance?" Holmes barked. Harry jumped in to calm his friend by saying that Joe's concern was that the materials, the formulas, might be copied and disseminated without any financial remuneration for those in its possession. By saying it that way he deftly avoided using the term 'owners of the formulas.'

"Well, that's not how we do things around here," Holmes said, rising to his feet and heading for his wine bar.

"If that's the way you want it, I'll take it to MIT," said Joe getting to his feet to leave.

"Wait, wait, gentlemen, please calm down and let's discuss how we can work together to ascertain exactly what we have in our possession and its relative value." Harry pleaded.

"I don't see how we can work under those restraints," Holmes said pouring himself a glass of sherry.

"Let's go, Harry, he thinks he's talking to a couple of his students," Joe said heading for the door.

"Joe, please, let's talk. We're here, we might as well hear what Dr. Holmes has to say."

Holmes took a sip of his sherry and returned to his chair. It seemed to Joe that the esteemed professor enjoyed a little bit of the fisticuffs. Harry waved Joe over to his seat saying, "Do you feel better now?" Joe sat without saying a word, content that Holmes understood where he was on the matter of the formulas' security.

As it turned out, that was the easy part. The next couple of hours were devoted to setting the parameters of who had access to the software, when they had access, and where. To set it in concrete, they drew up a 'Memorandum of Agreement' that each man signed. Holmes then called a couple of his postdoc students to carry the materials from Joe's car to a secure lab on the first floor. The lab's entrance was controlled by a keycard system, which monitored who entered and how long they stayed. In addition, the room was monitored by a video surveillance system that recorded everything that went on in the lab day or night. Confident that their materials would be safe, the topic changed to where Joe and Harry could find accommodations near the university. Dr. Holmes suggested a

B&B and even called the proprietor to hold two rooms for 'his guests'.

"You'd think that a university of this caliber would have several fine hotels for guests, but no, the town council thought better. It was their decree that hotels, regardless of the brand, would degrade the history and quaintness of the town," Holmes said in dismay.

As Joe and Harry went to depart, he said, "I'm happy we've thrashed it out and have come to a meeting of the minds. So, let's leave it as we discussed, and we'll be in touch as soon as we have something of substance to tell you, okay?"

After registering at the Castle Hill B&B, Joe and Harry went to a tavern the innkeeper suggested for dinner. Over drinks, Joe asked Harry of what he thought of Dr. Holmes.

"There are only a handful of institutions in the world that have the resources and talent necessary to interpret Zack's formulas. Princeton is one of them," Harry said, swirling his pinot noir.

"That's all well and good, but can we trust him?" Joe asked.

"I considered what you previously said about safeguards, and as I see it, it's his reputation in the field, it's what his colleagues think of him, that will keep him on the straight and narrow," Harry said.

"How long do you think it will take to get an idea as to the formulas' worth?" Joe asked.

"Without being smug, it will take as long as it takes," Harry said picking up his menu.

The next morning after a sumptuous English breakfast of fried eggs, sausage, bacon, fried toast, grilled tomatoes, baked beans, and black pudding, Joe and Harry decided to take a walk into town.

"I haven't had so much to eat since my father's wake," Joe said.

"What did your dad do?" Harry asked.

"We weren't close. He went his way and I went, well, I went into the Marines. But to answer your question, he was a factory worker and then at a few warehouses around Jersey." Joe said. "How about your dad?"

"As a kid he worked on a fishing boat in Crete," Harry said, "learned the ropes then borrowed some money to buy a small twenty-four-foot wooden wreck. Spent a year fixing it up until he put it into the water."

"That sounds like the American dream," Joe said.

"Not really. As soon as he got it out maybe 100 yards, it sank," Harry said with a smile.

"No shit?" Joe remarked.

"But my dad was an irascible man, and when there was a very low tide, he got some men to help him bring it ashore." Harry said.

"Then he saved the boat?" Joe said.

"Not really, he found so much rot that I think the boat is still somewhere on the coast, buried in the sand." Harry laughed.

"So, what did he do?" Joe asked.

"He went to work in my cousin's restaurant, and when he died my father inherited the place. That's the real American success story," Harry said.

Chapter 31: Max

When Max and Margery got to the funeral home the next morning, the fence materials had already been delivered to the site and the contractor had begun boring postholes with a large portable auger. Glen came over to tell them some good news.

"I sourced the plates in Pittsburg, Pennsylvania. They should be here tomorrow," he said.

"Oh, that's a relief!" Margery smiled.

"Come inside. I want to show you the video setup.

"Watch this," he said indoors, as he ran the first five minutes of video he'd shot of two of his crew pretending to be the rabbi and Madoff. Then the tape switched to Max and the look-alike in the New York studio. Although one could clearly differentiate the actors, the switch from live to recorded was, as they say in the trade, seamless and impossible to tell.

"Excellent," Margery said.

"Now we have to superimpose the images for size and position," Glen said as Franco, a member of his crew, rushed in, needing to talk to Glen in private. The men stepped outside to talk. Max and Margery could only wonder what the crisis was.

"He's got to get back home," Glen said shaking his head.

"What's the problem?" Margery asked.

"His kid's in the hospital. Got hit by a pickup while riding his bike to school," Glen said nervously pacing.

"What's his condition?" Max asked quietly.

"He doesn't know," Glen replied.

"Okay, let me get him a ticket. To Reno, right?" Margery asked.

"Yes, Reno," Glen said.

"What's his full name? Does he have a photo ID for TSA?"

Glen checked and gave Margery his full name. "Franco LaPoma, and yes, he has a Nevada driver's license."

After purchasing a boarding pass for Franco, Margery and Max hopped in their car to drive him to the airport.

On the ride to the airport Franco spoke to his wife on his cell phone in Spanish. When Margery asked him what his son's condition was, he merely shook his head saying his wife didn't know. When they arrived at the United departure terminal, Max asked Margery if she had any cash.

"I've got two hundred and twenty-five dollars," she said.

"I've got one-fifty," Max said.

Getting out of the car, Margery embraced the distraught Franco and stuffed the three hundred and seventy-five dollars and his plane tickets in his hand, saying, "We'll pray for your boy's recovery," which brought Franco to tears.

"Go, go directly to the gate," she said. "You'll miss your flight."

On the way back to the site, Max brought up the delicate subject that he and Margery had struggled with after they began living together: their mutual desire to have a child. In the beginning they tried but found to their regret that Margery was unable to conceive. They ultimately decided that they would devote their lives together to a loving relationship without the blessing of children.

"Hey, it's time to get another car," Margery reminded Max as they headed back to the site.

"Our getaway car?" Max replied.

"A vanilla one—something that will blend in and not call attention to it," Margery said.

"I guess that rules out a Jaguar?" Max joked.

"Definitely," Margery agreed. They stopped for coffee and picked up some auto circulars at a convenience store.

"I don't see anything. They're all dealer ads disguised as little old ladies who drive once around the block," Margery said.

"Let's try Craig's List," Max suggested. They stopped and parked under a tree so that both could scour Craig's List on their phones.

"I found a couple of cars that are old enough and meet our criteria for about forty-five hundred," Margery said.

"Get their phone numbers and we'll call them," Max suggested.

By the time they got back to the funeral home, Margery had spoken to a couple of Craig's Listers. One had another white Honda Accord just a stone's throw away.

With the privacy fence now up, Glen was marking up the lines his backhoe operator would follow in digging the trench. He had decided that the trench would be six feet deep and four feet wide. He had previously bored a two-inch test hole to see if he hit water at the six-foot depth, and thankfully the bit came up dry. In addition, by laying the four-by-six-foot steel plates side by side over the trench, he had roughly a one-foot grip on either side of it. The Bobcat would then cover the parking lot with two inches of topsoil and then four inches of three quarter inch crushed stone.

"You'd never know there was a trench beneath the parking lot," he told them.

Satisfied that Glen was doing his thing and not wanting to micromanage the construction process, Margery and Max went to inspect the Honda. Before doing so, they stopped at an ATM to get two hundred in cash. The Honda was parked alongside the road with a crooked 'For Sale' sign on it not more than fifteen minutes away. Parking behind it, they got out to inspect the car. At first glance it seemed to Margery that it was in good condition. Shortly after they arrived, a woman dressed in jeans, a denim work shirt, and cowboy boots strode over to say hello. After the customary handshakes, Max asked if they could take it for a spin.

"Here's the keys," she said getting into the backseat. "Where you from?" she asked trying to be folksy.

"Here and there," Max said, not offering up too much information.

"Why are you selling it?" Margery deftly asked to change the subject.

"Need a four-wheel drive to pull a camper," she said proudly.

Max put the car through the usual test drive, looking and listening for signs of trouble. He stopped to look under the hood, not because he knew what to look for but because that's what everyone does. The woman sat in the back seat trying to get to know the prospective buyers, but Margery was clever enough to deflect her overtures. She stuck to questioning the woman, not the other way around. Driving back to the house, Margery and Max conferred for a few moments and decided the car would fit the bill for the time being, knowing they would probably ditch it and get another car as soon as they got a few hundred miles from Butner.

"We'll take the car if you can leave the plates on it until we can get it registered," Max said.

"Oh, sure I can," the woman practically shouted, happy to know she'd sold the car.

"This is what we'll do. I'll give you one hundred dollars in cash to hold the car until tomorrow when we'll pay for it and pick it up," Margery said, getting out her wallet.

"You got a deal," the woman said, clearly thinking how lucky she was that they didn't even quibble about the price.

Max checked the VIN number on the registration and the car, then took out a pad and made out a bill of sale and had the woman sign it. The way they left it, they'd call tomorrow and set up a time to collect the car. Driving away, the whole process took less than an hour to complete.

"Everything should be that easy," Margery said.

"Let's go see the Prince," Max suggested. "I want to find out what's new from the warden."

The Prince invited them to join him for a late lunch at his hotel.

"He sure knows how to play his part," Max said as they left their car with the valet.

Making their way through a large atrium, they entered an annex in which many of the private suites were housed. The largest of which was the Presidential Suite where the Prince held court. Max realized that first impressions were important to seduce and set the stage for the con. In a way, it was their client Bernie Madoff who exemplified the art of the con. He's heard that most of Bernie's victims begged him to take their money so they could get in on the action. He smirked. If you looked wealthy enough, people would eat out of your hand.

"A red smoking jacket?" Max said, embracing the Prince.

"You like it?" he asked, leading them into his massive great room. "I got it at a consignment shop in the West Village. It's got to be thirty years ago. There was a time everyone I knew smoked, and drank, and smoked. That being said, can I offer you a drink?" he said as Miss Latex sashayed into the room.

"It's good to see you, Betty," Margery said embracing her.

They fixed their drinks and settled into overstuffed lounge chairs to discuss what progress, if any, there was from their local attorney and his quest for concessions for Madoff vis-à-vis Ruth's cremation.

"Yes, that's also been on my mind. According to our last conversation he was to meet with Warden Cecil Cummings yesterday and my calls to him have been unsuccessful," the Prince said.

"Is he ducking you?" Margery asked.

"Definitely, he may be embarrassed that he was unable to secure all our requests," he said.

"In any event, he's got to tell us where we stand with regards to our requests," Max said.

"I've given him enough rope up until this point. Now's the time to yank him over for a show and tell." Betty entered with a tray of hors d'oeuvres.

For the next several minutes the conversation drifted from the progress, or lack thereof, in their plans for possible venues they'd like to visit after their foray was complete. However, Max sensed that something was bothering the Prince and suggested getting some fresh air. Leaving Margery and Betty, the Prince escorted Max out onto the veranda where they could speak in private.

"What's bothering you?" Max asked.

"Can't tell but my nose smells a rat," he said sipping his drink.

"On our end?" Max asked.

"No, the good ol' boy, the attorney, Prescott Andrews," the Prince said.

"Be more specific," Max coaxed.

"Well, it wasn't exactly what he said that troubles me, it was a vague reference he made about Freda."

"Who's Freda?"

"That's what's bothering me. He wouldn't say. It was something he said to himself, not me."

"What does it mean? Is she his wife?" Max asked.

"No, his wife's name is Phyllis," the Prince said.

Both men looked at each other as if they were simultaneously reading each other's minds, saying in unison, "It's his mistress!"

Chapter 32: Joe

"Harry, come to the lab," the voice said at 8:30 a.m.

"Is that you, Holmes?" a sleepy Harry said into his iPhone.

"Yes, we have to talk," Holmes demanded.

"You're done?" Harry asked, sitting up on his bed and looking at his bedside clock.

"Just come over," Holmes said and hung up.

Harry stared at his phone for a few seconds thinking, He's never done that before. Harry went into his bathroom and washed his face and brushed his teeth. Awake, he called Joe to tell him that they had to go to the lab, pronto.

The beehive that was classes at Princeton was buzzing once again with fresh faces in colorful outfits.

"The kids have so much energy here," remarked Harry as they entered the quad leading to the lab.

"Well, don't get too close to them, they may be radioactive," Joe said.

One of Dr. Holmes' postgrads opened the door, asked who they were, and admitted them, then quickly closed the door behind them. In addition to Dr. Holmes, there were several other people in the lab, whom Holmes quickly introduced. Two were faculty, three were postgrads, and four others (three men and a woman) were curiously not identified. Behind Dr. Holmes were four large white boards with formulas written from top to bottom.

Looking at which, Harry murmured to Joe, "It's all Greek to me."

"Good morning, gentlemen, and thanks for coming so quickly to our meeting," Holmes began. "As you can see," he motioned to the white boards, "we've been hard at work and have, thanks to the people assembled before you, a breakthrough.

"I've asked the people responsible for this massive undertaking to explain what they found," he said smiling. "In laymen's terms." With that being said, a tweedy-looking gentleman stepped forward and introduced himself as Professor Mannheim in a pronounced Germanic accent. The professor elucidated that he had previously examined some of the formulas many years ago and was extremely impressed with their theory of quantum finance. He referred to it as the 'Quantum-Bose-Einstein Theory of Finance,' but he couched his remarks by saying, "It was what we call basic research, begging for an application. However, to be clear, the way it stood back then was nothing more than genius.

"Today," he hesitated, struggling to come up with the right English word or phrase to convey his utter amazement, "today, we analyzed these new formulas and, after running many simulations, have come, so to speak, full circle," he said, shaking his head.

"Yes, the application of these formulas will change the way commerce is conducted in the foreseeable future. From the classic scientific method of basic research to its application, these formulas make banks, insurance companies, venture capital companies, and Wall Street itself superfluous. They're not necessary in the world of tomorrow."

"Thank you, Professor Mannheim. Now I would like to introduce Professor Liebowitz, dean of the School of Economics." Holmes gave him the floor.

"Thank you for giving me the opportunity to address these remarkable formulas and their possible application in today's world markets," Professor Liebowitz began. "I wholeheartedly concur with my colleague Dr. Mannheim. Today's financial institutions on a grand scale do not contribute to the overall wealth and wellbeing of the individual citizen. Here in the United States twenty people—let me repeat that number—twenty people have more wealth than half of the American population. That's twenty people who have more wealth than one hundred and seventy million people combined. They are able to accomplish this largess by means of an unregulated shadow banking system where over an estimated one hundred trillion dollars is hidden in offshore banks. Briefly, the author of these remarkable formulas mathematically conceived of a system that put a price, and this was startling, on the value of commerce to humanity. In other words, what is the value of the product and/or service to society? To a capitalist this is pure heresy. To them, the ones with obscene wealth wish for a continuation of the status quo. In other words, leaving all the wealth in the hands of a few men as it is today."

"Thank you, Dr. Liebowitz. I would now like to call on Dr. Donna Wang, a postdoctoral student here at Princeton," Dr. Holmes said.

"Thank you, Dr. Holmes. I was a member of a team," she acknowledged several members of the audience, "who debated the relative impact the formulas would have if introduced into the market. It was a very contentious debate to say the least. We broke into two camps, those in favor of using the formulas and those who didn't favor their use. Both sides had good arguments for using and not using them. Using them meant the dismantlement of everything we now use in commerce and a redistribution of wealth. Using these formulas also creates a transparent system where wealth cannot be acquired by legal or illegal means and laundered through secret offshore tax havens. The team opposed to their use argued that the changes would be cataclysmic to everything in commerce regardless if the byproduct fostered graft and corruption. In addition, the share number of jobs that would be lost in banking and financial sectors would be monumental. They came to the conclusion that the US government wouldn't allow by fiat such a drastic change. Moreover, they said that Wall Street would do everything in their power to see that these formulas never see the light of day," she said.

"Thank you, Dr. Wang, and my colleagues and students, who spent many tireless hours pouring over very complicated materials and synthesizing them down into meaningful information we can understand. Bravo, you have done well," Holmes said, excusing them.

"Well, what do you think of it so far?" he asked Joe and Harry.

"Well, I would like to know what the formulas are worth," said Joe.

"Worth? They're priceless," Holmes said holding his head high.

"Holmes, what did you mean by 'so far'?" Harry asked.

By way of answering, Holmes asked another question. "Look at the worktable and tell me what you see or don't see."

Joe noticed it first. "Where's the other computer?"

"Exactly. The other computer is in another laboratory," Holmes said.

"What's going on, Holmes?" Harry asked angrily as he caught on.

"We believe the contents of the other computer are diametrically different from those on this computer," he said pointing to the Cray computer on the worktable.

"Say what? You lost me," Joe confessed.

"At this point in time, we have no idea what it all adds up to. It's just codes and formulas. Without a Rosetta stone, as it were, we can't translate what it says or does."

"So how does it stand?" Harry asked politely.

"I've reached out to a Professor Kolinsky at Stanford for help. He's a noted theoretician. I'm hoping he and his people can help us."

"Do you know him personally?" Joe asked.

"No, but some of my colleagues here have recommended him." Holmes said, letting it sink in before changing tacks. "In addition, it's time we spoke about the provenance of the formulas."

"What are you getting at?" Joe snapped. His patience was wearing thin.

"Who owns the formulas? Who has the rights, the legal rights, to them?" Holmes snapped back.

"Okay, calm down, both of you," Harry interjected. He turned to Holmes. "You knew full well when I brought you the formulas some time ago that they were given to me by Bernie Madoff."

"Yes, but that was because Madoff thought they were part of his NASDAQ algorithms. You remember at that time his formulas were the basis of the NASDAQ. He was the fucking chairman of the NASDAQ Stock Exchange," Holmes said, completely out of character in rebuttal.

"What are you guys talking about? Is it ours to sell or not?" Joe asked with some apprehension.

There followed several moments of reflection as the men thought of what to say.

"Actually, it's Bernie's call," Harry said. "Did Zack create the formulas as part of his employment at Bernie's company or were they something he dreamed up outside of his employment for Bernie?"

"That begs the issue of why Bernie had the formulas in his possession in the first place," Holmes said.

"Maybe he was just curious," Joe suggested.

"I don't know how a judge would rule on it, but we have a situation here, gentlemen," Holmes said.

"What if Bernie says that he didn't know about Zack's formulas?" Harry asked.

"That would be a lie." Holmes said.

"Only if he knew that you had evaluated them," Joe said.

"Gentlemen," Holmes warned, "don't go there. With regards to these formulas I will not give false testimony in a civil or criminal proceeding for any amount of money. I suggest, in light of the software author's death, that you confer with Bernie Madoff."

Harry looked at Joe. "Let me speak with my colleague, and we will get back to you this afternoon."

"Fine. I'll keep the computers under tight security here, but I'd like permission to see if we can, with the assistance of Professor Kolinsky and his people at Stanford, find out what these damned formulas do on the other computer," Holmes said.

"What, if anything, have you seen on the second Cray computer?" Harry asked.

"Overlapping compound algorithms on steroids," Holmes said.

"Is there such a thing?" asked Harry, confused.

"Nope, it's not in any of the literature, and it's unbelievably complex," Holmes said with a smile.

"You like it?" Joe asked.

"Joe, this is like something from another world, from an advanced civilization, not from mere mortals like us," Holmes said with a faraway look on his face.

Disappointed, Joe and Harry left the lab. They decided to assuage their fears that there was no pot of gold at the end of the rainbow by getting a stiff drink and a rare steak at the tavern they had dined at the night before. The first drink did little to help, but after the second round, things didn't seem so bleak.

"I'll call Bernie and set up a visit at his penitentiary in Butner, North Carolina," Harry said chewing on his rib eye.

"Should I come with you?" Joe asked.

"I don't think he'd see you, and I doubt they'd allow two unrelated visitors to see him. Remember it's a federal institution, with pages and pages of rules.

"I'll put a call in and see what I can do. In the interim I think we should let Holmes do his thing until we know what our options are. It wouldn't hurt if we asked him to compose a letter to Madoff on our behalf explaining his finds relative to the value of the formulas, especially since his team concluded that they were 'priceless.'"

"I guess you're right," Joe said. "We'd probably get the same advice if we brought the stuff to MIT."

With that the men raised their glasses on high and toasted to a better tomorrow.

Chapter 33: Max

The call Max got the next morning was a shock. "We've got to move Ruth," the Prince said.

"What?" Max automatically replied. "Say that again I thought I heard you say—"

"You heard me right. Prescott's just told me that his squeeze shot her mouth off that Ruth Madoff is in Butner," the Prince said.

"Who'd she tell?" Max asked.

"Who does a woman tell everything to?" the Prince asked.

"Who?" Max said thinking of her girlfriend or some stranger on a bus.

"Her hairdresser."

"Oh shit, not now!" Max cried.

"We have to manage the news, and the best way is to get Ruth out of sight," the Prince counseled.

"How did Prescott find out about the leak?" Max asked.

"He got a call from a reporter at the Raleigh News and Observer asking for a confirmation."

"Did he confirm or deny that Ruth was in Butner?" Max asked.

"He gave her a 'no comment' reply, which is in itself a tell that it's true.

"We have to move her now. I'll send my car to collect Ruth and Otto, while Levi, the Major, and His

Lady pack everything into Ruth's car and all head for your place."

"Where's the son of a bitch now?" Max asked thinking he'd like to strangle the moron.

"He's here in the hotel dining room waiting for me to tell him what to do," the Prince said.

"First ask him if he's made out his will. Because we're going to kill him."

"Easy, Big Mac," the Prince warned, "we still need him. He's got to tell the warden what he's done and ask for his forgiveness because guess who the reporter will call next?"

"The warden. Do you want me to tell Ruth?" Max asked starting to feel out of the loop.

"No, I brought him on board. It's only right for me to tell her," he said.

"Okay, then I'll head over to the site to prepare for the rehearsal. If it all goes well, Bernie will be a free man in a few days," Max said, feeling better that it was coming to an end.

Margery caught the tail end of the phone conversation and asked, "What's up? You look troubled."

"If it's not one thing, it's another. Our eminent attorney Prescott told his mistress that Ruth was in Butner and get this... a reporter is looking for info on where she is. Prince suggested moving Ruth here until we're ready to get Bernie out."

"No problem. We have four bedrooms," she said, wondering if there were enough linens.

"If you can wait until they arrive, I'd like to get back to the site and prepare for a rehearsal of the escape," Max said giving Margery a peck on her cheek. " I'll call you if I need Otto and Levi to rehearse their parts."

"Roger, Mr. Spielberg," Margery said.

The funeral home was a whole different place with the seven-foot privacy fence and gravel parking lot. Max was confident that no one would be able to tell that under the parking lot there was a tunnel stretching from seven feet under the building to six feet under the shed some fifty-five feet away.

"I've got to see what it looks like down there," Max said to Glen as he entered the crematorium.

"You'll like it, we just hung the LED battery-powered lanterns eight feet apart in the tunnel," Glen said as he brought him to a hole in the floor.

"We're fabricating a trapdoor to cover the hole, which will match the existing floor." He slid a ladder into the hole for Max to descend into the tunnel. "This is only temporary until we can build wooden steps on both ends of the tunnel."

The first thing Max thought when he stepped off the ladder onto the tunnel floor was how eerie it was looking down the fifty or so feet to the other end. He knew it was four feet by six feet, but it seemed tight and claustrophobic to him. "Thankfully," he said to himself, "I'll only be down here for twenty or thirty seconds."

"You okay?" Glen asked, peering down at Max.

"You did a great job," Max said climbing back up the ladder.

"It's a little tight down there, but think about it, there will be light at the end of the tunnel," Glen said.

"Are we ready for a test run?" Max asked.

"Still trying to get some of the kinks out. How about tomorrow?" Glen said.

"Okay, let me know." Max said. He went on to share news of the unfortunate leak with his contractor.

"Do you think they'll come here?" asked Glen.

"No, he doesn't know anything about what we're doing here," Max said to reassure him. "Remember, you and your boys will already be two thousand miles away when this thing goes down. How are the pyro guys doing?" he asked.

"They're pros, but there's no real way to test the system without burning the place down," Glen said.

"Good thing you've told me. In that case, I'll bring some matches," Max said with a crooked smile.

It was at that point that Max received a call from Margery.

"Ruth's here and wants to know if we should go ahead with the plan in light of the press snooping around," she said.

"What did you tell her?" Max asked.

"I told her that it's still on schedule and Bernie will be with us soon."

"Excellent, I've just descended into the tunnel. It looks ready for Broadway," Max said trying to sound upbeat.

"When are you doing the run-through?" Margery asked.

"Glen wants another day," he said.

"Then if all's well, Act One is only a few days away."

"I'm hoping that it turns out that all's well that ends well, as someone famous once said," Max joked.

"Anything new from the Prince and the village idiot?"

"Not yet, he's told Prescott to see the warden, explain what he's done, and beg his forgiveness," Max said.

"Do you think they'll find Ruth's house?" Margery asked.

"I think they'll start with the obvious places, local hotels, motels, and bed-and-breakfasts. Then maybe apartment rentals, although that's a stretch in a rural community like Butner. After exhausting that, house rentals. Any way you look at it, it will take a while and a lot of legwork to find Ruth's house," Max said.

"What do you think?" Margery asked.

"Only time will tell, my love."

"Well, keep me informed," she said.

Max volunteered to pick up subs for the crew at a local Italian restaurant. While he waited for his order to be filled, he sat back, and for the first time in a long time, he thought about where Margery and he would end up after the gig was over. They'd played with thoughts of North Africa, Asia, and Europe, targeting those countries without extradition treaties, but Max's idea of an escape was rooted in the US. He would love to find a secluded house by the sea with a deep-water dock to tie up a fifty-foot yacht. There they could enjoy the sea, the sand, and each other. Life was too short to gallivant all over the world looking over your shoulder. The less exposure, the better, he thought. The ones that get caught flaunt their money and eventually draw attention to themselves.

In addition, the feds would probably offer a king's ransom for their capture, adding to the necessity to lie low until things cool down. Max regretted that they'd spent so much time contemplating what others should do without nailing down a safe haven for themselves. He decided that tonight he'd discuss the subject with Margery and they would pick a place, any place safe, and figure out how to get there.

On his way back to deliver the subs, Max received a call from the Prince. It turned out that Prescott met with the warden, and according to Prescott, he spilled his guts about the mistress, his marriage, the lies, and other unspeakable sins. The warden said he accepted his repentance, and they prayed together right there in the warden's office.

"Amazing what honesty can do for the soul," Max said.

"I've changed my mind about the man, too," the Prince said. "He's officially off my shit list."

"Where are you now?" Max asked.

"Waiting for my driver to return from your place."

"Good. Wait for me. There's something I want to bounce off you," Max said.

"Can you give me a heads-up?" the Prince asked.

"It's a bit awkward and it may sound funny to you, but Margery and I haven't decided where to go after we spring Bernie," Max said.

"Come on over and we'll share a single malt together," the Prince said.

When Betty opened the door to Max her first question was, "How do you like your scotch?"

"Bring your drink outside," the Prince said as she handed Max a single malt on the rocks. "So, my dear boy, you haven't set a course to the promised land?" He said raising his glass to toast his new arrival.

"As sad as it seems, we're still debating where to hang our hats."

"It's a little late in the game but not impossible if you can answer one question," the Prince said.

"Shoot," said Max.

"Is it for now or forever?"

"What do you mean?"

"The place you want to go," he said. "Is it forever?"

"Huh. We never thought of it like that," Max said.

"Exactly. If you think of the place as the one and only place you'll spend the rest of your life, it makes choosing a place impossible. One place cannot possibly fulfill all your wishes."

"I think I see where you're going. In other words, choose a place that fulfills our needs now with an eye towards another place down the road if necessary," Max said.

"By George!" the Prince crowed. "I think he's got it."

Chapter 34: Joe

When Harry met Joe several hours later it was not with the good news Joe had anticipated. Harry had hit a brick wall in his attempt to see Madoff.

"It's bureaucratic bullshit with a cherry on top," Harry said.

"What did they tell you?" Joe asked.

"Well, first of all, Madoff has to submit Form 263-77 two weeks prior to the visit. In addition, he's allowed a certain number of visits each month depending on some other cockamamie rule. When I asked for clarification, they told me to go to their website and read the rules for visiting inmates. So, I asked them if I could leave a message for Madoff. The guard said, 'We're not his secretary,' and hung up."

"So, what's the next step?" Joe asked.

"To be honest, I did go to their website and reviewed the rules for visiting inmates. There are two exceptions. One is immediate family members and the other is his attorney," Harry said.

"Do you know who his attorney is?" Joe said sensing this might be an avenue to get to Madoff.

"Yes, I read up on the trial and found an attorney named Ken Bernstein represented Madoff. Best of all, he has an office on Park Avenue."

"Did you call him?" Joe asked, moving closer.

"I did, but his secretary said he was out and took my phone number," Harry said.

"Did you tell her that it was about Madoff?" Joe asked.

"Of course not! He'd never call if it was about Madoff. He's probably been bombarded with requests over the years."

"Then what—how are we going to see him?" Joe asked nervously.

"We need a attorney to represent us in a Wall Street million-dollar scam we perpetrated," Harry said.

"No, a multimillion-dollar scam," Joe shot back.

"No, a multi-billion dollar scam," Harry said, laughing.

"What company should we tell him we defrauded?" Joe asked.

"We won't unless he agrees to take our case."

"Excellent, my good man, I think I'm rubbing off on you. One day you'll hang your shingle out on the Isle of Crete as the Numero Uno Con Man in the world," Joe said shaking his head.

It didn't take long until Bernstein's secretary called back with several questions.

"Gentlemen, may I have your names and who referred you? Can you please tell me the nature of your requirements for legal counsel?" On she went, with a typical battery used to screen potential clients without asking them if they could pay five hundred to a thousand dollars an hour for a high-priced Park Avenue attorney.

"Let me cut to the chase," Joe said. "My partner and I are involved in a multimillion-dollar stock embezzlement case, and trust me, we can afford your firm's services. Now please be good enough to tell Bernstein that we'd like to see him tomorrow. You have my cell number. I would appreciate a call back today," Joe said and cut the connection.

"He'll call back," he said confidently.

"I hope you're right, since he's the only one who can get us to Madoff," Harry said.

Just as Joe had predicted, Bernstein's secretary called to say that "Mr. Bernstein can see you tomorrow at the end of the day. Say, four o'clock?"

"We'll be there at four," Joe said. Then he turned to give Harry a high-five.

At precisely 3:45 p.m. the following day, Joe and Harry were in the lobby of 200 Park Avenue, a fifty-eight-story glass and steel behemoth, peering at a large directory of the names of companies and individuals who had offices in the building.

"There he is, fiftieth floor, Suite 5070," Joe said making a mental note of the suite number.

"How do you want to play it?" Joe asked.

"If he doesn't call security to throw us out, let's stick to the facts as we know them," Harry said.

"Did you do a background check?" Joe asked, watching the elevator's numbers flying up and down.

"Columbia Law, did a stint at Justice and retired from the Treasury Department. He's no lightweight, and I'll bet you dimes to dollars he'll check out our story," Harry said ushering Joe onto an elevator heading up.

Bernstein's outer office was both spacious and tastefully decorated in glass and stainless steel, in the same motif as the building itself. Situated on the fiftieth floor, the reception area had a commanding view of LaGuardia Airport. On a clear day, one could imagine seeing as far out as the White Cliffs of Dover across the ocean. What struck them as they waited were the Audubon paintings of birds on the walls. Harry pointed to one and said that it was probably worth thousands of dollars. At precisely four, a secretary brought them to Bernstein's corner office, which also boasted a breathtaking view.

"Gentlemen, how can I help you?" Bernstein asked, shaking their hands.

"Sir, we are here under false pretenses," Harry began. This took Bernstein by surprise. He sat back and placed his fingertips together waiting for an explanation. What followed was a concise recap of what the men had done and why they did it.

When Bernstein had processed what he had heard, he asked,

"What do you want out of it?"

"The reward for returning the investors' money," Joe said.

"You mean to tell me that these formulas are worth billions of dollars?" Bernstein asked.

"According to our experts, they're priceless," Harry said placing Dr. Holmes' letter to Madoff in front of Bernstein. Bernstein picked up the letter and briefly read it.

"And what about Bernie? What does he get?" Bernstein asked.

"A presidential pardon," Harry said.

Bernstein snorted. "You think it's that easy?"

"Do you know what would happen if we auctioned the formulas off? To China, Great Britain, Russia, or the Saudis? They'd use it as leverage in their dealings with Wall Street," Harry said.

"What he's trying to say, in so many words, is that it would be a shitstorm!" Joe said in his best Jersey speak.

This was followed by several moments in which Bernstein sifted, scratched, weighed, dissected, and analyzed this multifaceted proposal. Nothing in his thirty-odd years of practicing law had he ever had such a confusing dilemma. Here he had a client now serving a 150-year sentence, a formula of unknown provenance, a team of experts from Princeton of all places claiming the formulas were priceless, a way of restoring billions of dollars to Madoff's investors, and all he had to do was convince the Treasury Department to secretly buy the formulas and a law-and-order president to pardon public enemy number one? Piece of cake!

"And where are these formulas?" Bernstein asked.

"They are under lock and key at Princeton," Joe said.

"Well—" Bernstein started to say, but then Harry, looking at Joe, said, "And that's not all."

"You mean there's more!? What is this, a ten-part series?" Bernstein said in frustration.

"What we just spoke about is on one Cray Computer. It holds the Quantum-Bose-Einstein formulas we just described, but there's another Cray Computer in the mix at Princeton."

"Tell me Einstein isn't part of the equation?" Bernstein said, beginning to laugh.

"No, but it probably involves some of his theories," Harry said. "The second computer has not been fully analyzed at this point in time, and Professor Holmes has brought in a Professor Kolinsky and his people at Stanford to check it out. It was Professor Holmes' impression that the formulas on this second computer held a great deal of promise. He said the formulas had the ability to run something called 'overlapping compound algorithms' so fast that he said they were on steroids."

"Gentlemen, that's a lot to digest in one session. Let me review what was said, let me do a little due diligence, speak to Mr. Madoff and some of your references, and I'll give you my decision after I have all the facts. Okay?" Bernstein said.

"You can actually speak with Madoff in prison?" Joe asked.

"Yes, under the federal system, an attorney may speak with his client by phone without anyone listening or recording the conversation," Bernstein said bringing the meeting to an end.

"I think that went well," Joe said in the elevator.

"Well, he didn't throw us out," Harry replied.

"Where did you come up with the idea of a reward?" Joe asked.

"I made it up," Harry said.

232 | *The Hunt for Madoff's Treasure*

Joe couldn't believe what he just heard. "Man, you're slick," he said as the elevator reached the lobby. "Where to now?"

"Let's catch a cab and have a drink at The Palm onThird Avenue," Harry said.

The Palm was mobbed at that hour, so the boys decided to grab a beer at an old popular saloon, The Blarney Stone, just two blocks down on Second Avenue. Saddling up to the bar on a couple of greasy stools Harry and Joe had the bartender pull two pints of Guinness on draft. Another great thing about The Blarney Stone was that at happy hour you could fill up on an endless supply of appetizers. Filling their plates with chicken wings, meatballs, deviled eggs, and bread, there was no reason to buy dinner that night. Satisfied that they had done as much as they could, they bid each other goodbye with Harry heading to his hotel on Sixth Ave and Joe to his car parked on the West End.

On the ride home Joe called Patty to check on the kids.

"Hello," she answered on the first ring.

"Hey, hon, how you doing?" Joe asked.

"I'm always afraid of answering the phone because your phone number is different every time," Patty said.

"Yeah, I'm using a burner because I'm in New York," he said. "Are the girls okay?"

"Yes, but they want to go home," Patty said.

"Not right now, I've got to check if it's safe. Maybe in a few days," Joe said.

"You mean they haven't caught him yet?" Patty asked, incredulous.

"I'll check on it tomorrow."

"Are you going home?" Patty asked.

"Yeah, I should be there in about thirty minutes."

"Okay," she said. "Call me tonight before you go to sleep."

The traffic was pretty light, so it took him only twenty minutes to get to his street. As usual he made a pass of the house to see if he had any uninvited guests waiting for him. He knew most of the neighbors' cars. Nothing looked out of place except for a black Caddy at the end of the street. That stood out like a sore thumb, he thought. Best to circle around to make sure.

As he did, bingo, there was someone sitting at the wheel in the dark smoking. He couldn't get the license plate in the dark, so he drove away. Stopping around the corner he called the Morristown Police Department and told them there was a suspicious car parked on his street. He gave them the house number and waited until a patrol car arrived and followed it down the block. The police car stopped alongside the Caddy. The officer approached the driver with his hand on his revolver. After a brief conversation Joe saw that he had returned to his patrol car with the driver's license and registration to run a check, when out of the blue the Caddy revved to life and raced away.

The patrolman dove in his car in hot pursuit of the fleeing motorist, strobe lights flashing and siren blasting. Joe parked several houses away, and after retrieving his 9mm Glock from under his seat, he approached the back of his house. He had to assume the assassin left his backup in the car.

Joe silently opened the back door and listened for any movement. He crept through the mudroom on all fours to the doorway leading into the kitchen. He pressed his back to the wall and raised his Glock while he reached with his other hand for the light switch. He clicked the lights on, but no one was there. Relieved he lowered his gun when he heard a noise and caught a glimpse of someone darting through the front door. With his gun extended in front of him, he raced through the front door and spotted a figure dressed all in black running between the houses.

"Stop or I'll shoot," cried Joe in hot pursuit, but whoever the intruder was, he was much faster than an out-of-shape former NYPD detective. Stopping for breath, Joe called the police station again to tell them that one of the subjects was on foot in the neighborhood and probably armed. In a few minutes, two patrol cars came racing down the street. Joe, holding his old detectives badge over his head, stopped one of the cars to give them a description and to be careful because the person they were chasing was an armed killer. Both men understood shaking their heads and headed off to find the suspect.

Joe once again entered his house through the back door with his gun raised, just in case, but the house was empty. He called the police station and spoke to the sergeant on duty, advising him that the hit men may be working out of the Majestic Hotel in Atlantic City. Joe sat at the kitchen table, coming down from his adrenaline rush and nursing a bottle of Michelob. He thought that it was by the grace of God and his own good instinct that his wife and kids were not at home. In that moment, he decided that he'd never tell them of what went down that night.

Chapter 35: Max

The next morning was a bit chaotic at Max and Margery's house. Their new guests, all five of them, seemed to be roaming around the house. Doors were opened and closed, toilets were flushed, showers were started, voices rang out, and plates were clattered onto the table.

"Is it safe to go to the bathroom?" Margery whispered to Max.

"You'll never know until you try," Max replied, glancing at his iPhone.

"I thought I heard it buzzing. What does it say?" Margery asked. Max tried to read his text, but without glasses, it was just a blur.

"Here give it to me," Margery said taking the phone. "Oh, it's from Glen. It says, 'It's show time at the bakery.' Isn't that a bit macabre?" she said, tossing the phone in Max's direction. She snuck out of the bedroom and came back to tell Max that the coast was clear and that he should join her for a twosome in the shower. Refreshed and squeaky clean they joined the others in the kitchen where Chef Otto was serving breakfast.

"I love to cook," Otto said in his best Russian-British accent, "but your lack of culinary spices makes everything I cook quite bland. I couldn't even find any saffron, a condiment that every kitchen should have."

"I'm sorry, but we got just the basics without any thought to spices," Margery said in her defense.

"Oh, don't let him fool you, Margery," Ruth said. "The only meal he's perfected is breakfast, and that's usually bagels, cream cheese, and lox."

"And you like it?" Otto shot back with a smile.

"Yes, I confess, it's excellent," replied Ruth.

"Otto, after breakfast I need you for the rehearsal back at the funeral home," Max said, taking some coffee.

"We take Levi, too?" Otto asked.

"Yes, he'll be in the getaway car."

"Almost curtain time," the Major said, from where he sat farther down the table.

"Yes, the first act is only days away," said Max.

"I'm concerned that with the press poking around they may uncover our plans. Do you think it's wise to go ahead or wait until we're sure they will not discover our plans?" Ruth said.

"At this point in time I can assure you that no one is aware of our plans. The longer we wait, the greater the possibility that they'll stumble upon something that we're not aware of," Max said.

"You're confident that you've covered all your tracks?" Ruth asked.

"I wouldn't attempt it if I wasn't sure," Max said. The tension was building. The longer they waited, the possibility of a mistake became more likely.

"Meeting time! We have to take a meeting, gentlemen," Max said as he entered the funeral home. He grabbed some chairs to place in a circle.

"You got my text, I see," Glen said sitting down beside Max.

"We're going to do a run-through this morning, but I first want to emphasize that it will be done carefully, looking for ways to improve," Max said, taking out a steno book.

"Let's begin with Madoff's arrival. Madoff will be brought into the crematorium where the rabbi will be waiting. The rabbi will close the door and proceed to the podium with Madoff to his left facing the video camera. The rabbi will place a white shawl over Madoff's shoulders and a black yarmulke on his head. The rabbi will reach over and tear the breast pocket of his suit. The moment the rabbi tears the pocket, the video recorder will start a five-minute countdown from the live, real-time image to the prerecorded video shot in New York. Are we all on the same page?" Max asked.

"What's the thing with tearing the pocket?" Glen asked.

"It's a sign that your loved one has been torn from your heart," Otto said. "How does the video recorder know when to start its countdown?" he asked in turn.

"It's fuckin' magic," says Glen.

"No," Max said. "I'll be wearing a watch that, when I push a button, will signal the recorder to start the countdown. It will vibrate when the five minutes is over, and the prerecorded program will begin its twelve minute run." Max showed them his watch.

"Looks like a real watch," Otto said.

"It is, it's a Timex with 007 features," Max said with a smile. "So, the rabbi feels the watch vibrate knowing that whatever Madoff and he do from then on will be invisible to anyone outside of the crematorium. This is when Otto, who has been waiting in the tunnel, will open the trap door in the floor, bolt the doors to the hallway, then assist Madoff and the rabbi into the tunnel. Otto will close the trapdoor and lead Madoff and the rabbi to the end of the tunnel, which will be lit by battery-powered LED lamps, to a ladder up into the shed. It is my estimate that from the time Otto opens the trapdoor to the crematorium to the time we're all in our getaway cars, it will take four minutes. Any questions or comments before we make a trial run? None? Then let's get into position. Levi to your car, Otto into the tunnel via the shed, and Glen with me into the crematorium," Max barked like a drill sergeant.

During the first run-through several mistakes occurred. Glen's yarmulke kept falling off, Max forgot to unwind the Torah, Otto had trouble closing the trapdoor in the shed. Max fell running in the tunnel and cut his knee, and time-wise it took five minutes and thirty-two seconds to accomplish. Once in his car Margery tied a handkerchief around Max's knee and helped him back up the hill to the funeral home for a recap of the results.

"Needless to say, we have some work to do," he said nursing his knee. "Questions and comments?"

"How do you keep the little hat on?" Glen asked.

"You can use a bobby pin," Otto suggested.

"I forgot that the Torah wasn't already open," Max confessed.

"I was all thumbs with those trapdoors, too," Otto said.

"I'm going to leave a collapsible chair in the tunnel to change clothes," Glen said.

"Are you ready for a video run-through?" Maurice asked.

"Not yet," Max said.

The second run went much better and even shaved thirty seconds off their first try. Glen used some gaffer's tape to keep the yarmulkes on their heads, and Max limped as fast as he could through the claustrophobic tunnel without falling.

"Okay, all systems are go for liftoff!" he proclaimed from the control room as Maurice adjusted the video camera. As the actors took their places, Maurice went live, signaling the five-minute real-time portion by sending a vibration to Max, who remembered to unroll the Torah as it was on the tape in New York. Max and Glen pretended to read from the Torah, motioning to each other for the five-minute period until Max felt his watch vibrate again telling him that the video recorder was now playing the prerecorded tape shot with the look-alike at the production company in New York. Otto popped out of the tunnel to bolt the doors and help Max and Glen into the tunnel. The chair placed in the tunnel was an aid in changing clothes.

Everything went smoothly until they had trouble replacing the door to the outside of the shed. Glen said he'd trim the opening to allow for the door to be closed properly. They had cut an additional thirty-six seconds off their original run-through. Gathering for a looksee at the five-minute recording of Glen and Max and the switch to the twelve-minute recording, the team saw a few areas to improve on in the next take. But before doing so, Max ordered lunch for everyone and sent Levi to pick it up. Max realized that the transition from the live feed to the prerecorded video had to be seamless or the jig was up. The time differential, the difference of twenty or thirty seconds, was inconsequential in the grand scheme of things. After lunch and eager to do it again, everyone took their places and ran through their parts without a glitch. They hadn't cut any time off their record, but they completed their mission and felt confident that he next time they did it, Madoff would be free!

On the way back to the house, Max stopped at an Italian restaurant and ordered a variety of meals to bring back for everyone. Sitting around a crowded table of food and people, Ruth asked how everything went.

"It started off like a Chinese fire drill and ended up as smooth as the Silk Road," Max said with his mouth full of pasta.

"Otto, what do you think?" Ruth asked her loyal bodyguard.

"He's right, there were some rough edges, but after a few tries we got our collective acts together. We can do it."

It seemed that, to Ruth, hearing it from her friend and trusted adviser eased her fears and gave her the support she needed to go through with the escape plan.

"Oh, for an espresso and a biscotti," Otto mused to everyone's delight.

Chapter 36: Joe

The next morning Joe received an unexpected call from Eisenstaedt advising him that Sergio's body had been found in a reputed mob safe house in the New Jersey Meadowlands. He also wanted to know why Joe had missed an important meeting at the office, a meeting at which he was to be introduced to his fellow members of Waters' white-collar crime division. Joe then explained the circumstances leading up to the last night's visitors and their intent to kill him and his family. Eisenstaedt was shocked to hear how close Joe had come to being killed, and the forethought he had used to protect his family by sending them into hiding.

"Why didn't you tell me of the danger you were in?" he asked.

"It's a long story, but for now, with Sergio out of the picture his hit men will scatter," Joe said.

"You know, I may not have ever said this, but I care deeply about my people. It may sound old-fashioned, but I consider you as family," Eisenstaedt said.

"Boss, I appreciate everything you've done for me, and I guess I thought that I had to do it my way. Granted, it was risky. I've learned it was also foolhardy putting the wife and kids in harm's way, but I promise you that I'll think twice before doing anything like that again."

"Are they still in hiding? Your wife and your two little girls?" Eisenstaedt asked.

"Yes, I spoke with them last night and plan on seeing them this afternoon," Joe said.

"Good, take care of them and make sure they're safe. That's your number one priority," Eisenstaedt said.

"I will, boss, and I'll be back as soon as I feel they're not in danger," Joe said, recognizing that Eisenstaedt was on his side and he shouldn't go it alone all the time.

He called Harry to ask if he'd heard anything from Bernstein.

"Nothing. I hope he's got time to follow up on what we discussed," Harry said.

"Is it too early to put his feet to the fire?" Joe asked.

"It's only been a day. In the meanwhile let's keep our powder dry and wait for his call, okay?"

"Call me if you hear anything," Joe said. He chose not to tell him about last night's close call with the two assassins.

What Harry and Joe didn't know was that Bernstein was busy reading their dossiers and interviewing Professors Holmes at Princeton and Kolinsky at Stanford by way of Skype. Bernstein then called Leon Kahn, the court-appointed trustee in charge of the Madoff bankruptcy case, to discuss a possible restitution, but found him disinterested due to the fact that it was in his best interest to prolong payments to the investors while he reaped obscene legal fees. He later learned that Kahn and a group of his friends had billed the government over $710 million in legal fees despite the fact that, after several years, not a penny had been returned to the defrauded investors. With a new sense of urgency, Bernstein hoped that his client could clear up the provenance of the formulas. He also knew that there was a right way and wrong way to contact an inmate in a federal penitentiary, and being Mr. Nice Guy would get him nowhere.

"This is Ken Bernstein, attorney of record to inmate #706052, Bernard Madoff, requesting a collect call back to 212-555-6611," he said sounding very officious. He received a decidedly different reception than Harry had the day before. He was advised that Madoff would be free to return his call at 3:00 p.m. EST, and at precisely three, Madoff was on a phone in the prison returning Bernstein's call.

"What's up, counselor?" Madoff asked.

"I'm working on a plan to bring restitution to the investors," Bernstein said.

"How are you going to do that?" Madoff asked.

"Let's talk about Zack's software," Bernstein said.

"What about it?" Madoff replied. Sensing that this was a sore subject, Bernstein eased into the topic of provenance, assuming that it was not the property of Madoff's company.

"Well, some of his formulas are worth a great deal of money. I think we should claim that they were created while he was employed by your firm," he said.

"How much money?" Madoff asked.

"To the right buyer, billions," said Bernstein.

"So, if it's mine, what good would that do me?" Madoff asked.

"Leverage in a plea for a pardon," Bernstein said.

"Do you think we have a chance?" Madoff asked, now interested.

"It would go a long way to help our chances. Right now the trustee is the only one making money. He's recovered over five billion dollars from offshore banks and hasn't given a penny to the investors. Meanwhile he's raking in 710 million dollars in fees for himself and a few chosen law firms who do his bidding."

"I've heard the son of a bitch was playing both ends against the middle. What do you want to know?" Madoff said.

"Everything!" Bernstein said. Madoff then told Bernstein the whole story of what Zack did from the first day he started to the day he died. It was a story of how he loved and nurtured a boy he took under his wing, and how he helped Bernie fly to the heights of the financial world, ultimately resulting in the creation of the NASDAQ Stock Exchange with him as its chairman. Bernstein was impressed by Madoff's sincerity and told him that, armed with his new understanding of the situation, he would be going forward to press his case for a pardon by selling the formulas contingent on Madoff's release.

The next day Bernstein called a meeting of his associates and staff to discuss the Bernard Madoff case. He explained to them the facts that he had at his disposal with an eye towards the restitution of the investors' legitimate losses and a plea for leniency and time served for Bernard Madoff—in other words, a presidential pardon. There were a lot of oohs and aahs when he mentioned the pardon, but the way Bernstein presented his argument, it sounded like a win-win for everyone. That being said, he cautioned everyone in the room to consider their discussion a hot potato politically speaking and to avoid any discussion of their plans.

Armed with a way to repay the investors who lost their savings, Bernstein called his friends at the Justice Department, one of whom was now the second ranking deputy in the Criminal Division, Roger Goodell. Goodell was genuinely happy to hear from Bernstein until the topic of Madoff's pardon came up. But Bernstein had a good argument for Madoff's pardon and after a half-hour Goodell said he'd run it by his people.

"No promises," he said, though he promised to give it "a good shot." Sensing that Goodell might have trouble convincing the Attorney General as to the idea of backing an unpopular political case, Bernstein thought that the formulas and their potential American buyers might be able to push the ball across the goal line.

He then called Professor Kolinsky at Stanford to ask: "During our recent conversation you mentioned that several companies would be very interested in purchasing the formulas and that if auctioned off, billions of dollars could be realized by the owners of the formulas. Could you tell me who some of these companies are?"

"These formulas on the second Cray computer would be a godsend to the manufacturers of autonomous self-driving cars," Kolinsky said, "some of which are pouring billions into software research for which these formulas bring real-life solutions. What the formulas do—no, let me backtrack a moment. The conventional wisdom is to develop a formula, express it as a algorithmic code to solve a problem. What the second Cray does is run thousands of overlapping algorithmic codes simultaneously, and this is the genius of it, they come at it from different directions, so to speak, all working on the same problem. I can't understand how it does it, but it's like they talk to each other until they solve the problem. If you have a powerful enough mainframe, it's done within the wink of an eye. Some of my kids believe that the inventor was an alien because no one on earth has the intellect to conceive of such a program. Crazy, huh?" Kolinsky said.

"And who could use these formulas?" Bernstein asked again.

"To name a few: Tesla, GM, Toyota, and Ford would give anything to acquire these groundbreaking Artificial Intelligence advances. Between you and me, I'd put my money on Ford. They have the resolve to produce an advanced self-driving car and not a 'me-too version' of someone else's design."

Antsy, Joe called Bernstein to see where they stood. He was told by Bernstein's secretary that he was out and would call him back. Joe left his cell number as he drove to the Poconos to see his wife and kids. Just to be on the safe side, he wanted Patty to stay put for a couple more days. It started to rain as he got off the interstate making driving on the hilly country roads challenging. In addition to the leaves covering the roads, rainwater and hairpin curves caused his car to slide here and there, testing his nerves. When he finally got to Patty's cottage the girls were just sitting down for dinner.

"Why didn't you call me?" she asked running over to give him a big hug.

"I thought it would be a nice surprise. Hey," he said giving the girls a squeeze.

"Sit down, I'll make you a plate," she said as Joe reached for his phone.

"It's Harry, let me see what he wants," Joe said as he went out onto the porch. "Any news?"

"Plenty, where are you?" Harry asked.

"I'm out in the Poconos with my family," Joe said.

"When can you get back to the city?" Harry asked.

"I just got here not ten minutes ago," Joe said.

"Well, I just spoke to Bernstein, and he wants us in his office tomorrow."

"Oh shit, what did he say?" Joe asked, thinking the change of plans wouldn't go over well with Patty.

"He said, and without going into too many details, that there's been an important development. He wants to know what we want out of bringing the formulas to his attention."

"What does he mean bring the formulas to HIS attention?" Joe said angrily.

"I don't know, but if we want to protect our interest, we'd better show up tomorrow at ten," Harry said.

"I don't like it. I think he's doing an end around on us," Joe said in disgust.

"You'll meet me at his office tomorrow at 10:00 a.m.?" Harry asked.

"I'll be there," Joe said preparing a story in his mind to tell Patty.

Chapter 37: Max

The news hit Max like a lightning bolt from the sky.

"STAND DOWN UNTIL FURTHER NOTICE - CONFIRM RECEIPT OF MESSAGE."

Why was Sy cancelling the operation at the eleventh hour? Max could not believe this. Was there a snitch that gave the plot away? Are they on to us? Should we scatter into the wind? But before composing a reply, he had to speak to Margery.

"Do you need anything at Walgreen's?" she asked as she picked up the phone.

"We have to speak," Max said with great urgency.

"Can you tell me on the phone?" she inquired.

"Sy's put a stop to the operation," he said in a whisper.

"I didn't hear you, did you say—"

"Yes, his words were: 'Stand down until further notice,'" he said. When Margery didn't respond, Max repeated the Email.

"I got it the first time. I was thinking what could have brought him to cancel the plan," Margery replied.

"I haven't got a clue!" Max said in frustration.

"Have you told anyone?" Margery asked.

"No," Max murmured.

"Don't do anything until we meet with the Prince," she said.

"Okay, I'll call him and tell him we're coming over for a cabinet meeting," Max said.

The Prince, being the Prince, welcomed Max and a few minutes later Margery, with a pitcher of Ramos Gin Fizz and a platter of crab cake hush puppies. After a sip of the welcomed libation Max got right to the point.

"Sy, he's my boss, he pulled the plug on our operation," Max said, looking to the Prince for his reaction.

The Prince seemed unfazed. "Try the crab cakes. They're served at the Commander's Palace in New Orleans."

"What did we do wrong?" Margery asked, not one to lose her train of thought.

"Probably nothing. It might be something completely unrelated to what we're doing here in Butner," he said.

"Like what?" Max shot back.

"Well, there's something I didn't tell you because it seemed beyond the bounds of our plans. I heard through the grapevine that a large agency based in New York sent an investigator to Florida recently, looking for a Madoff associate. Since his assignment was to track down Madoff's alleged money laundering, I didn't see any connection," the Prince said.

"You think he got wind of our plans?" Max asked.

"I don't see how."

"Then what?" Margery interjected.

"Only your boss, what's his name, Sy knows," the Prince said tasting a Crab Cake.

"What should we tell the others?" Margery asked.

"Look, if he's cancelled the gig, we're all the richer and wiser," Prince said. When no one picked one up on their own, he insisted on passing the tray of crab cakes around.

Max and Margery decided that they were going to tell Glen next and met him at the funeral home.

"What's so important that you can't tell me over the phone?" he said exasperatedly.

"It's over—that's what!" Max exclaimed.

"What's over?" Glen asked.

"That's it, that's all we know. 'Stand down' were our instructions," Margery said.

"Then what do we do now?"

"I'll respond to my boss' email for clarification and instructions," Max said, "but if it's just the end, I'll have everyone pack up and get out of Dodge."

"But this place is a time bomb. We can't leave it as is," Glen said.

"When I give you the word, get the boys to pull the pyro, reconnect the sprinklers, and dump the props in the tunnel," Max said.

"What about the tunnel?" Glen asked.

Max sighed. "Fuck it, it's just a trench."

"What about transportation home?"

"Go first class," Margery suggested. "You deserve it."

"Oh, one last thing, get the DVD from the video recorder," Max said. Glen retrieved the disc for him. Before they left, Max and Margery crafted a carefully worded response to Sy's email asking for clarification and instructions, pointing out that they had been planning on executing the escape plan the coming weekend, a mere three days out. If they missed this opportunity, they would have to cancel the operation.

"At least we put him on notice! " Margery said as she pressed send.

When they returned to their house they found a note from the Major saying that they went to a nearby park for a picnic and to feed some ducks. In addition, Ruth, Otto, and Levi were also out. A quick look around told them that something was wrong. Seriously wrong.

"It looks like Ruth and company have done a runner, cleared out, lock, stock, and barrel," Margery said.

"What the fuck's going on?" Max said pulling his hair.

"Did she orchestrate the whole thing, the STAND DOWN ORDER?" Margery asked no one in particular.

"To cut and run at the eleventh hour without a word? Smacks of collusion," Max said taking Margery by the hand.

"Where are we going?" she asked as Max opened the car door for her.

"The airport," he said as they fastened their seatbelts.

Max and Margery raced to the Raleigh Airport. Entering the hangar area for private planes, he saw to their mutual dismay Sy's Lear taxiing out to the runway.

"They were in such a hurry they left the Mercedes at the hangar," Margery said pointing to the black Mercedes 600 parked in the temporary waiting lot.

"Fuck it. We're breaking camp, and everyone is free to go," Max said banging the steering wheel with his hand.

While driving off from the airport Margery called Glen and confirmed that the operation was cancelled. He could go ahead with the deconstruction. Glen told them that he'd follow through with what they spoke about and said, "If you're ever in Reno, call me. I know a great spot for fly fishing."

When told about the Ruth's impromptu exit by Learjet, the Major was relieved and philosophic. "Sometimes the best performances go unseen." He also mused that, "This was not a time for despair but for celebration."

"Good idea," Max said. "Let's meet at the Prince's place and celebrate the show's closing."

"Black tie?" the Major jested.

"Nah, come as you are."

Max called the Prince and advised him of the cancellation of the operation and asked him to put together a party to celebrate the successful if unexpected conclusion of their operation.

"Most assuredly, El Capitan. I'll pull out all the stops," the Prince said joyously.

Later that day, with the gang all there, the Prince raised his glass of Dom Pérignon to toast the successful outcome of a perilous but fruitful enterprise. To that, all stood and downed the bubbly grape as the Prince declared, "Bottoms up!"

The dinner that he had arranged was literally fit for a king. Chilled oysters on the half shell with a dollop of beluga caviar, a Caesar salad with white anchovies, a Chateaubriand with root vegetables, and to finish it off, Flaming Cherries Jubilee. After dinner Max unbuttoned his belt as he relaxed on a comfortable high-backed lounge chair and opened the conversation by asking what his collection of nefarious associates planned to do with their newfound riches.

The Prince started off by saying that he'd like to relocate to a warmer clime.

"Where would that be?" Max asked.

"Palm Beach, of course," said the Prince.

"Why there?" Margery asked.

"For a very good reason. Do you know the story of Willie Sutton?" the Prince asked with a sinister grin.

"Willie was a bank robber—not a very good one, by the way—since he was usually caught spending the loot at places like the Copacabana on gin and wicked women. Invariably he'd be caught and paraded by the press in handcuffs with flashbulbs bursting, on his way to be booked for another heist. But being a clever sort, Willie would find a way to escape and do it all over again. However, during one of his famous perp walks a reporter stopped him and asked, 'Why do you keep robbing banks, Willy?'

"To which Willie turned, thought about the question, and responded, 'Cause that's where the money is.' Does that answer your question?"

"What about you, Betty?" Max asked.

"I want to immerse myself in fashion and the arts: the Boston Symphony during the summer in Tangelwood, the Pilobolus Dance Troupe at Jacobs Pillow, the Picasso exhibit at the Prado in Madrid, the Metropolitan Opera, and I've been studying costume design at the New School... Oh, I could go on and on." Betty said, running out of breath.

"A tour de force!" said Max.

"Wonderful! It sounds like you've given it a great deal of thought," Margery said.

"Atta girl, save me a seat on the runway," the Prince said.

"Major, where do you plan to go?" Max asked.

"Not very far from home. We adore our life in Manhattan, and now that this money isn't connected to a crime, we can stay there! This newfound fortune will give My Lady and me the luxury of not worrying where the next buck comes from. The theater is and has always been my life's greatest pleasure, and I don't wish to give it up regardless of how much money we'll now have at our disposal. But now I'll have the luxury of being able to pick and choose my roles without thinking of how much money I'll be paid. If I want, I'll work for free because I can. I also know that I'm a bit too long in the tooth to play Barefoot in the Park, but I'm ripe enough to play many, many roles that call for a mature gentleman. So there, does that answer your question?" the Major said, sipping his brandy.

"For you, my friend, the curtain will never fall," Max said. "Lady Sally, it's your turn on stage. Hit your mark!"

"Like my love," she said, looking at the Major, "my life also revolves around the theater. As soon as we return to Manhattan I'll be looking for a venue to establish our own repertory group. I see a small theater with maybe fifty to seventy-five seats. I want the audience to breathe in the actors' energy and passion. I want to pull them into the plot by being close and intimate with the action. Those theaters uptown have to have audiences in the thousands to afford the rent. Did you ever attend a performance where the seats were so far from the stage and the actors were so small you needed binoculars just to see them? That's not what the theater's all about! Go to the Globe in London. The actors are right in front of you, close enough to touch. You feel their energy. The magic of the theater is that it's personal. You're swept up into the plot and you care about the actors. Sometimes it's life or death," she said.

"Bravo, my love," the Major said giving her a standing ovation.

"Well that's a hard act to follow. Would you like to go, my dear?" Max said to Margery.

"No, I prefer to close the show," Margery said.

"Okay, then let's hear from Glen," he said.

"Honestly, I haven't given it too much thought. Maybe out of fear, you know, like something will go wrong. So I don't try to get my hopes up too high. But now, all bets are off. I plan to find a place to open a hunting and fishing lodge. That's what I'd like to do," Glen said raising his glass to toast his colleagues in crime.

"Excellent! I might one day take you up on fly fishing lessons." Max said. "Well, I guess it's my turn in the barrel." He turned to look at Margery. "I'd like to spend some time seeing the world with Margery. Not to say that living in New York has not been interesting, but there are faraway places I've dreamed of visiting and having my love, my life's partner, as my traveling companion would be my desire." Max toasted Margery who came over and gave him a hug.

It was her turn to wish upon a star. She acknowledged her desire to see the world with her lover and also said, "What I'm looking forward to is a place by the sea. High enough to not be swept away by a storm but low enough to allow a friendly path to the beach where I can walk my Cavalier King Charles Spaniels in and out of the surf. A home where Max can lay in his hammock at night and gaze at the heavens while I watch gushy love stories on the Hallmark Channel."

"It will soon come to be, my love, very soon," Max said.

Chapter 38: Joe

The first thing Joe saw when he entered Bernstein's sleek reception room was Harry standing by one of the room's four-by-eight-foot, plate-glass, floor-to-ceiling windows with its towering view of the Port of New York.

"Thinking of taking a cruise?" Joe said as he approached Harry.

"There's a ship down there waiting to take me to my estate on Crete? I wish," said Harry.

"If we play our cards right..." Joe tapered off as the receptionist entered the room.

"Can you please tell Bernstein that Mr. Mancuso and Mr. Sarandopolis are here?" Harry said to the serious-looking receptionist.

After cooling their heels for over a half an hour, Joe approached the receptionist again who was transcribing a document from her earphones and said to her, "Tell Bernstein that he's got five minutes to see us or we walk. Do you hear me?" He leaned in and pressed both palms on her desk for emphasis. At this, she ripped her earbuds out and marched out of the room in a huff.

"Do you think that was appropriate?" Harry asked.

"Fuck him. That's an old ploy they use to get the upper hand. Keep 'em waiting and they'll eventually eat out of your hand," Joe said with some authority.

"How should we handle this?" Harry asked.

"Well, we can play Good Cop, Bad Cop," Joe suggested.

"On the phone he intimated that he's looking for a number from us," Harry said.

"What? A million, a billion? Who the hell knows?" Joe shot back, looking at his watch.

"Do you really want to walk if he—?"

Joe put up his hand and reiterated. "Fuckin' A, right out the door. We can play the game, too. If you're willing to walk, he'll think twice about screwing with us," he said as the receptionist reappeared in the doorway, inviting them to follow her to the conference room.

"Good morning, gentlemen," Bernstein said rising from his chair on the opposite side of a long, plate-glass conference table supported by a no-nonsense stainless-steel frame. Joe noticed that Bernstein had positioned himself with his back to the rising sun, putting his guests in its unavoidable glare. He was planning to come at them like a fighter pilot using the sun to blind them from his attack.

"Please have your receptionist draw the blinds," he said. "The glare is unacceptable." He refused to sit until this happened.

Bernstein, realizing that his ploy hadn't created the effect he'd intended, walked over to a control panel mounted on the wall, and after he pushed a button, a string of vertical blinds appeared to block the morning sun.

"Is that better?" Bernstein asked as he motioned for them to sit.

"I've asked you here to discuss the disposition of Madoff's materials." Bernstein said, making himself comfortable. Instantly Harry and Joe realized that Bernstein's pronouncement of 'Madoff's materials' was said to put them outside the realm of any ownership of the materials, vis-à-vis the priceless formulas.

"Where are you coming from? We have the stuff, and you don't," Joe said.

"That may be true at this point in time, but as an employee of Madoff's firm—"

"Bullshit," Joe interrupted. "Zack created the formulas outside of his employment. Why are you even going down this road?"

"Because I've spoken with my client, and he contends that Zack was employed by him to create the formulas," Bernstein stated.

"Really, do you want to hand these formulas to that rat bastard trustee to do what he wants with them?" Harry said, getting hot under the collar himself.

Bernstein, an avid sailor, then took another tack. Figuratively steering into the wind he let his sails billow for a while. At the last moment, before losing control, he turned to ask, "What do you want for the formulas?"

Taken by surprise, Harry looked to Joe who looked to Harry. They didn't know how to respond. They had never figured out between themselves what they actually wanted for the Zack's stuff.

"Fifty million for each one of us," Joe blurted out looking Bernstein in the eye.

"You want one hundred million dollars?" Bernstein asked pushing back from the table.

"Exactamente, counselor," Joe said.

"That's out of the question," Bernstein said rising.

Joe, an old hand at gaming, sensed that this was just another ploy, another one of Bernstein's maneuvers to keep them off balance.

"Come on, Harry, we'll find another customer for the formulas," he said getting to his feet and heading for the door. Harry realized what Joe was doing: playing the bad cop. He almost smiled. It was his turn as good cop to bring everyone back to the table.

"Wait ,my compatriot, what are you offering?" Harry said to Bernstein.

"I say we take a brief recess. I'll send in for some coffee and be back in a few moments," Bernstein said as both men tacitly agreed and returned to their seats.

"What did they say?" Ruth Madoff asked as Bernstein entered his office.

"They want a hundred million," Bernstein replied.

"What are they, delusional?" Ruth said.

"On the contrary, they know what the formulas are worth."

"No, no, no. No way. We're so close to getting Bernie out. I've already dropped ten million on a band of clowns, and now this?" Ruth said aggravated.

"I told you from the very beginning not to rely on Sy. He brought in a bunch of amateurs," Bernstein said.

"Well, what was I to do? Wait 150 years?" Ruth said dismissively.

"Relax, Mrs. Madoff, we have to respond to their demands and—"

"They don't care!" Ruth cried.

"Wait, calm down, Ruth," Bernstein said realizing that he was losing control of the situation on both ends.

"I want to meet them," she demanded.

"I would not advise that."

"What are you afraid of?" Ruth said, getting out of her chair.

"Ruth, I'm telling you, you don't go face to face, not until we broker a deal, farshtaist?"

You give them an inch and the next thing you know, they'll be back for the keys to your car and the keys to your house. It never ends!" she cried looking for the door even as Bernstein blocked her path.

"Tell you what. I'm going to tell them that we'd like time to consider their proposal, and then meet in the conference room after lunch. At say two p.m."

Ruth shrugged off Bernstein's hands and walked towards the windows shaking her head. "You can't win in this life. We made a mistake, a terrible mistake, and God knows we've paid for it. I need my husband back," she said pressing her forehead against the window.

"Please sit. I'll be right back. I'm going to tell them we'll adjourn until after lunch," he said heading back to the conference room.

He popped his head into the doorway. "Gentlemen, we want time to consider your proposal and believe that we should continue the discussion after lunch. Say two o'clock?"

"Who's 'we'?" Joe asked.

"My client," Bernstein responded.

"Ya mean Bernie?" Joe said.

"In a way, yes," Bernstein said trying to extricate himself from continuing down this line of questions.

"Counselor, it's either yes or no," Harry shot back.

"That's all I can say at this point in time," Bernstein said.

"What's this cloak and dagger shit?" Joe asked looking at Harry.

"Frankly, you don't need to know," Bernstein said showing them the door.

"We'll be back at two, and this time we want some answers," Joe said before leaving the room.

Back in his office, Ruth was perusing her iPhone for messages.

"I've scheduled our meeting for this afternoon. Let's grab a bite on the rooftop," he suggested.

When Ruth didn't respond, he picked up the phone and asked his secretary to make a reservation for lunch. He thought that some food and fresh air might stir her from her anger and lead to some productive and rational attempts to solve their problem. He knew from experience that putting the parties together would only lead to chaos. In other words, it was a time for a time-out.

The restaurant was busy, and they had to wait several minutes for a table, but the sky was clear, the sun was peeking through the giant high-rises, and the rumble of the traffic below was muffled by the melodies of Joni Mitchell. Who could ask for a better venue to take a deep breath and clear the mind of negative thoughts?

Bernstein ordered a glass of pinot noir and Ruth an unsweetened ice tea. As Bernstein sipped his wine he couldn't remember how many times he'd brought warring clients to this rooftop restaurant to let off steam. It was something about an office setting that got the gall flowing, so whenever the opportunity arose, it was up to the rooftop he'd go with his clients in tow.

"How was the fish?" Bernstein asked.

"I couldn't even taste it." Ruth said.

"Want some coffee?" Bernstein asked.

"No, I'd rather know what you're going to do to bring closure to this nightmare," Ruth uttered.

"I have to convince them that it's easier to deal with us rather than the court-appointed trustee," he said.

"How are you going to do that?" Ruth asked.

"It all boils down to provenance. Who owns the rights to these formulas? If we can get them to see how mishugas, how crazy it is to sell stolen property, especially to a very few select clients who have the resources to use and apply these sophisticated formulas... Remember, Professors Holmes and Kolinsky—from Princeton and Stanford, no less—are speaking with the Ford Motor Company in Dearborn, Michigan, to sell these formulas from Bernie. The number one question on their minds, on Ford's mind, is who owns the formulas," Bernstein said in a very measured and clinical manner.

"How much will it cost me, and how can I be assured that they'll go away and never come back?" Ruth asked.

"All I can do is draw up a document that if they break the agreement we can take them to the cleaners," Bernstein said as a matter of fact.

"What will it take to make them go away?" Ruth said, watching a large black bird effortlessly floating on the thermals cut a path between the office buildings.

"Five each," Bernstein lied, picking a number out of thin air.

"Five million each?" Ruth said with a twisted smile. "And if they refuse?"

"We walk!" Bernstein said asking for the check.

"Fuck them. I hope they refuse and we can bring criminal charges against them for theft," Ruth said easing herself out of her chair and preparing to go to war.

Chapter 39: Max

When Max and Margery took their seats on Delta Flight #324 to LaGuardia their minds were filled with where to spend their $3.2 million. They had already confessed their plans to their coconspirators the previous day, and with great anticipation they looked forward to carrying them out. However, as the prophet often warned, 'Sometimes the best horse never gets out of the gate,' and this was the case of Margery's seaside dream. In retrospect, New York had too much going for it: the arts, the people, the food, the styles, and the ability to come and go at will twenty-four hours a day. The house by the sea was a dream, but honestly, after a while one has to wake up to reality and smell what the tide brings in—it would also bore her to death! But she didn't have to throw the baby out with the bathwater. She could still have her dog, a Cavalier King Charles Spaniel. A lovely little Blenheim girl to hold and love, just like Madeline, the dog she had as a child growing up in Sussex, England.

Max, on the other hand, who was never keen on the idea of a desolate life by the sea, relished the thought of traveling with Margery and seeing and exploring the marvelous sights, sounds, and smells of faraway places. Since money was no longer an obstacle, they could do it in style.

When Max arrived home later that day, he found Margery comparing photos of Cavalier King Charles Spaniels on her laptop.

"They all look the same," he said looking over Margery's shoulder.

"They're bred to follow the lines of previous champions going back hundreds of years in England, hence the reference to King Charles II," she said.

"Are they apartment dogs?" asked Max.

"They'll survive in any environment as long as they get lots of love," she said.

"That's not a problem in this household," Max said with a smile.

"Good. Then we'll visit some breeders. And, by the way, my dear, I think you have a message from you-know-who." Margery pointed to his computer.

"He's maybe responding to my questions as to his stand-down message," Max said.

"I think it was fortuitous to cancel the operation when he did. I had my doubts that Ruth was up to the challenges of going on the lam," Margery said.

However, when Max retrieved the encoded message from Sy

it merely said, "We must meet."

"What do you think he wants?" Margery asked, getting up to look at the message.

"It's hard to predict what's on Sy's mind. I'll respond asking for clarification, you know, where and when to meet," Max said beginning to send Sy his message.

"Wait—let's discuss what you should say," Margery suggested getting a bottle of water out of the fridge. "This is the perfect opportunity to grill him on his reason for cancelling the operation," she said.

"Why should we go there? As the Prince said, we're richer and wiser."

"But don't you want to know the why of it all?" asked Margery.

"Not really. I'm sure he had his reasons, and if he wants to tell me, fine. Otherwise I'm not going down that road, especially if I don't know where it leads," Max said.

"What if he wants to suck you into another 'Mission Impossible'?" she asked.

"I'll pull a Nancy Reagan and just say no!" said Max.

Twenty minutes later Sy's email directed Max to meet him at the historic Cypress Hills National Cemetery at nine that evening. Sy had brought Max to the cemetery once before, but only after he was stoned, to visit Max's cousin Howie's grave. When Max read the message to Margery, she said, He's off his bloody rocker! First the 'Stand Down' from out of the blue, now a graveyard rendezvous."

"I'd better get ready," Max said looking for his wallet and keys.

"Uber it," Margery suggested.

"Good idea. To bring an uninvited witness."

It was a first for the Uber driver, Hassan.

"A cemetery?" he asked.

"Yes, it's an old military cemetery," Max said.

"Isn't it a bit late for a funeral?" Hassan remarked, sounding concerned.

"Death has no office hours," Max replied.

"What if the gates are locked?" Hassan asked.

"I know someone who has a key," Max said, and sure enough, the gates were wide open.

"Drive around to the back," Max instructed Hassan. "That's them over there," he said as Sy's black limo came into sight.

"Park behind the limo and do exactly as they say," Max cautioned Hassan. "Don't worry. It's a matter of security. You'll be okay as long as you do what they say."

"I think I should leave," Hassan said getting worried.

"No, just wait," Max said passing a hundred-dollar bill to Hassan. Hassan looked at the cash, wondering if that's all his life was worth to his passenger.

"No, no, it's too late, Hassan. Trust me and you'll be okay," Max said as two large men dressed all in black approached from either side, aiming tactical flashlights at their car.

"I must go now," Hassan said as he tried to maneuver his car around one of Sy's security men.

"Stop," cried the security man producing a 9mm Berretta from out of nowhere. He took a shooting stance directly in front of the car while training the Berretta's red laser beam directly at Hassan's chest. Hassan jammed on his brakes and collapsed, placing his head on his steering wheel, awaiting his immanent demise.

"He's my Uber driver," Max said to Sy's men as he slowly exited the car with his hands raised.

"Not too smart. If he kept coming I would have shot," said one of the men in black.

"Tell him to get out of the car slowly," the man nearest to Hassan said. Max poked his head in the car to tell Hassan to get out slowly with his hands above his head.

"Hassan, they want to frisk you for weapons. Please do as they say and all will be okay," Max said softly, seeing that Hassan was crying. The security men performed the usual pat-down and used a wand to detect the presence of any recording device on both men. In Hassan's case they also swabbed his hands and checked the swab for gunshot residue with some space-age gadget they had in the trunk of the limo. Once cleared, Max was told to join Sy at Howie's gravesite while Hassan was told to sit on the ground in front of his car's headlights.

Max walked down a long line of crosses to find Sy sitting on an aluminum beach chair facing a gravestone shaped in the Star of David.

"What's all the hullabaloo?" Sy said, slurring his words. Max knew that Sy was off in La-La Land and that he had to tread carefully while the narcotic had a hold of Sy's mind.

"Sy... Sy, what do you need me for?" Max asked trying to get his attention.

"You know what day this is?" Sy asked, pointing towards the grave.

"No, why is today special?" Max asked trying to keep it simple.

"You forget—forgot?" Sy said angrily mixing up his words. When Max didn't immediately answer, he said, "It's Howie's birthday. That's what day it is, stupid." He shook his head.

"I'm sorry, no disrespect, I forgot," Max said ashamed of his ignorance.

"You probably didn't even bring him a present, did you?" Sy said getting a pink rubber ball from a brown paper bag sitting next to his chair. "This was all we needed back then, to play stickball or stoop ball or whatever it was. A little ball, a Spalding," Sy said, emphasizing 'ding.'

"I remember playing stoop ball in Brooklyn when I was a kid," Max said in all sincerity. Both men then went silent as the dreams of their childhood flashed before their eyes.

"She wants the money, she always wants money, the money we put away for a rainy day," Sy said trying to bounce the ball on the grass. Max, mindful that this might be his last and only chance to discover who the elusive sponsor was, chose his words carefully so as not to needlessly upset Sy's train of thought.

"Isn't that just like a woman?" he said.

"But I told her I had to justify it to my people. I have to show them something... something that affects their bottom line."

"Exactly," Max exclaimed. "There's no free lunch!"

"Bernie said that I should give her the money but..." Sy said, fading off into dreamland.

It was Ruth, Max said to himself. It was always Ruth. Now what money is he talking about? Max glanced at his iPhone and decided to give it a few minutes before waking Sy from his stupor.

As it turned out, this wasn't necessary. All of a sudden, Sy awoke with all his faculties and barked, "Tell Bernstein that we'll wire the money to him and he should deliver the 'Wall Street' computer to my office. It'll get me off the hook." He fumbled in his pocket before handing Bernstein's business card to Max.

"Certainly, Sy," Max responded, thinking, What the hell does a computer have to do with the price of tea?

"And tell him, the feeders have to be fed," Sy said.

"What?" Max asked.

"Tell Bernstein, he'll know."

"Who's the feeders?" Max asked.

"Our bank, you idiot," Sy said getting irritated by the questions.

"Sorry, I just wanted it to be clear," Max said in his defense.

"If he's free, they get their cut. Understand?" Sy said.

"Is Madoff free?" asked Max.

"Never mind. Do your job, and keep your mouth shut."

Unable to bounce the Spalding on the grass, Sy placed the ball back in its paper bag. Getting down on his knees, he carefully tucked the bag between the fresh flowers he brought and Howie's grave marker. Seeing how lovingly Sy cared about his childhood friend had a deep effect on what Max thought about this supposedly ruthless Wall Street titan.

Sy then rose to his feet, using the grave marker as a crutch. Stopping for an instant; he bent down to touch the Star and said, "I love you, Howie, and I'll never forget you," with tears in his eyes. He straightened to attention, took a deep breath, and saluted Private First-Class Howard Shapiro's grave.

Both men slowly made their way to their cars without saying another word. Sy's bodyguards took their seats up front and swiftly drove off. Max glanced over at Hassan who had gotten to his feet and was brushing the wet grass from his pants. He noticed that Hassan had wet his pants in the encounter.

"You okay?" Max asked.

"Can we get out of here?" Hassan asked.

"The Devil's gone back in his hole," Max said as they drove off,

trying to find their way out of the cemetery before the Devil came to get them.

Chapter 40: Joe

At two, Harry and Joe were already in the conference room, nervously pacing in front of the windows, making sure that when Bernstein entered the room, they could take the seats at the table with their backs to the midday sun.

"Good afternoon," Bernstein said as he entered the conference room, holding a stack of papers in his hand for effect. Harry and Joe took their seats to the amusement of Bernstein who recognized their immature tit for tat. Bernstein began his opening remarks by making some small talk to give the impression that he'd spent his time during the recess trying to convince his client as to the necessity of recognizing their position.

This struck Harry as disingenuous. Why bother with the charade? However, Bernstein did get in some salient points in a roundabout way as to the limited number of prospects for the formulas and their potential reluctance to acquire 'stolen property,' which Bernstein hyped whenever mentioning the formulas. Ultimately, faced with the reality of their position, a quick small fortune, compared to a large, distant, possible fortune was a no-brainer. Take the money and run made more sense, so they took the ten-million-dollar offer: five million for Harry and five million for Joe.

That being done, the two sides laid out their conditions. Bernstein's conditions called for the delivery of Cray Computer #1, which contained the 'Wall Street Formulas,' and all associated external backup devices and collateral documents to his office by 2:00 p.m. the following day. In addition, both Harry and Joe were to sign an agreement that stipulated severe penalties if they reneged on the agreement. It also carried with it a nondisclosure agreement on the terms and conditions of the agreements. They also agreed that they had no rights, ownership, or title to Cray Computer #2, its formulas, backup devices, or documentation.

For their part, Harry and Joe stipulated that the payments be made separately: five million to Harry Sarandopolis and five million to Joe Mancuso. The payments were to be made simultaneously by wire transfer to designated bank accounts upon the delivery of the Cray Computer #1. In addition, they sought relief from taxation by requiring that the transaction be private and off the books, and finally, they asked that Bernstein sign a nondisclosure agreement as to the details regarding the terms and conditions of the transaction. With that being done, they agreed to meet back at the conference room the next day to transfer the property and receive confirmation that the funds were transferred to Harry and Joe's designated accounts.

As they left Bernstein's office, clearly walking on air, they stopped to call Dr. Holmes at Princeton. They would be collecting Cray #1 the next morning at ten. However, when Harry asked about the disposition of Cray #2, Holmes told him that he'd discuss the matter when they met.

"Is there a problem?" Harry asked.

"No, it's just a bit hush-hush. I'll tell you all about it tomorrow," Holmes said.

At the meeting the next day at Princeton, Holmes told them that the Cray #2, the quantum Artificial Intelligence computer, was being used as a bargaining chip for the release of Bernie Madoff. It seems that the court-appointed trustee has been engorging himself and his cronies to the tune of almost one billion dollars in fees to the detriment of the investors who had legitimate claims to the Ponzi scheme.

"It's very close and not for dissemination until the fat lady sings, okay?" Holmes said, directing a couple of his students to pack up the Cray #1, its backups and docs.

"When will you know?" Joe asked.

"They're all at Ford now running simulations on the software. If all goes well, Ford will purchase the software for $7.4 billion, the exact amount necessary for the full restitution of Bernie's indebtedness. If and when that happens, the President will pardon Bernie," Holmes said.

"So, what will you get out of the deal?" Joe asked.

"Me? Nothing, so to speak, except maybe a flight to Dearborn and back on their corporate jet, a free stay at the Hyatt Hotel, and a few meals. Now Kolinsky's a different matter. If he plays his cards right, he's in for a big payday. I think they'll offer him a position to head up research for Ford's Autonomous Self-Driving Car," Holmes said licking his lips.

On their way back to New York, Harry called his attorney in Miami on the car's speakerphone and outlined the agreements that they'd need drawn up for presentation at the forthcoming meeting. The attorney told them he'd draw up several agreements for their perusal and email them to Harry. "Pick whatever suits your fancy," said his attorney.

Their next stop was the branch office of the very bank Harry eluded to on his boat, UIC, the United Interbank Consortium, where they opened provisional wealth management accounts.

"You know that the minimum deposit to open a wealth management account is one million dollars?" the young, attractively tailored woman emphasized.

"Yep," said Joe, and he asked for the bank's routing number.

"You realize that once the funds are transferred to us, we will have to meet with you to discuss your requirements before we do anything," she said.

"I understand, and I'll be back," Joe said.

Once they both had routing and account numbers, it was off to Bernstein's office to deliver the Cray #1 'Wall Street Computer,' backup drives, and documentation. Borrowing a cart from building security, they wheeled their treasure into the elevator and up to Bernstein's office just as the clock struck two. This time the receptionist hurried them into the conference room where Bernstein and another man were waiting for them.

"This is Matt Dyson, who will verify the software for us," Bernstein said. Harry and Joe nodded agreement and decided to spend their time reviewing the various agreements Harry's attorney had sent them. Bernstein asked if they wanted anything to drink, and both men asked for bottled water. Bernstein then left the room to see his client, Ruth Madoff, who was cooling her heels in his office, desperately longing for a cigarette.

"This is a non-smoking office, Ruth," Bernstein softly explained.

"How long will it take?" she asked.

"I don't know. It depends on what he finds. Look, he's a computer expert and mathematician, but quantum finance is exceedingly complicated, and he's said it's beyond his pay grade."

When Bernstein returned to the conference room, Harry and Joe had agreed upon one of the versions the attorney sent, but Joe sensed something in the air. He couldn't explain it. It was the way the expert kept looking at his monitor. Joe knew there was a problem before the expert started to speak.

"May we speak in private?" the expert requested of Bernstein.

"What the hell's going on?" Joe asked.

"Let me speak with—" Bernstein started to say when he was interrupted by Joe.

"If you've got something to say, I want to hear it," Joe demanded.

"Mr. Mancuso, this man works for me, not you," Bernstein replied.

"Okay, let's keep our eye on the prize, gentlemen. Bernie's fate might depend on our resolution of this matter," said Harry.

"What is it?" Bernstein asked the expert.

"The, ah, contents, the formulas on the hard drive are consistent with the Bose-Einstein quantum model. However," he paused to find the right words, "the formulas were locked, unlocked, and locked recently. It looks like, based on the timeline, they were downloaded recently. They've probably been copied." Everyone looked at each other when Joe owned up to the fact that he had the files copied.

"Well, in that case, you'll have to produce the copies," Bernstein said putting the transaction on hold until the copies could be delivered to the meeting. However due to the time it would be impossible to retrieve the copies from Joe's safety deposit box at the bank until nine the next morning, which they decided to do. In the interim, Bernstein had the unenviable task of telling Ruth Madoff the bad news.

"Why didn't you tell me you'd backed up the files?" Harry asked angrily in the elevator.

"Relax, I was playing it safe," Joe said.

"Still you should have told me. Instead I looked like an idiot." Harry looked away.

"I overreached on this one, so, I owe you a dinner, okay?" Joe said putting his arm around Harry's neck. Once they hit the street, Harry took a rain check on dinner afraid by celebrating he'd spook the deal.

"Go get the backup stuff and we'll meet here tomorrow... at what time?" Harry asked.

"I'll pick up the stuff at nine and should be in the city by ten at the latest. Ten-thirty in the conference room?"

"Good for me, and don't make more copies," Harry said getting into a taxi.

When Joe got home somewhat early that day Patty wasn't there to quiz him on where he went and what he did. It was refreshing to get home and not be interrogated for once, but that was Patty. He'd given her a lot of shit along the way to deal with, and she'd stuck with him. Now for once in his life he could repay her for all the years of aggravation and sorrow. He'd decided to turn over a new leaf and think of someone other than himself. Since she didn't know about their newfound wealth, he figured that he'd wait for the appropriate time and place to tell her. He'd already thought about getting a house in Montclair, a bit chichi for him, but it had the best public schools in the state. In addition, he liked working at Waters, even though he could technically retire. Eisenstaedt was a straight shooter and actually cared about his men and women in the field. The NYPD had been big and autocratic from top to bottom; it was like being in the Marines all over again. Then it hit him. He liked, no, loved being a family man with a wife who loved him and two adorable little girls who wanted nothing more than all the love he could give. It was so fuckin' corny he almost cried.

The next morning Joe was up at seven to retrieve the Cray backup drives and copies of Zack's documentation from his bank. When he took his box into a private cubicle, he opened it and peered down one last time at probably a billion dollars' worth of formulas. For a millisecond, he thought what a waste it was to give it up, but then he shook the thought from his mind. He put the stuff in a brown paper bag and headed for a new day in the life of Joe Mancuso, private eye.

"You've got everything?" Harry asked when he joined him in the law office.

"It's here in this bag with my lunch," Joe said opening the bag for Harry to see. From there on everything went relatively smoothly. They all agreed on the terms and conditions of the transfer. Joining the Cray #1 computer with the 'Wall Street' formulas were two sets of backup drives and two sets of documentation. In addition, Bernstein received one set of backup drives and documentation for the Cray #2 now at the Ford Motor Company. Bernstein then handed over confirmation that five million dollars was transferred electronically to Harry Sarandopolis and Joe Mancuso, respectively. With the business amicably concluded, Bernstein called Ruth Madoff to tell her that the eagle had landed and that she should contact Sy for the delivery instructions of the Cray #1 and its accessories. Bernstein also contacted Dr. Holmes at Princeton to advise him that he was sending additional items associated with the Cray #2 by courier.

The boys, now part of the nouveau riche, shared a cab to their new bank to confer with their wealth management advisors.

With their super-secret account numbers and passwords, the boys were treated like royalty. Upon verification that they were who they said they were, the Pearly Gates opened to a new plush world, where a mere five million dollars is considered a piss-hole in the snow. Is this how the rich and very rich are catered to? Joe thought. He was amazed at how open and frank his wealth manager was in detailing how the bank went about laundering money.

"Oh yes, we have many small depositors like you," he confessed. After Joe signed some papers explaining the fees for their services, they got down to business. His manager recommended the 'Silver Service Plan,' which allowed for a lower fee for domestic transactions through an offshore bank credit card. When asked the name of the corresponding bank, he was told that it was part of a chain of banks throughout the world.

"Not to worry your head about, the chain controls over a trillion dollars in assets for people just like you."

After leaving the bank the boys strolled over to a coffee shop down the street to compare notes.

"Did they push the 'Silver Plan' on you?" Harry asked.

"Yep, they said the fees were cheaper on domestic transactions," Joe said.

"Yeah, they told me the same thing, but I'm moving back to Crete and need the flexibility to make international transactions." Harry said ordering a glass of iced coffee.

"When are you leaving?" Joe inquired.

"As soon as I get back to Miami and sell my boat. You know the best thing about boats?" Harry asked.

"The time you buy it, and more importantly, when you sell it," Joe answered.

"Exactly. A boat's a hole in the water where you pour your hard-earned cash! What are you going to do now that you're rich?" he asked Joe.

"I'm going to keep working at Waters. I thought that detective work was menial, but I've learned a lot as a NYPD detective and at Waters I can apply it to my new position in the white-collar crime division," Joe said, getting the check and stating out loud for everyone to hear, "It's on me, Dad."

Out on the street, they embraced and gave each other the obligatory command to 'keep in touch.'

Chapter 41: Max

Meanwhile, on the other side of the country—well, almost other side—Glen had decided that Reno, Nevada, the divorce capital of the good old U.S.A. and he had irrevocable differences. A separation was needed. It was time, he thought, that he should plunge headfirst into the river of life and swim upstream to the place of his birth, Rockport, Maine, 'the prettiest town in America' according to Forbes Magazine. The mere thought of the little harbor with its multicolored fishing boats and the eclectic catch of shops, restaurants, taverns, and bed-and-breakfasts took his breath away.

He knew, he just knew, that Rockport was just the place to reestablish his lifelong dream of a hunting and fishing lodge. So, he set about finding a place, and to his surprise; he found a recent listing for an old farm. It was up for sale for less than a mil. It was a steal, he thought. The land alone, some 125 acres, was worth at least $250,000. As he scanned the listing, he remembered the boys he grew up with that worked the farm. They had these Oreo cows, pitch-black coats with a bright white ring around its waist. They were Belted Galloway cattle from Scotland. The more he thought about it, the more excited he became. He just had to put an offer in before it was sold. He immediately called the listing broker to ask if the property was still on the market.

"Hello, are you the listing broker for Prescott Farm?" he asked.

"No, but I can help you," the woman on the phone said.

"I'm interested in putting in an offer," Glen said. The woman took down his name, address, and phone number and asked why a person living in Reno, Nevada, was interested in a property in Maine.

"I'm a purebred Mainer," he said.

"I should tell you that there have been several offers, but the heirs have not made a decision yet," she said.

"Is the property in probate?" Glen asked.

"No, they're free to sell it, but there's been talk that they don't want to sell it to an 'outsider,'" she said in confidence.

"What's the highest bid?" he asked.

"Right now, it stands at $829,000."

"In that case, I want to submit a full-price offer, $849,000.00."

"All right," she said getting his email address to send him a form to complete and their address to send a 10% deposit to be held in escrow.

"When will I know?" Glen asked excitedly.

"Well, we can't bring the offer to the heirs until we receive your paperwork and deposit," she said, "but I will tell the listing broker, Ms. Brooks, that you plan to put in a full-price offer."

"Please do so and tell her I'll be on the next plane from Reno to Portland. By the way, tell her I'm not an outsider," he said proudly.

Once home the Major was back in his element. It was as if he'd never left. He loved the city and the special place the theater held in the hearts of the New Yorker. In fact, there were many messages from friends regarding auditions

"It's by Pinter, an amazing theatrical experience, and you'll be perfect for it."

"Call me, where are you? It's the first time Other Desert Cities will be performed in the Village, and the role of Lyman Wyeth was made for you."

Meanwhile his Lady, Sally Lipton, found to her dismay that securing an affordable venue for her repertory company did not take into consideration the gentrification of Greenwich Village. Dilapidated buildings that once went for a song were now commanding eight figure prices. However, an actor, a real actor, never believes a bad review. They show up, hit their mark, and with head raised high, they catch the spotlight and follow their dream, never looking back, only moving forward.

"If I can't buy, rent, or lease a building, I'll become a director and let the producer worry about the bills," she said. And so she did, to the acclaim of audiences throughout the Village.

The Prince of Second Avenue, a man for all seasons, had to put his plans for a warmer clime on hold when he received an offer even a prince could not refuse. Larry Silberstein, the CEO of the exclusive, LSCS Ltd, clothing stores asked him to establish a line of men's clothes for the one percent. Here was an opportunity to hire the crème de la crème of designers, artists, and staff for the sole purpose of designing wardrobes for the rich and those who want to look rich. His paramour, Betty Owens, a student of Dawn Mostow, the world-renowned latex costume designer, planned to open a boutique in Soho offering handcrafted latex garments for the trade, the theater, and the fashionista. To cap it all off, rumors have it that the Tavern on the Green in Central Park, has booked a wedding reception for two hundred guests under the names of Perry & Owens for June of this year.

Meanwhile down in North Carolina the day started out looking overcast and dreary. The forecast called for a high of seventy-two and a low of fifty-nine with scattered clouds and a hint of thunderstorms. At 8:00 a.m., there was a single car parked in the visitor's lot at the Butner Federal Penitentiary, a black Mercedes Benz 600. In the driver's seat was a stocky man wearing a short-sleeved white shirt opened at the neckline and khaki cargo pants. In the back seat, smoking a Marlboro was a gray-haired woman wearing a dark brown pants suit and dark sunglasses. At precisely eight minutes after eight, a gray-haired man wearing a black suit slowly opened the door of the administration building and froze as a clap of thunder shook the ground. Stepping out onto the walkway, he was engulfed in a blinding ray of sunlight. The burst of light cast a long shadow that followed him as he made his way to the parking lot. Stopping for only an instant, the man took in the prison one last time, then turned and never looked back.

That was the last anyone would ever see of Bernard and Ruth Madoff.

Epilogue

Several months later Clarence was out of his warm, comfy, king-sized memory foam bed. He had things to do; he wasn't going to waste his time in retirement sitting around his house. The sooner he'd accomplished his tasks on his list, the more time he could devote to his correspondence with the kids and grandkids. Being a prison guard at the courthouse in Brooklyn for almost thirty years had taught him that idleness was not good for the mind or the body. The second item on his list, which was a carryover from the week before, was a problem: what to do with the herbs wilting in his window box? It was very confusing. One person on the 'Don't kill your houseplants' side had suggested watering the herbs only once a week; another cautioned that too much sunlight burned delicate herbs. He had already tried their suggestions to no avail. Shrugging his shoulders, he picked up the flower box and unceremoniously dropped it in the waste bin.

"Good riddance," he said to the empty spot the flower box had occupied. Clarence could afford the luxury of buying herbs at the market whenever he needed them for his tomato and mozzarella caprese salad

"Just pick up a bag of basil, that's what I'll do," he said to himself.

Clarence had prepared for his eventual retirement wisely. Fifteen years ago, before living in Williamsburg was chic, he'd purchased a two-family brownstone on a nice, tree-lined street just a ten-minute walk to the subway. He took the ground floor for himself and rented out the upper floor to a succession of tenants until he found a young attorney at the courthouse and rented it to her and her husband. Now, with his second floor rented, his pension, and social security, he had enough money to live comfortably as long as his health insurance took care of the expenses associated with growing old.

But that was about to change when someone rang his doorbell.

"Who can that be at this hour?" Clarence said as he put on his spectacles to look at the digital clock on his stovetop range.

"It's eight-thirty," Clarence said, squinting to make out the clocks little red digits. He made his way through the kitchen to his living room window just in time to see a yellow cab drive away. Fixing his bathrobe, Clarence opened the door expecting to see someone on his doorstep, but no, the cab had left him a box. Bringing it into the house, he put it on the kitchen table to see who sent it. Adjusting his glasses, he saw his name and address in large bold letters but no return address, which made him suspicious.

"Did I order anything recently?" he asked himself.

"Can't remember," he answered himself.

"And who delivers packages by taxi?" he murmured, growing concerned. He gingerly picked up the box to get a better look at it and noticed a grease stain on one side. He carefully returned the box to the kitchen table and sat on a chair to think what to do.

"Do I have any enemies that want to harm me?"

"Was it from one of the nutty inmates I supervised at the courthouse?" He pushed back from the table.

"Came in a Yellow Cab...could it be a time bomb?" He crept closer to listen if it was ticking. "Can't hear anything, but maybe the bomber muffled the sound of the clock, or it's a silent digital device."

He debated the idea that he should call the bomb squad, but decided it might be premature. Best give it a forensic looksee, he told himself. So, he got out a sharp paring knife and ever so slowly cut the packing tape and stuck a finger under the lid feeling for a tripwire. Satisfied that there wasn't a wire underneath, he opened the lid and saw a Styrofoam box inside next to a Tyvek envelope.

"Well, what do we have here, a box within a box?" Getting his courage up he took the Styrofoam box out and placed it alongside the other box. Starting to perspire, Clarence decided to take a timeout and retreated to the living room to collect his thoughts.

"What am I getting myself so nervous about? It's probably a gift of some kind.

"Or maybe it really is a bomb. In that case I'll put in the bathtub and fill it with water." Clarence felt good. He'd thought it through and come to a rational decision. Clarence got up, marched into the bathroom, and sat on the toilet seat. He started filling the bathtub with water.

It took a long time, he thought, but it had to be done. When the bathtub was half full, he took the Styrofoam box into the bathroom, and to his dismay couldn't submerge it in the tub. No matter how he pushed it under the water, it popped up to the surface. The Styrofoam was too buoyant to sink. So, he decided to rethink the matter.

"Eureka!" he said to himself a little while later. "I'll cut holes in the Styrofoam and flood the inside, drowning the explosive.

"What to use? What to use?" he thought.

Looking through his silverware drawer he found the perfect utensil to bore into the box—a grapefruit knife! Getting down on his knees, he held the box down as hard as he could and began boring holes in the top and sides of the box, when suddenly smoke began spitting out of the holes.

Clarence jumped to his feet and tore out of the bathroom wondering if he should really call the bomb squad or the fire department or the police or all of the above. Luckily, he knew that his tenants were at work, along with most of his immediate neighbors. Clarence went into the kitchen determined to figure the situation out once and for all while the box in the tub did its thing. Whatever it was in the Styrofoam box was probably toast by now. Meanwhile he took the Tyvek envelope out of the carton and slowly cut it open. He poured the contents on the table. At first he wasn't sure if he saw what he saw. Crisp, new hundred-dollar bills cascaded all over the table and the floor. "Oh my God what have I done?" he thought.

"You've delivered the drugs to the wrong house," he said to the box.

"There must be thousands and thousands of dollars here," he thought as he scooped the money back into the Tyvek bag. He went into the bathroom to clean up the mess, thinking that the crime scene guys wouldn't like what he did to their evidence. The Styrofoam box had stopped spitting and he was able to lift the cover off to examine the drugs—probably cocaine, he surmised. But what he saw looked like a small white takeout container.

He opened the soggy container and knew immediately he'd made a big, big mistake. It wasn't drugs, it was a container of ice cream and the residue around the container was dry ice. He sat down at the kitchen table holding a container of melting ice cream, feeling like an old fool when he noticed scribbled on the bottom of the box a cryptic message:

"White King to Pawn 4." Under it was written BLM107@gmail.com, and he knew immediately who sent the mysterious package. It could have only come from Bernard L. Madoff, prisoner 107. The gobbledygook at the top was a classic opening chess move. It was the exact move Bernie had used to capture the center of the chessboard when they played chess at night.

Clarence knew that Bernie had been pardoned and that no one knew of his whereabouts, but this...this was a message in a bottle. This was Bernie's way of reaching out from God knows where for someone who shared a tragic part of his life and survived. Yes, Clarence knew that Bernie had done terrible things, but life made him and his family pay for his wrongful deeds in spades. Clarence was also a spiritual person and believed deeply that in certain circumstances there had to be a measure of forgiveness in life. Otherwise we're forever doomed by the errors of our past.

Putting everything aside, Clarence found his chess set on the top shelf in his closet and placed it on the kitchen table. He then set the pieces in their positions on the board, and as Bernie's message indicated, moved the white queen's pawn to the fourth position from the queen. Now it was his move. What should he do? Play it safe or attack? Clarence stared at the board and grasped the black queen's knight placing it on Bishop 3. He was to attack, and from then on, it was every man for himself. The game would go on and on and on, until the 'Man' killed the lights.

About The Author

After an exciting professional life, Phil Sills has settled down to the simple pleasures of family and friends where he writes, lectures, and paints.

You may also enjoy his previous Max Rosen book, Ghosts of Sackett Lake.